RETURN OF THE GUN

BY

R B CONROY

CCB Publishing
British Columbia, Canada

Return of the Gun

Copyright ©2008 by R B Conroy
ISBN-13   978-1-926585-09-3
First Edition

Library and Archives Canada Cataloguing in Publication

Conroy, R B, 1944-
Return of the gun / written by R B Conroy. – 1st ed.
ISBN 978-1-926585-09-3
I. Title.
PS3603.O57R57 2008   813'.6   C2008-906629-4

Cover image by Alton Vance: www.NHisLight.com

Publisher: CCB Publishing
British Columbia, Canada
www.ccbpublishing.com

WITH LOVE TO MY WIFE CHERYL,

Thank you for believing in me.

and

TO MY EDITOR AMANDA WOODIEL,

Thank you for your keen insights and great editing.

Chapter 1

The large boulders formed a narrow path as the lone rider struggled down the rocky knoll. Glimpses of a sparkling stream flashed ahead as he wove his way through the dark passageway. Soon a sandy basin was in sight. The trail broke open as the traveler spurred his steed forward into the flowing river, swollen by a morning rain. The mare whinnied and pranced nervously in the water, then calmed and began to drink. The rider dropped off, crouched down and began to sip water from cupped hands.

"Freeze!" A voice shot out from the jagged rocks near the water's edge.

Startled by the loud voice, the man froze. The water slowly drained through his thick fingers.

"Now put 'em up, mister, nice and easy. Any quick moves, and you're a dead man!"

The wary journeyman stood slowly, arms raised.

"Now move away from that rifle, pronto!"

The man glanced to the right at his Winchester in the saddle holster, tempted to go for it.

Suddenly, another voice shouted from the far side.

"You heard 'im! Get movin'!"

Reluctantly, the traveler moved sideways in the stream, away from his horse and rifle. His eyes darted left and right trying desperately to get a look at his tormentors. "I don't want any trouble, fellas—just passin' through," he shouted. His mind was racing. Alone and vulnerable, he wanted to get these cowards before they got him.

Without warning, the robber to his left dropped down out of the rocks and bolted toward the stream. The water flew as he stomped through the shallow rivulet to the horse, yanked the saddlebag open and dug inside.

The traveler watched from the corner of his eye. "Nothin' in there, mister. You're wasting your time."

"Shut him up!" the thief shouted to his cohort.

A gun hammer clicked; the victim spun right as a dark figure ran toward him from the other side, six gun in hand. Unexpectedly, the charging man slipped on the mossy bank and stumbled briefly, his arms flailing backward as he tried desperately to right himself. The savvy trekker saw his chance and yanked a Bowie knife from his waist sash and flung it hard toward the wobbly attacker.

"Uhgg!" The bandit groaned in agony as the sharp-edged blade drove deep into his chest. Wide-eyed, he grabbed the huge knife with both hands, rocking side to side in a desperate attempt to yank the dagger free. He staggered forward, moaning, his face filled with horror. He took a few more steps and then fell backwards on the muddy shore. His thick chest heaved violently and then went still with the knife's ivory handle pointing to the heavens.

"One down," the angry prey muttered.

"What the—?" the man by the saddlebag shouted as he watched his partner fall to the turf. Startled, he jerked up from the bag and reached for his gun. Like a flash, the knife thrower charged through the water toward the thief. The back of his hand slammed hard against the side of the varmint's head. The powerful blow knocked the robber senseless; he bounced off of the horse and fell hard to his knees. Disoriented, his six gun fired harmlessly toward the sky as he teetered momentarily and then fell in the shallow water. The attacker grabbed the frayed collar on his cotton shirt and yanked him up to eye level.

"I been ridin' hard all day. I'm tired, thirsty, and hot. All I needed was a couple of no good sidewinders like you two tryin' to rob me. Makes me real mad!" he shouted. "You understand?"

The terrified robber nodded his head as blood trickled down his cheek. The victim, now aggressor, squeezed harder on his collar.

"What's your name, mister?"

"W…Wes Harger."

Surprised at the name, the big man's angry face broke into a grin. "Wes Harger, ya say! Well, I'll be damned! I thought your ugly mug looked familiar! I hung your wanted poster all over Mesquite County a while back. You're wanted for bushwackin' that stagecoach driver down Amarillo way. Pretty good price on your head if I remember right—'bout five hundred dollars." He shoved the frightened scoundrel to the ground. "Stay put!" he ordered.

The slender robber dropped to the ground and rolled back on his elbows; his eyes darted up and down the man's face. "I know who you are now. I wasn't sure, but now I know!"

"You talk too much, Harger!"

"Yeah, you're Sheriff Jon Stoudenmire from Arizona Territory. I know who ya are. I was passin' through Logan's Crossing last winter when you took out Zing Fuller at the Barbee Saloon!"

"It's former Sheriff anyhow," Stoudenmire barked as he slid his rifle out of the saddle holster. "Now shut up and tell me about your dead friend over there. Is he wanted for anything?"

"Naw, he just got out of the pen for beatin' some whore to death in Las Cruces."

"Nice fella."

The man smirked. "That was really somethin' the way you blew that Fuller fella away. I never seen anything like it."

Trying to ignore the persistent road agent, Stoudenmire carefully fed cartridges into the loading port on his Winchester.

"How many men have you killed, Stoudenmire? Ten? Twenty? I could tell that he wasn't the first," the jumpy man pressed on.

Jon's eyes narrowed. He pushed the last cartridge in, cocked it and spun the rifle toward the annoying scallywag. "I told you to shut up!"

"Don't shoot!" Harger screamed, arms raised.

"I oughta, but not today." Jon slowly released the hammer and let the gun fall to his forearm.

Harger looked puzzled.

"Ya might say this is your lucky day," Jon barked as he walked over by the stream and yanked the bloody knife out of the dead man's chest. He washed it in the clear water and stuck it back in his sash. He strolled over to the robber. "We're only a day's ride from Skeleton Pass, Harger, and your poster didn't say dead or alive. You're no good to me dead, so I guess I'm gonna have to take you with me. I'm a little short of ready cash anyhow—I could use the spending money."

Jon grabbed hold of the mouthy mudsill's shirt and yanked him to his feet. The man's heart was pounding hard against Jon's fist as he dragged him over to his horse. A small shovel hung just below the back of the saddle. Jon unstrapped it and handed it to the jittery scoundrel.

"Take this and get busy!" Confused, the thief stood stock still. Irritated, Jon planted his big boot on the man's behind and shoved him toward the rocks. "There's a good spot right over there. We got a grave to dig—get at it!"

Harger stumbled over to the rocks, dropped to his knees and quickly began carving a hole in the ground. Dirt flew as he dug feverishly in the sandy soil.

Jon reached in his vest pocket, pulled out a cigar and stuck it between his teeth. A yellow flame exploded as he struck a match across his belt buckle. He took a hard drag and exhaled; failed attempts at smoke rings broke apart in the soft desert breeze. Falling back against a nearby rock, he gazed up at the pink desert sky. Just for a moment, while admiring the cloudless sky, he could almost see the deep green vines in his beautiful vineyard blowing in the soft ocean breezes. *Looks like a California sky,* he thought. A contented smile broke out on his handsome face as thoughts of his distant paradise rushed through his mind. The smile quickly faded when he looked back at Harger.

"How ya coming over there?" he barked.

"I'm getting close, I reckon."

"Hurry it up. I ain't got all night."

Dirt flew for a few more seconds and then stopped. Exhausted and sweating profusely, the gravedigger hurried over, grabbed the dead man under his arms, dragged him over and dropped him in the grave. The limp body folded up neatly as it fell into the narrow hole. Dust plumed up as Harger covered the grave. He dabbed sweat from his brow with a grimy handkerchief and scanned the area near the gravesite. He spotted a long stick lying by some nearby rocks. He snatched up the sturdy stick, snapped it in two and drove the shovel's edge in the top of one half. He lifted the shovel and pounded the other piece in the split end to form a cross. Shoulders slumped from fatigue, he pounded the makeshift cross on the front of the grave with the back of the shovel and stepped back to admire his handiwork.

"Toss the shovel over here and then say a few words," Jon ordered.

The man scowled as the shovel bounced near Jon's feet; he was obviously not accustomed to such ceremony. He struggled for words.

"Dear…uh…uh…"

"Keep quiet!" Jon said disgustedly, "I'll do it." Jon pushed away from the rock and walked over next to the skinny varmint.

"Take your hat off and bow your head."

He did as ordered.

Jon removed his hat. His chin dropped to his chest. "May the Lord have mercy on this man's tortured soul. Amen." Jon pulled handcuffs left over from his lawman days from his back pocket. "Put your hands together and put 'em behind your back," he ordered. The cuffs clicked shut. He led the man over to the riverbank near a small Joshua tree and shoved him to the ground.

"Stay put," Jon ordered as he scavenged around some nearby bushes for twigs and sticks. He tossed the sticks in a pile and struck a match. The bone dry twigs burst into flames. Jon hurriedly picked up some larger kindling and threw it on the flames.

"I'll make us some grub and then we'll ride out in the morning, Harger."

The other man nodded and glanced up at the sheriff. "If I'd known it was you back there, Stoudenmire, I wouldn't a tried to rob ya."

"I guess I'm supposed to feel better now."

"Well, I suppose not, but what's a big shot sheriff like you doin' way out here in the Sonoran Desert all by yourself anyhow? Ya musta screwed up or something!"

"Yeah, you're right, Harger. I did screw up."

"I knew it," he said. A cocky smile broke out on the robber's face.

"I screwed up all right—I shoulda killed ya a while ago when I had the chance." Jon grinned at the scowling Harger. Jon unstrapped his saddlebag and pulled out bacon, grits, coffee, a cast iron skillet, and a small metal coffeepot. It wasn't long before the scent of fried bacon, grits and fresh coffee filled the air.

Jon grabbed a metal spoon and scraped some bacon and grits onto a tin plate and handed it to Harger. He filled his own plate, crossed his legs and sat down by the fire. The two hungry men ate quietly, wasting no time in cleaning their plates.

After dinner, Jon led the robber over and cuffed him

to a tree. He gathered up the utensils and dishes, quickly washed them in the river and stuffed them back in his saddlebag. He unstrapped his bedroll and spread it on the cold ground. The eerie sounds of the great horned owl filled the air as he crawled under the blanket and got ready for a night's sleep.

"Better get some shuteye, Harger—we got a big day tomorrow," Jon barked.

Harger grumbled as his head disappeared under the blanket.

Jon lay wide-eyed, staring up at the starry night, unable to find sleep. His thoughts took him back to his childhood. The chilling voice of his father calling him a coward after a beating by a much older boy raced through his mind. Still trying to prove his father wrong, the cruel admonishment drove him forward with great fury and brutality in times of battle. But his loving mother's urgings always to be kind to others confused and tormented him. Tough on the outside, Jon bemoaned such violent incidents, and he always would. It was part and parcel of being Jon Stoudenmire—a notorious gunman and deeply conflicted man. After tossing and turning for what seemed an eternity, his eyes finally fell shut as he drifted off to sleep on the cold desert floor.

- - - - -

"Wake up," Jon shouted as he kicked Harger's boots. "We gotta get goin'."

Harger grimaced. His dirty fingers rubbed his crusty eyes. "What about breakfast?" he carped.

"What about it?" Jon asked.

"Ain't we havin' breakfast?"

"This isn't some fancy hotel, Harger. Besides, we don't have time. Here, eat this," Jon said as he tossed the man a strip of jerky.

Harger bit off a chew as the men gathered up their gear, quickly mounted up and rode off toward Skeleton Pass, a long day's ride through the hot desert.

Chapter 2

It was about sundown when the men reached the outskirts of Skeleton's Pass. Jon paused on a rocky knoll overlooking the bustling outpost, an important watering hole along the Gila trail to California. He glanced back at his long-faced prisoner.

"Ever been here before, Harger?"

"I've passed through a couple of times."

"They got a hotel here?"

"Yeah. It's at the other end of town."

"Let's ride on in," Jon ordered. "It's gettin' on toward sundown and I wanna be sure to get a room for the night. You'll be stayin' at the county jail."

Harger frowned.

Jon surveyed the popular settlement as they passed through the outskirts of town. He saw a blacksmith's shop, stable, bank, telegraph office, stage depot, small general store, saloon, jail, assorted other businesses and the hotel. As they rode on in, the riderless horse garnered a few stares from the curious townsfolk. Suddenly, Jon pulled hard on Babe's reins; the big steed came to a stop in front of the county jail. The front door swung open. A tall man wearing a badge stepped out on the boardwalk and greeted them.

"Evenin', fellas."

"Evenin'," Jon replied as he quickly dismounted and wrapped the leather straps around the hitching post.

The man stepped off of the boardwalk and extended his hand. "Marshal Ned Brown," he said, smiling.

Jon reached forward for a quick shake. "Jon Stoudenmire, Marshal. Pleased to meet ya."

The marshal's faced broke into a big smile. "Well, I'll be damned. The famous Sheriff Stoudenmire, right here in Skeleton Pass. May I ask what brings a man like you to our little corner of the world?"

Red-faced, Jon quietly replied, "Just passin' through on my way to California."

"Looks like ya had a little trouble along the way." The sheriff glanced at the empty horse and the cuffed man.

"Yeah. I stopped to water yesterday and this fella here and his friend were hidin' in the rocks near the river. First thing I knew, they were tryin' to bushwhack me."

"Hmmm, is that so? What's the lowlife's name?" Brown asked.

"Wes Harger," Jon replied. "You probably heard of him."

"Hmmm…yes…yes, I think I have. Didn't he shoot that stagecoach driver down Texas way?"

"Sure enough did, from point blank."

The marshal frowned. "Looks like you lost one," he said as he nodded at the empty horse. "I'm sure you're not using that beautiful buckskin for a pack horse."

"You're right about that. This varmint's partner came at me from the rocks near the river with pistol in hand, so I introduced him to my Bowie knife. We gave him a proper burial next to the river yesterday. Harger here probably knows his name." Jon eyes shot toward Harger.

"Slim Jernigan," Harger grunted.

"'Nother bad one," the marshal replied. "Ya did us all a favor puttin' him in the ground."

"Yeah, that's what I figured."

"Let's go inside, gentlemen." The marshal pushed the door open. Jon helped Harger down and led him inside.

Jon ducked under the doorway of the small adobe building, pushing a grumbling Harger ahead of him. He looked around; there were two cells and a couple of desks, a black pot belly stove and a supply room. Pens and paper sat on both desks; from this he figured Brown must have at least a part-time deputy. The sound of a man snoring drifted out of one of the cells. The other one was empty.

"Put him right there in that empty cell, Jon," Brown ordered.

"Say hi to your new home, Harger," Jon said as he grabbed the skinny robber by the cuffs and led him across the room.

Harger stumbled to the door and glanced in the small enclosure. "I been in better jails than this," he grumbled.

"Quit your bellyaching!" the marshal barked. "The food's good and the tarantulas only come out at night."

Jon grinned; he was starting to like the friendly lawman.

The marshal slammed the iron door shut and locked it. The key chain rattled as he tossed it on the peg and then ducked behind his desk.

"The bank's closed for the day, Jon, so I'll go down first thing in the mornin' and get your reward money. In the meantime, I'll run the horses down to the stables and make sure they get some good grooming. There's a hotel just down the street a ways if you're lookin' for a room."

"Thanks, Marshal. I guess you're just kinda takin' care of everything."

"It's my pleasure, Sheriff," he replied as he slid a tattered log book out of the desk drawer. He opened it as he glanced up at Jon. "My deputy will be in after a while to spell me. How 'bout I meet ya down at the Oasis Saloon for dinner in about an hour? It's right across from the hotel."

"It will be a pleasure, Marshal." Jon slid his pocket watch out of his vest pocket and checked the time. "See ya at seven."

The marshal nodded as he dipped the pen in the ink well and logged the prisoner's name in the frayed book.

Jon quickly exited the jail and jumped down next to Babe. He untied his saddlebags and tossed them over his shoulder. He patted her on the hindquarters and started down the busy street toward the hotel.

"Sheriff Stoudenmire!" Marshal Brown shouted from the doorway, pen in hand.

Jon stopped and turned in the street. "Yeah, Ned?"

"The hotel clerk's name is Elijah. Tell him the room's on me."

"Much obliged," Jon said as he resumed his trek to the hotel. He felt the stares of some of the locals as he made his way down the dusty street. Another indicator that his reputation had preceded him, it was becoming a familiar dance but not one he appreciated. Soon the faded sign atop the three-story hotel building was in sight; he hopped up on the wooden boardwalk and stepped inside.

"Howdy, stranger." A smiling clerk looked up from the front desk and greeted Jon as he ambled in.

"Howdy." Jon scanned the lobby. A few guests were talking quietly on two large leather sofas located just to the left of the desk; otherwise, it was empty. He turned back to the clerk. "I'd guess you're Elijah?"

"Yes, yes, I'm Elijah, and you're Mr.—?"

"Stoudenmire," Jon said as he approached the desk.

The diminutive desk clerk paused for a moment and looked over the top of the small round glasses hanging on the end of his narrow nose.

"Is that Jon Stoudenmire?" he asked politely.

"Yes, that's right."

"From down Arizona way?"

"Why do you ask?" Jon replied quickly, annoyed by the continuing questioning from the inquisitive clerk.

"I've just heard about you, that's all," the clerk replied in a wheedling voice.

"Is that so? And just what have you heard?" Jon wanted to know just what people were saying about him.

"Rumor is you rode into a mining town out in the Arizona desert and single-handedly took on a whole rat's nest full of hired guns. They say you're no one to trifle with when you get riled up. Some say you might have killed upwards of a dozen men." The clerk's eyes blinked rapidly as he peeked over his glasses at Jon.

"Don't believe everything you hear, Elijah. I had plenty of help, and I sure didn't kill twelve men. But you're right about one thing, Elijah."

"What's that?" The nosey clerk replied.

"I do get riled at times, and right now I'm damned tired and wanting a room in the worst way. You understand?"

"Why…uh, yes sir, I do… your room is coming right up." The clerk quickly grabbed a key from the wooden slot. "Room 210, just at the top of the stairs."

Jon frowned as he glanced up at the rooms. "Got anything with a view of the street?"

"Yes, yes, we do, Mr. Stoudenmire. Let's see, room 230 is open." The clerk poked the first key back in the slot, grabbed the key for 230 and laid it on the counter.

"Marshal Brown said he'd take care of the room," Jon said as he snatched up the key and headed for the stairs.

"No problem, Mr. Stoudenmire. I'll take it up with him." The clerk smiled broadly.

Jon hurried up to his room to clean up a little. He tossed his saddlebags on the featherbed and splashed water on his hot face from a nearby pan. He grabbed a towel off of the bedpost, patted dry, untied his saddlebag and carefully pulled out a gray silk shirt. He slipped on the shirt, splashed some cologne on his cheeks and headed for the Oasis Saloon. Still dry from his trip, a couple of shots of whiskey sounded real good right now.

Jon dodged a couple of potholes in the heavily traveled street, jumped up on the boardwalk and pushed slowly through the swinging doors of the saloon. He looked around; the folks looked peaceable enough. A man in a plaid vest pounded out "Turkey in the Straw" on the upright piano as Jon walked slowly toward the end of the long oak bar. The roulette wheels, faro tables, and poker games were at full throttle as he leaned against the bar. "Shot of Early Times, please," Jon said quietly.

"Comin' right up," the bartender replied. "My name's Jess Landis. Welcome to the Oasis."

"Pleasure to meet you, Jess. I'm Jon."

The bartender gave Jon a friendly nod. "Staying in town long?"

"Naw, I'm just passin' through. I'll be trekkin' on toward California in the morning."

Jon felt a bump on his arm as one of the whores in the bar pushed in next to him. She smelled of cheap perfume and laudanum. Swashes of rouge on her pale cheeks couldn't hide her dark, tired eyes. Her round, well-shaped bosom was precariously close to falling out of the top of her white cotton dress as she leaned toward Jon. Her face looked young—too young. "Buy a girl a drink?" she smiled awkwardly, batting her long eyelashes.

"Set her up, Jess."

"Usual?" Jess asked.

"What else?" she asked in a voice too glib to be confident.

Jess quickly poured a glass of Merlot and set it on the bar. She smiled at Jon as she lifted the glass to her thin lips. "Where ya from, honey?" She took a sip and gently pushed her knee against Jon's thigh.

"I'm from a lot of places, darlin'. How about—"

Suddenly, the wine glass crashed on the bar as the whore screamed and jumped back. Jon's back went stiff as the cold metal of a gun barrel pressed hard against his skull. There were more screams; chairs scattered across the floor as the patrons scurried out of the way. The piano stopped. The saloon went stone quiet.

"Remember me, Stoudenmire?" A strong hand grabbed Jon's chin and pulled it around as the gun pressed hard against the back of his head.

Jon's anger grew as he looked into the face of the bearded man. His eyes shot up and down, trying desperately to figure out who he was. Nothing looked familiar until he looked at those eyes—those black, wicked eyes he had seen years earlier in that saloon in Cheyenne, Wyoming.

"Will Sledge. Remember me? Your worst nightmare just came true." The iniquitous man laughed as his bony fingers slid roughly off Jon's chin. He grabbed the handkerchief on Jon's neck and yanked hard.

Jon was livid as the handkerchief cut into his neck. As he gasped for breath, he thought back to that day in Cheyenne. Sledge and a companion had come there to seek revenge against Jon for beating his older brother nearly to death a couple of years earlier in a buffalo camp in the Dakota Territory. After threatening Jon in a local saloon, the two men were quickly disarmed by an alert local sheriff. Wanting some closure, Jon goaded them into a fistfight, two against one out in the street. It was a brutal affair with Jon administering quite a beating to both men. Humiliated in front of the whole town, the badly beaten Sledge vowed revenge.

"I never gave up lookin' for you, Stoudenmire, but I was always just one step behind. Then I ran into some trouble down Abilene way. I choked a man to death and they gave me five to ten in a Kansas prison. I spent a

lotta time in jail—all I could think about was finding
you and killing you. My brother never recovered from
the beatin' you gave him in the Dakota Territory. He
died a few years later. You beat him unmerciful, you
never gave him a chance. He was the only family I had,
and you took him away from me. Now you're gonna
die!"

A portly, unshaven man standing just behind Sledge
cracked a wicked smile.

Jon glanced to his left as the bartender Jess moved
carefully along the bar. He reached down ever so easily
and pulled up a sawed off shotgun and laid it carefully
on the bar.

"The man's not armed, mister," Jess said calmly. The
hammer clicked on the shotgun. "Pull your gun down
nice and easy and put it back in its holster. And tell
your friend there to keep real still. One false move out
of either one of you, and I'll blow your damn heads
off."

Jon could tell this young barkeep meant business and
so could Sledge.

"Keep still, Red," Sledge commanded his stubby
partner. Then a nasty grin broke out on his face. "Don't
worry bartender, I wasn't planning on shootin' him in
here anyway. I want a fair fight." He pulled the gun
away from Jon's head, let loose of the bandanna and
stepped back. He dropped his gun in his holster.

Jon turned slowly around; he stared angrily at his old
nemesis. "I vowed I'd never carry again, Sledge. But for
you, I'm gonna make an exception. You need killin'."
There were groans from the crowd as Sledge knocked a
table aside, giving the men more room for their
showdown.

"Give him a gun, Red," Sledge hollered.

His partner pulled an extra six gun from his sash, set it on the bar next to Jon and quickly stepped back.

"Pick it up, Stoudenmire," Will ordered.

"I'm not stupid, Sledge. If I touch that gun, you'll blast me to the heavens," Jon said calmly. "Fight me like a man, Will, face to face out in the street."

Sledge paused and cackled, an ugly shrill little laugh. "I don't care where I kill ya, Stoudenmire. Street's fine." The cruel man sneered at Jon as he stepped backwards through the swinging doors, pushing Red behind him.

Jon yanked out his Bowie knife and dropped it on the bar. He grabbed the six gun and stuffed it in his sash as he tipped his hat down and walked outside. "I should have killed that bastard when I had the chance," he mumbled.

Spurs jingled as the patrons hurried toward the door to watch the fight. Jess eased the hammer down on the shotgun and set it back under the bar.

Jon scanned the street as he pushed through the batwing doors. Sledge stopped in the middle of the rutted road and turned toward Jon. The sun was quickly setting below the tops of the wood frame buildings. With the building blocking the glare from the sun, Jon would have a clear shot. Suddenly, he heard a familiar voice.

"Evenin', Jon."

Surprised, Jon spun to face Marshal Brown, just arriving for dinner.

"What's going on here?" Brown asked.

"Sorry, Ned. I ran into a little problem." He nodded toward the menacing Sledge standing feet apart, hands poised above guns in the middle of the street. "Didn't mean to bring trouble to your town, Marshal."

"Why don't we all sit down and—?"

Jon interrupted the marshal. "Ned, this man's been trailin' me for years. He doesn't want to talk. If I don't take him out here, I'm gonna be looking over my shoulder for the rest of my life."

The two were interrupted by Will's gravelly voice. "What's the hold up, Stoudenmire—you gettin' cold feet?"

Jon glanced back at the marshal. The marshal grimaced. "Go ahead and take the son-of-a-bitch, Jon. I'll watch your backside."

Jon ambled slowly to the center of the street. He yanked the gun out one last time and spun the cylinder to be sure it was fully loaded, a ceremony he performed without fail before every shootout. Then he tucked the gun back in the sash for a crossover draw. He opened and shut his hands, trying to relax his fingers as he turned to face the determined Sledge. Unafraid, Jon lived for these moments, mano e mano, out in the street with a nasty killer. He wanted Will Sledge dead in the worst way.

"Can you see me okay, Jon? I know you're gettin' kind of old." A hoarse laugh followed as the nasty critter smirked at Jon.

"I'm plenty close enough, Sledge," Jon growled.

"Got a bead on 'im, Red," Sledge yelled at his partner, trying to distract Jon.

"Stay out of this, Red," Marshal Brown bellowed.

"Ain't my fight." Red raised his hands and stepped backwards.

"That's okay, Marshal. I can kill two snakes as easy as one!" Jon barked.

The snake comment enraged Sledge. His skinny hand dropped down as he went for his gun.

Jon drew like a flash, cocked the hammer and pressed hard on the trigger. Yellow flames shot out from the barrel; smoke filled the air. He fired two more quick shots. The crowd screamed as Jon's bullets blasted into Sledge's chest. Wide-eyed, he blew backward, skidded on the dusty street and fell still. His head dropped to the side as blood oozed from the smoking bullet holes in the center of his chest. The shocked crowd was numb as Marshal Brown rushed out to the street, gun drawn. He swung it toward Red.

"Don't do anything stupid," he shouted.

Red pushed his hands even higher at the marshal's command.

Jon ran toward Sledge's lifeless body, six gun smoking. He looked down at the fallen man, his face red with anger. For a horrifying moment as he gazed at Sledge's lifeless face, he saw his own father's narrow evil face instead—the same face that had terrified him as a boy. A firm slap on the back brought him out of the excruciating trance.

"Great shooting, Jon!" Marshal Brown exclaimed.

Eyes glazed over with anger, Jon tried to compose himself. "Th…thanks, Marshal."

"Take the body down to the coroner's office," Marshal Brown shouted at his fast approaching deputy.

Sledge's shaken partner mounted up and turned to ride out of town. "Here!" Jon shouted as he tossed him the Peacemaker. Red caught the warm gun in midair, stuck it back in his holster and spurred his steed forward to the edge of town.

The marshal looked back at Jon. "Are you okay,

Jon?"

"Yeah, I'll be fine," Jon said quietly.

"How about a drink?"

"Sounds good."

The two men turned and walked toward the Oasis. They pushed through the doors and Marshal Brown nodded to the right. "Over there." He pointed to a table in the corner of the room, slightly elevated and bordered by a shiny gold banister. "That's kind of my little slice of heaven." The marshal smiled. "Jess made it for me and my deputies. He likes to have the law around here as much as possible."

As the two men ambled over to Ned's special table, Jon thought of the promise he had made to his true love Elizabeth, back in the Arizona Territory. Contemplating marriage and tired of all of the violence, he had promised the lovely saloon owner that his gun fighting days were behind him. Jon's thoughts were suddenly interrupted by the approaching barkeep as the two men stepped up on the red carpet and sat down.

"Whiskey?" Jess asked.

"Sounds good," the marshal replied. Jon nodded his approval.

"Let me know when you want to order dinner." Jess said as the two thick glasses banged against the tabletop. The bartender splashed in the whiskey and hurried back to the bar.

Jon pushed his hat back on his forehead, reached inside his vest pocket and pulled out a Havana. "Smoke?" he offered as he lifted it toward the marshal.

"No thanks, Jon. I'm tryin' to quit," he laughed.

"Do you mind?"

"No, no. Please, go right ahead."

"Thanks." Jon lit up, took a hard drag and exhaled.

"That Sledge fella seemed like a real bad sort," Brown said.

"Yeah, he was a bad hombre all right, and he needed killin'. It's just…" Jon hesitated.

"Just what?" The curious marshal leaned forward.

"Well, it's just that I made a promise never to fight again to a very special someone back in Arizona." Jon's brow furrowed as he watched the brown liquid swirl in his glass.

Brown looked sympathetically toward Jon. "Is that why you're not packin' and all?"

Jon frowned. "Sure enough is."

"A noble gesture indeed, my friend," the marshal replied, "but it seems a little risky for a man of your reputation. It only stands to reason that there are going to be a few more Will Sledges out there."

Jon grimaced. "I guess so, Ned. I'm just hopin' that when I get over those mountains that most of the bad stuff will stay behind me."

"Well, let's hope so, my friend," said the marshal, lifting his glass. "Here's to you and that pretty girl back in Arizona!" The two men downed their shots.

"You ridin' out in the morning?" Ned asked.

"I'm plannin' on it, Marshal."

"It's been a pleasure gettin' to know ya, Jon!"

"Same to ya, Ned." Jon smiled warmly. "And since you got my room, it's my turn to fork over for dinner."

"I give up Sheriff." The marshal playfully raised his hands above his head.

The flickering light of the kerosene lamp danced over the faces of the two tough men as they drank and broke bread together. The room darkened as they spoke of mutual acquaintances and past adventures. It was in the wee hours of the morning when Jon reluctantly bid farewell to his new friend and retired to his room at the Far End Hotel.

He staggered as he climbed up to the boardwalk and shoved through the partially open door of the Far End. The banister creaked as the big man pulled himself up the stairs and wobbled down the hall to his room. He fumbled for the key, stuck it in the slot, and the door fell open. The dull light from the street lamps spilled through the milky window frame and formed yellow squares on the floor. The back of his foot banged the door shut as he stumbled over and fell on the soft bed. Conflicted by his broken promise to Elizabeth, he stared blankly at the ceiling. Drunk and tired, he soon fell fast asleep.

- - - - -

"Hiya! Hiya! Get movin', you damn stubborn mules," the loud voice bellowed from the street below, waking Jon from a deep sleep. It was late morning; the weary gunhand had overslept. He rolled out of bed and quickly washed up. He gathered up his things, hurried downstairs and hustled over to the livery stable.

As Jon approached the stables, he could see Babe prancing nervously out front as the stable hand ran a dandy brush through her coat. She was groomed, fed and ready to go. Jon flipped a ten dollar gold piece to the hand and mounted up to leave. He was surprised when he heard the marshal's voice.

"Mornin', Jon."

"Mornin', Ned." Jon smiled, happy to see the fast-

Everything

approaching marshal.

"Looks like ya overslept a little, big guy."

"Yeah—seems this fella kept me up past my bedtime last night." Both men smiled.

The marshal reached into his shirt pocket and yanked out a wad of cash. He peeled off several bills and handed them to Jon. "Here's your five hundred dollar reward and fifty dollars for the extra horse you brought in yesterday."

"'Preciate it," said Jon as he stuffed the cash inside his vest pocket.

"Be careful Jon—the Paiutes have been going off the reservation lately. For some reason, they're pretty riled up. They've left more than a few scalps out in the desert."

"Thanks for the warning." Jon paused as he glanced over at the marshal. "I sure hope our trails cross again, partner."

"Back at ya, buddy," the marshal replied warmly.

Anxious to make up for lost time, Jon spun around and rode toward the general store to grab some supplies. He pulled up and hurried inside. After stuffing his saddlebags full of flour, bacon, beans, and beef jerky, he settled up. The owner tossed the money in the register, the money drawer banged shut as Jon hurried out the side door toward the well. The excess water drained off the heavy pouches as he struggled to the front and tossed them over Babe's hindquarters. The big steed reared up on her hind legs and leapt forward toward the desert. Jon's long, difficult journey through California had resumed.

Chapter 3

The cool wind felt good against Jon's dry, parched skin. The exhausting ride over the mountains and up the California coast was nearing its end as he pushed several miles inland on the final leg of the trip. Evening was falling as he wove his way along a low mountain pass. He would soon be arriving at El Cabrera, a mining town just a short distance from his vineyard. All he needed was a little grub and a good night's sleep; he would ride on to his winery in the morning.

"Whoa, girl, whoa!" Jon pulled gently on the reins. The mare's ears pricked up as the sounds of music and loud voices blared out to the countryside from the bawdy town. An occasional gunshot echoed up the ridge. Marshal Brown had warned Jon that El Cabrera had become a wild and lawless town since the discovery of gold some years ago.

"Let's go, girl." Jon prodded his weary steed down the trail toward the bustling mining town. As he reached the final incline toward the rowdy outpost, more gunshots rang out, giving Jon pause. Alarmed, he pulled up and reflected on his recent brushes with death—the bloody fight with the robbers near the stream, the incident at the saloon in Skeleton's Pass. He could almost feel the cool barrel of Will Sledge's six gun pressing against his skull. If not for the bartender's quick action, Sledge would have shot him close up. Then there was the ominous warning from Marshal Brown that there would be more Will Sledges out there. Also, his growing reputation made him a special target for every young gunslinger trying to make a name for himself. But it wasn't the danger that troubled him the most; it was the vow he had made to Elizabeth. It was a vow he took seriously, but recent events were causing him to revisit that pledge. What good was such a vow if he ended up dead? He knew it would be terribly dangerous for a man of his reputation in El Cabrera. The thought of some coward putting a bullet in his belly while he stood unarmed and helpless was more than he could bear.

Tormented, the famed gunman grimaced as he dismounted, unstrapped his saddlebag and dug inside for the leather pouch. Heart pounding, he reached inside and took out a heavily worn gun belt holding two ivory handled Colts. He quickly stuffed the leather pouch back in the saddlebag. He was stoic as he pulled back his black duster and slid the gun belt around his waist. He pushed the nose of the belt through the buckle and yanked it tight. "Forgive me, Libby," he whispered as he mounted up and spurred Babe forward to El Cabrera, his trusty Colts once again bouncing at his side.

Piano music poured from the window of the local saloon as Jon rode into town. Loud voices blurted out from inside the bawdy bar. "Sounds like the boys are havin' a good time," Jon whispered.

Suddenly the doors of the saloon flung open, and a young man flew out of the door and tumbled onto the dusty street near Jon. Babe reared; the cowboy rolled just out of range of her giant hooves as they crashed to the ground. Wide-eyed, the youngster hopped to his feet.

"You go to hell—I'm not selling out!" His face flushed red as he shouted toward the saloon. The rocking saloon doors banged open again; three men came charging out toward their victim. The terrified youngster was soon surrounded; the men were shouting insults and shoving him.

"You got a big mouth, Sonny. Now let's see what else you got!" A skinny cowboy with a thick scar above his right eye grabbed the youngster by the collar.

Jon could feel himself becoming more and more upset as he watched the ugly scene unfold in front of him. The veteran gun hand was tired from a long day's ride, he was in no mood for bullies. He felt he could stay silent no longer.

"Let 'im go!" Jon barked.

Startled by the sound of the stranger's voice, the scarred man spun around in the street. His black, beady eyes glared at Jon. "This ain't none of your affair, partner. Just butt out!"

"Three on one is always my affair, partner."

"I guess you didn't hear me! I said shut your trap and get on down the road!" The surly man spit on the ground near Jon.

Jon winced; the disagreeable poke had gone too far. He pulled back the sides of his long duster, displaying his six guns. "I'm tellin' you for the last time, mister. Let the boy be!" The sight of Jon's guns appeared to alarm the cocky scallywag—suddenly he went for his gun.

Like a flash, Jon drew and blasted a shot toward the bully. Sparks flew as the gun tumbled out of the attacker's hand and bounced to the ground. Jon quickly fired two more shots; the bullets ricocheted off of the gun's metal cylinder, knocking it out of reach of the nasty man. The gathering crowd screamed as Jon wheeled around, six gun smoking, to confront the other culprits.

"You son-of-a-bitches stay away from that boy! One false move out of either one of ya, and I'll blow ya away." The men quickly backed off.

Jon wheeled toward the skinny man. "You're lucky I went for your shootin' hand, partner. Most days I woulda let you have it. I guess I'm in a good mood."

Visibly shaken by the speed and fury of Jon's attack, the frightened man cowered in the street.

"Go pick up your gun, and get the hell out of here. If I see ya within fifty feet of this young fella again, I'll shoot first and ask questions later!"

The man gathered up his gun as he and the others scrambled to get out of the way. They'd seen enough of the big stranger and his smoking six gun.

The shocked youngster watched as the nasty cowpokes hustled on down the road, tails between their legs.

"Ya all right?" Jon asked.

"Yeah, I guess I am," the youngster replied shyly. Dust flew as he smacked his hat against his dirty leather chaps.

"I'm gonna be stayin' in town for the night young fella. You let me know if those boys bother ya again." Jon smiled at the grateful boy.

"Thank ya, mister. I sure will." The shy youngster's mouth curled up in a smile.

Jon tipped his hat, reined Babe around and rode toward the center of town. A man's voice barked out from the porch at the Dead End Saloon. "That's one tough hombre! I hope I never run into him!" the man exclaimed as the crowd hurried back inside to reclaim their spots at the faro and blackjack tables.

Tired and hungry, Jon pulled a strip of jerky from his shirt pocket, bit it off and chewed it hard.

His body aching, he saw the Callahan Boardinghouse sign on down the road a piece. He gently spurred Babe toward the two-story building. The small boarding-house was right in the middle of town, just two doors down from the Dead End Saloon. *Perfect,* he thought as he pulled up and jumped down. As he tied up to the hitching post, a familiar voice shouted out from the darkening street.

"My oh my, sure surprised to see you in these parts! Last time I heard, you were hiding out in the Kansas Territory after shootin' that deputy sheriff in Hays City."

"Well, I know I'm tired, and my mind could be playin' tricks on me, but that sounds like that nasty ole cousin a mine, Cliff Stone." Beaming, Jon turned to face his greeter. "Well I'll be damned, it is you! How the heck are ya, Cliff?" Jon extended his hand toward his smiling kin.

The two shook and shared a hard hug. "I can't believe it's you, Jon. It's so good to see you! We had a lot of good times back in Indiana."

"Sure did, Cliff. I'll never forget 'em."

"We were just kids then—it's been a while."

Jon nodded. "Ya look good, cus. You've put on a few, but you were always a little too skinny."

Cliff grinned. "That was quite a show you just put on over at the Dead End. I was watching from the porch of the general store. Kinda reminded me of that time back in Indiana when you took care of that bully at the county fair. I could've handled it, but you jumped on 'im before I had a chance!"

"Maybe so, but you were just a little shaver. I had to do somethin', or ya probably woulda got your butt kicked."

"That's for sure," Cliff laughed. "It's quite a surprise seeing you way out here in California, Jon. What brought you out this way?"

Jon leaned back against the hitching post. "Since those Indiana days, Cliff, I've pretty much been all over the place. Travelin' from town to town just doin' odd jobs and a little gambling here and there. And I've been in my fair share of scrapes along the way. Never one to back down, I'm sorry to say I've been in a number of gunfights. Unfortunately, a few men have died." Jon glanced at Cliff for his reaction. Cliff was calm, showing little emotion at Jon's revelations.

Jon went on."I only killed in self defense or to protect a friend. A good man need not fear me. But my fightin' has bought me a reputation. That reputation wears you down after a while. You're never sure when some coward is gonna try and put a bullet in your back."

Jon paused, grinding his boot into the dusty road. "Years ago, I bought a vineyard near here with the money I saved in my early days at the buffalo camps," he continued. "A while back, I decided to give up my fightin' days and head out to that little slice of heaven. I'm almost there now," Jon smiled.

"How about you, Cliff? I thought you'd have about three hundred head and a nice wife by now!" As Jon looked over at the sturdy man Cliff had become, he remembered the good kid back in Indiana, the one who read the Bible in Sunday School and never sassed his parents. The one the other parents wanted their ornery little cusses to be like. The kid everyone wanted to play with at recess. Jon had to admit there were times back then when he was getting a whuppin' from his mean father that he was a bit jealous of his popular cousin.

A nervous smile broke out on Cliff's friendly face as he replied. "Well, that was my plan all right, but it hasn't worked out that way. Ma died of consumption about three years after you left. Pa was so lonely that he went to drinkin' and eventually lost the farm. He died of a broken heart a short time later, so I took off. I headed for Abilene. After a short time there, I moved on to Hayes City and found a job working on the railroad. I tried ranchin' a couple of times, but the drought got me both times. Then it happened."

Jon's eyebrows rose.

"I had some trouble."

"Trouble? Why, you were the one who always avoided trouble, Cliff. What happened?"

"I went over to the Oriental there in Hays one evening to do a little gambling. Short time later, I was invited to join a game of blackjack. After several hands, I was sure one of the boys was cheating. When I called him on it, he got real mad and went for his gun. Problem was, I saw it coming. Quick as a flash, I grabbed the six gun out of the guy's holster next to me."

"Guy next to ya, huh? That's impressive!"

"I blasted away at the cheatin' dog. He fell hard to the floor. With the help of one of the whores in the bar, I vamoosed out the back door. I don't know if I'm a wanted man or not. I just needed to get as far away from that town as I could. I rode and rode, never looking back, just keepin' on. After a few stops in between, I ended up here in El Cabrera, and I've been mining ever since. Not what I planned on, but I guess that's the way life is."

"Well I'll be, cousin Cliff is runnin' from the law!" Jon chuckled as he poked him playfully in the shoulder.

"Just trying to keep up with you, Big Jon. You were always my hero, you know."

Both men joined in a raucous belly laugh. Jon could have talked all evening, but Cliff had some things to get done.

"It's great seeing you, Jon, but I better run. I got some errands to run before everything closes. Why don't we get together later?" Cliff looked at Jon with great anticipation.

"Sounds good to me, Cliff—maybe we can get a bite at the Dead End later on."

"It would take a herd of wild horses to keep me away!" Cliff said eagerly. His black mare whinnied as he reined her backward toward the center of town.

Alone and tired from his long journey, Jon couldn't wait to meet Cliff. But first he needed to grab a room and a quick bath.

Chapter 4

"Can I help you, sir?" The lovely lady glanced up from the counter as Jon hustled into the boardinghouse. Jon slowed dramatically on his way to check-in, taken aback by the beauty of the friendly lady behind the counter. She was tall, just a few inches shorter than Jon, with dark flowing hair and a classically beautiful face adorned by gorgeous brown eyes framed by carefully manicured eyebrows. Her pink calico dress fit snuggly, accentuating her trim, curvy figure. Her smile seemed to warm up the entire room. Jon tried to collect himself and say something, but she beat him to the punch.

"I'm Maggie Callahan. Welcome to El Cabrera, Mr....?"

"Oh...uh, Stoudenmire, Jon Stoudenmire." A red-faced Jon went on. "Forgive me for fumbling, ma'am, it's just that I wasn't expecting to see a...uh..."

"A woman at the desk. Is that what you're trying to say?" the smiling owner replied.

"Yes ma'am, especially one as lovely as you, Miss Callahan," Jon said politely as he tipped his hat.

"Why thank you, Mr. Stoudenmire. How nice. Now, can I get you a room?"

"Yes, of course. I need a room on the second floor and at the end of the hall if at all possible."

She turned; her lovely hand gently slid a key out of the rack. "Room 201 at the end of the hall as you requested." She paused for a moment and looked down at Jon's Colts. "I've worked long and hard to build my business, Mr. Stoudenmire. I don't need any trouble here," she said firmly as she dropped the key into Jon's hand.

"I understand, Miss Callahan, I surely do. I'm not lookin' for trouble from anybody."

She raised her chin and smiled politely at the anxious gunman. "And that will be five dollars, please."

Jon nervously poked around in his pocket, pulled out a five dollar gold piece and set it on the counter. His weathered, handsome face broke into a smile as he gathered up his belongings and headed up the narrow staircase to his room. He stepped inside, tossed his things on the bed in the corner of the room and glanced out the window at the street below. *Busy little town,* he thought as he wheeled around and hurried out.

As he passed the desk on his way out the front door, he tipped his hat politely to the stunning Miss Callahan; she smiled warmly. Jon quickly untied Babe from the hitching post and walked her down to the livery stable to get her some oats and well-deserved grooming. As Jon approached the stable, he could see a shadowy figure showing a horse just inside the front entrance.

"Evenin'," Jon said loud enough so the man could hear. The aging stable hand looked around, somewhat startled by the unexpected voice.

"Evenin'. What can I do for ya?"

"Can you work another one into your schedule?"

"Sure can, Mister. That's one of the prettiest palominos I've ever seen." He laid the horse's hoof on the ground and walked over to greet Jon.

"Thank ya kindly!" Jon said as they shook. "And if ya don't mind, sir, I need a little advice."

"Fire away! My wife tells me I'm good at giving advice."

Jon grinned. "Ya got a bathhouse here in town? I'm needin' a haircut and a bath real bad."

"Sure 'nough do. There's a barber shop around the corner and he's got a few tubs in the back." The hand walked over and took the reins from Jon and led Babe into the stable.

"We had a long ride today. She got plenty hot out there—she might need a little extra time."

"No problem, Mister. I'll give her all the time she needs. Now, why don't you quit fussin' about your horse and get on outta here and relax a little bit? I promise I'll take real good care of her." His mouth curled up in a friendly grin.

Jon turned and headed for the bathhouse. His legs were stiff from the many hours of riding along those narrow mountain passes. It felt good to walk and stretch for a minute.

Several people seemed to recognize Jon from the earlier gunplay at the Dead End as he walked down the dusty street. Soon he was in front of the bath-house. He looked up at the well worn sign: "Harper's Barbershop." As Jon jumped up on the boardwalk and hurried in, he noticed another sign advertising "Shave, haircut, and bath, four bits."

Chapter 5

Jon felt like a new man as he bumped the door open to the Dead End Saloon and strolled inside. The place was full of life and kind of fancy. There was a long mahogany bar pushed up against the back wall. A large mirror with beveled glass hung behind the bar. Several gambling tables, faro tables, and roulette tables filled the center area. On the far side, there was a long oak stairway that led up to the painted ladies' rooms. A honky-tonk piano sat in the corner of the room near the bottom of the stairs. The talented piano player was at full throttle when Jon arrived. *Not a bad place to hang out*, he thought.

Jon moved slowly toward the long bar. It was lined up from end to end with all sorts of humanity: miners, cowboys, gamblers, rustlers, and a few Mexican cattle herders and, as always, the hookers, conmen, gunmen, outlaws, and rounders. After his earlier fight with the cowboys, he wasn't looking for any grief from anyone. A few drinks and some grub with Cliff was all he was looking for on this warm spring night.

On the way to the end of the bar, Jon caught a glimpse of a gentleman in a fancy suit talking with some gamers at a faro table. As Jon leaned up against the bar, the man looked at him. He nodded to the faro players and walked toward Jon.

"Howdy, stranger. I'm Lou Stanton. This here den of iniquity belongs to me," he joked as his hand reached forward for a shake.

"Jon Stoudenmire." The two men shook hands.

"Yes, I know," Stanton replied. "When you chased off those fellas this morning, some of the local folks recognized you."

"Hmmm, is that so?" Jon frowned.

"Yeah, word travels slow over the mountains, but it eventually gets here. They say you're not one to trifle with."

Jon grimaced. "I don't want any trouble, Lou. I'm just in for the night. I'm headin' out in the mornin'. Got some friends in Vinegar Bend."

"Uh-huh. Vinegar Bend, ya say. That's not too far—just a few hours ride from here."

"Yep, I'm almost there!" Jon smiled.

Lou hesitated. "Let me give you a little advice, Stoudenmire. Watch your backside. There's some tough hombres around here, and they'd like nothin' better than to fill you full of lead. They'd become famous overnight."

"Thanks for the warning, Lou, but like I said, I'm not stayin' long, just passin' through."

Lou glanced at Jon's six guns and smiled.

"Just for protection," Jon said quickly.

"Well, I guess a man like you can't be too careful!"
Lou turned and walked quickly back to the gambling
tables.

Jon shaded his eyes as the swinging door pushed
open. Cliff hurried in and made his way to the bar.
Several of the men in the casino spoke to him as he
wound through the tables. He was obviously well
known and well liked in El Cabrera.

"Sorry, Jon. Got held up at the bank," Cliff sighed as
he fell against the bar.

"No problem, cus. I thought you might have
changed your mind or something."

"No way! I wouldn't have missed this dinner for
anything. We've got a lot of catching up to do."

"Yeah, I guess we do, Cliff," Jon said as he tossed
down a shot of whiskey. "Seems like you know about
everybody in town."

"I've been around a while. I know my share of
folks all right. There's some good ones and some bad
ones, just like any other place." The bartender slid a
shot of whiskey in front of Cliff.

"Wish I could stay long enough to meet some of the
folks, but I'm gonna light a shuck out of here in the
morning. I'm anxious to see how my vineyard's doin'."

"Well, you don't need to be in such an all-fired
hurry, Jon. That vineyard isn't going anywhere."

"Yeah, I know. I guess I'm just anxious to get there.
I'm sure I'll be back to El Cabrera from time to time for
supplies and such. And by the way, Cliff, kinda keep this
vineyard thing under your hat for the time being. People
will figure it out sooner or later, but for right now I'd
like to keep it quiet. I need some time to build a cabin

and get things around out there. A man with my reputation can't be too careful."

"My lips are sealed, cus. How about some grub?"

"Sounds good. I could eat a horse."

"Why don't we go over to that table in the corner of the room and see if we can keep you out of trouble for a while?" Cliff smacked his lips and set the empty shot glass on the table.

"Lead the way. And please don't say hi to everybody in the room, okay? I wanna eat before midnight. I'm hungry!"

"I'll try, but I'm pretty popular, ya know," Cliff joked.

Jon smacked him lightly on the head. "You haven't changed a bit—still cocky as ever."

The men wove across the room to the corner table. As they got near, Jon spoke up. "Mind if I sit against the wall, Cliff? One never knows when some angry relative of one of the men I've shot might show up and try to plug me in the back. Just like Jack McCall did to my friend Wild Bill in Deadwood a few years back."

"No problem."

Cliff waved at the bartender; he hurried over.

"Howdy, boys." He looked at Jon. "I didn't get a chance to introduce myself when you were at the bar. My name's Jake, and I guess you're not too picky about the company you keep," he joked.

"Pleasure, Jake," Jon replied. "And yeah, you're right—I'm not real picky! I take it you know this hombre."

"'Fraid so, and I wish we had more Cliff Stones around here. We would be a lot better off."

"That goes both ways, Jake," replied the younger cousin.

"Well, as soon as you fellas get done with your love fest," Jon grunted, "I'd like to order some grub."

"Sorry, partner. What's your pleasure? I got a bunch of T-bones on the grill, and they're really tender tonight."

"Sounds good!" the two old friends said in unison.

"Bring us a bottle of your best whiskey, Jake, and put it on my tab," Cliff ordered.

"Will do, Cliff. The steaks'll be up shortly." Jake hurried over to the bar and returned promptly with a bottle of whiskey and a couple of shot glasses. He splashed the brownish spirits into the thick glasses, set the bottle down and scurried off.

The whiskey kept flowing as the two old friends began to reminisce about the old days as kids back in Indiana. Soon they were conversing quite freely, laughing and joking about their days working and playing on the lush farmlands of the Midwest.

"The way you took on those boys in front of the Dead End today didn't surprise me at all, Jon. You were never one to mess with, even as a kid. I guess I can kinda understand how ya got your reputation and all—must be nice to be well known."

"Not really," Jon frowned. "That reputation isn't what it's cracked up to be. Like I said earlier, I never know when some lowlife's gonna try to put a bullet in my back for killin' some friend or relative of his. And then there's the youngsters looking for a reputation at my expense. I gotta be on my toes all the time."

"Hmmm…," Cliff replied. "Like the old saying goes, 'walk a mile in my boots.'"

"Guess so."

"Dinner's served!" Jake announced as the steaming T-bones hit the table.

Jon inhaled deeply; the big T-bone steak with fried potatoes, pinto beans and onions sure smelled great after weeks of biscuits, bacon and beef jerky.

"Thanks, Jake," Cliff said. The conversation stalled as the hungry men dove into the tasty vittles.

- - - - -

The fork rattled as Jon dropped it on the empty plate. He leaned back, reached inside his vest pocket and pulled out a cigar. Looking contented, he bit off the tip, struck a match along his jeans, leaned down and took a couple of hard drags.

"Don't mind if I do," Cliff barked.

Slightly embarrassed, Jon looked over at Cliff. "Sorry." Jon dug another cigar out of his vest pocket and tossed it to Cliff. The red embers burned brightly as Jon took a hard drag and pointed the hot end at Cliff. Cliff leaned forward, his cheeks pruned as the hot coals spread to his cigar. The smoke curled above his head as he exhaled. "Good cigar," he sighed. He carefully picked a loose piece of tobacco from his tongue and flipped it onto the wood floor. "You were always chasin' the girls as a youngster, Jon. I'm surprised some sweet little filly hasn't got a rope around you by now."

"Marriage just never seemed in the cards for me, Cliff. Bouncin' around the way I do, it just didn't seem right. Until—"

An interested Cliff interrupted. "Until what?"

"Until I finally found a girl that could put up with me. She's from down Arizona way, and she's pretty as a picture. Elizabeth's her name, but I call her Libby. She did a darn good job of meltin' this ole heart of mine."

"I hope to meet her someday."

"You'll get your chance. Soon as I get things squared away out at the vineyard, I'm going to send for her."

"Here's to Libby." Cliff raised his glass, and the two men downed the shots.

"How about you, Cliff? Anybody round here kind of trippin' your trigger?" Jon spilled more whiskey into the empty glasses.

"Naw, not really. I've done my share of courting since I been here, but so far nothing's really worked out."

"That Maggie Callahan's a good looker. How 'bout her?"

Cliff squirmed in his seat. "Maggie and I took a couple buggy rides, had a couple a dinners together, that's all. Nothin' ever came of it."

"Oh well, there's other fish in the pond." Jon could tell he had hit a sore spot with Maggie. It was obvious that Cliff had stronger feelings for her than he was letting on.

Not surprisingly, Cliff seemed anxious to change the subject. "Traveling like you do, I'll bet you've ran into some well known gunslingers along the way. You said earlier you knew Wild Bill."

"Oh yeah, I've met a few. Like everybody else who gets around."

"Ever gone one on one with any of 'em?" Cliff's eyebrows rose.

"Not really. We kind of avoid fighting one another—kind of a mutual respect thing, I guess. Plus, when you fight someone like John Wesley Hardin, there's a good chance you're gonna end up dead."

Cliff pushed on. "I don't get around much anymore, Jon. I kinda been stuck here in El Cabrera for a number of years. It can get plenty rowdy around here at times, but for the most part it's just the same ole, same ole. I could sure use a good story. How about it?"

Jon grimaced. His mother always taught him it was impolite to talk about oneself, but the alcohol was taking effect. He took another swig. "I got one or two, I guess."

"I got all night, my friend. Fire away." Cliff sat up in his chair.

"Okay, cus, I'll tell you one, but you gotta promise you'll never ask me again. I'm not much on talkin' about myself."

"Ya got my word!"

Jon fell back in his chair and took a drag on his Havana. A plume of smoke drifted slowly to the ceiling. He was quiet for a while as if in deep thought and then spoke slowly.

"A while back, I was travelin' down the Santa Fe Trail on my way to California. I'd been ridin' hard for several days and decided to stop in Las Vegas, New Mexico, and stock up a little. It was a good gaming town, so I decided to spend some time there, do a little gambling and so on.

"I found a good hotel, took a hot bath and headed for a nearby saloon to try and find a game of stud. A short time later, three cowhands came in lookin' for a fourth, so I joined 'em. After we started playin', my tooth started botherin' me again."

"Your tooth?"

"Yeah, I chipped a tooth during a fight in Hays, Kansas, a few months earlier, and it was really startin' to hurt. Just as I was dragging in a small pot, the bartender poured me a heapin' mug of beer fresh out of the root cellar. I took a big swig of that cool beer, and it ran smack dab into my achin' tooth. The pain shot clean through my body. I jumped clear outta my chair yelping and hollerin'. The other players were laughin' like crazy.

"'Get on down to the dentist!' one of them shouted.

"'Where the hell is he?' I hollered.

"'At the north end of town, right next to the telegraph office.'

"I rushed outta there fast as a jack rabbit, jumped on Babe, and headed for the north end of town. The telegraph office sign and the small building next door were soon in sight. There was a buggy out front. I was heartbroken—I thought there was someone in front of me. But luckily for me, when I hopped down and hurried inside, the big leather dentist's chair was empty. I looked around the room for the doctor, but he was nowhere to be found. Just then, the back door popped open and this fella hurried in, holding a small metal pan. The sun was bright behind him so he was kind of in the shadows.

"He said hello, slammed the door and pointed toward the chair. Still hurtin' like crazy, I jumped in that chair like a flash. He started rummaging around on the counter behind me. The scent of expensive cologne filled the air.

"He asked what the problem was. I explained about the chipped tooth and how the pain shot clear through me when I took that swig of cool beer. He looked at me and kind of chuckled. All of a sudden, my seat fell back, and I was staring straight at the ceiling.

"I told him I was Jon Stoudenmire and stuck my hand back over my shoulder for a shake.

"'John Holliday,' he said. 'Glad to meet ya.' He reached back with his left hand, squeezed my fingers and shook my hand."

"John who?" Cliff shouted.

Jon smiled at his excited cousin. "As he bent over me, I got a better look at him. There was no doubt about it. It was none other than the famous man killer Doctor John Holliday, bending over me and gettin' ready to pull my tooth."

"Well, if that just don't beat all!"

"Yeah, I was plenty surprised all right. I thought he'd given up dentistry a long time ago. I sure didn't expect to see him in Las Vegas that day. Maybe he wanted to give dentistry one more shot, or he was tryin' to go straight or something. I dunno."

"Go on." Cliff was getting impatient.

"He stuck his finger in my mouth and looked around a minute. He shook his head and told me it was going to have to come out. He handed me a bottle of whiskey and ask me to take a couple of swigs.

"I grabbed the bottle and kind of hesitated.

"He noticed my reluctance and tried to explain. He said whiskey was the only pain killer he had, and it was strictly for customers only—he never drank out of it.

"So then I took a couple of big swigs."

"Why'd ya wait to take a drink?"

"Everybody knows Doc's got consumption—I was too young to die!" Jon laughed.

"Oh yeah, I guess so," Cliff said.

"He looked kinda dragged out, pale and all. Nothing like I expected, but I guess when you're sick like he is, you don't look too good. But I tell ya, those blue eyes of his had a mean look to 'em. I could see a killer there in those eyes.

"He stepped away and started digging through a pile of dental tools or something on that table behind me. Then he told me to grab hold of the sides of the chair. Then the skinny critter climbed on top of me and stuck this god-awful lookin' pair of pliers way down in my mouth and started yankin' on that tooth. I thought his eyeballs were gonna pop out of his head. All of the sudden, he jumped off of the chair and started waving that bloody tooth around. He was like a kid in a candy store! I couldn't believe how excited he got. He stuck it in front of me so I could get at good look at it. He dropped it in a metal pan on the table, washed his hands again and stuffed a whole wad of cotton in my mouth."

"How'd he do?"

"I'll have to say, for as shaky as he was, he did a pretty damn good job. It didn't hurt near as bad as I thought it would. And surprisingly, he didn't get a drop of my blood on that fancy silk shirt and tie he was wearin'.

"After a couple of minutes, he pulled that big piece of cotton out of my mouth, pulled the side of my mouth open and looked inside. After stuffing a smaller piece of cotton in, he told me to shut my mouth.

"He reached down for the handle on the chair and gave it a yank. He was stronger than I expected. The chair popped up, and he looked over at me and smiled. Then he said something that really surprised me. He looked me straight in the eye and said that he had always wanted to meet me. He said Wyatt told him a few years ago that I was one tough son-of-a-bitch. My face got a little red when he said that."

"As red as it is now?" Cliff quipped.

"Yeah, I guess so," the embarrassed gunman replied.

"What happened next?"

"Then he told me that he and his long time girl, Kate, better known as Big Nose Kate, got in one whale of a fight back in Dodge, so he left town and headed for Colorado. He said he landed in Trinidad, where a young gunhand named Kid Colton badgered him into a fight. In an attempt to defend himself, he shot him dead. Fearing reprisals from the locals, he didn't linger long in Trinidad. He packed up and headed out for New Mexico Territory. He said he was tired of all the killing and hoping for a new beginning, so he thought he'd try dentistry again. Then he kind of sighed, dumped my tooth in a trash can and walked over to the front door. Looking a little down, he grabbed the most expensive lookin' suit coat I've ever seen off the hook on the door and slipped it on. As I was climbing out of the chair, I asked him how business was going.

"Frowning, he said not very good. He said he was closing up and that he had opened a small saloon down on Center Street. And then to my surprise, he asked me to join him for a game of stud that night."

"Tell me it ain't true, cus! You and Doc Holliday in a card game!"

"Yeah, I was pretty much shocked all right. I told him I had a few things to do, and I would join him later.

"He nodded and laid his hand on my shoulder as we walked out the front door. He locked the door and strolled toward the center of town. Still tryin' to absorb the whole affair, I just stood for a minute and watched him walk away. This bad man, legendary killer of the West, turned out to be a likeable, well-spoken man."

"That's really somethin'," Cliff exclaimed.

"Yeah, but it didn't take long for me to see the other side of Doc Holliday."

"Oh yeah? What happened?"

"Well, after I ran all my errands, I headed on down to Center Street and Doc's place for that game of stud. I moseyed on in. He saw me right away and motioned me over to his table. He had a chair waitin' on me. He introduced me to the other players and then proceeded to deal. One of the players was a local gunman named Mike Gordon. He was joking and laughing with the other fellows. He seemed to be pretty popular. Doc seemed annoyed by him. I nodded at everyone and took my seat."

"In a card game with the Doc. That's somethin'." Cliff shook his head. "Could he play?"

"Yeah, he knew his cards all right, but he acted different than he did in his office. He seemed nervous and kinda edgy, and his eyes had a dark look to 'em. He was drinking quite a bit and not near as friendly. I guess a skinny rich kid from Valdosta, Georgia, had to be on his guard all the time.

"I played for a few hours, lost a little and called it a day. Doc stood up to say goodbye to me. I told him I was leavin' for California in the morning, and he wished me safe passage. He put his poker face back on and rejoined the game.

"The next morning, I got up early and headed down to the livery stable to pick up Babe. I stopped by the hardware store and picked up some supplies and then started to ride out. As I rode down Center Street, gunfire and screaming erupted inside Doc's saloon. As I got closer, I saw Doc come staggering out of the swinging doors with his six guns a smokin'. He stumbled off the boardwalk and almost ran into me. Surprised, he looked up at me with bloodshot eyes. He smiled a little when he saw it was me and lowered the gun. I'll tell ya, Cliff, I'll never forget the look on his face that morning for as long as I live. It wasn't anger or hatred—it was remorse and sadness on his face."

"Ya think he felt bad about shooting that hombre?"

"Sure seemed like it," Jon replied. "I asked how it happened, and he told me Gordon had accused him of cheating and went for his gun. Doc beat him to the punch and blasted him three times at close range. He said it was an awful sight. He literally blew his guts out. He knew the town would be after him, so he ran out of the saloon. Haggard and tired, Doc smelled of whiskey, stale cigars, and cologne.

"Then he turned and started walking real fast toward his horse. I reined around and rode next to him. I leaned down and asked him where he was headin'.

"He said the word 'Dodge' quietly so nobody would hear. I nodded as he dropped his guns in their holsters and quickly mounted up. I felt honored that he trusted me enough to tell me where he was goin'.

"As he mounted up, I jumped down and grabbed a pouch of water off Babe and tossed it over his horse's hindquarters. Then I quickly stuffed some flour and bacon into his saddlebags.

"He said 'Bless you, my friend,' as he spun around and rode off toward Dodge.

"Several people came running out of the saloon waving their six guns. Like I said, Gordon was a popular guy. The local folks were more than a little bit upset by his killing."

"Why'd they wait so long to come after him?" Cliff queried.

"Gordon was more than likely the only gunman in there. The rest of them were probably just normal folks. They really didn't want any part of Doc Holliday.

"One of the men asked me if I knew where Doc went, and I didn't say anything. The man just stared at me for a minute and then looked up and down the street. Doc had left town on one of the finest quarter horses I've ever seen. Even in his drunken state, he was a fine horseman. There's no way they would ever catch him. Several others rushed out to the street, waving their guns and shouting, but none gave chase. It was all for show. Disheartened by the loss of their friend, they dropped their guns in their holsters and walked back in the saloon. One of the men shouted 'Good riddance' over his shoulder.

"I quickly rode back to the general store, picked up another bag of water and other supplies and headed out for California again."

"That's one whale of a story, Jon."

Jon sat back in his chair. "Yeah, he's quite a guy. After only a short time with him, I can see why Wyatt liked him so much. There was somethin' about him, an honesty or somethin' most people never see."

"I bet Gordon didn't see it," Cliff quipped.

"Guess not," Jon replied.

"I hear Doc had a big shootout down Tombstone way not too long ago."

"Yeah, I heard about that," Jon replied. "I guess some cowboys got shot up pretty bad."

Jon has really changed, Cliff thought. Since he last saw him, Jon had become a hardened gunman. Just the kind of man that he and the others miners needed to take on George Stanton and his gang of hired guns. Cliff had a hunch.

"If you don't mind, Jon, I would like to take a couple a minutes and tell you a little bit about what's going on around here."

Jon smiled. "You were patient enough during my story, cus. Go ahead."

"Well, as you may know, this town is pretty well dependent on the nearby gold mines for its survival."

Jon nodded.

"The original vein on the side of a nearby mountain was discovered and mined by a man named George Stanton. Everything was going just great for Mr. Stanton in the beginning. In fact, it went so well that he was thinking of expanding and looking for gold in some nearby areas. Only problem was, he was a little short of capital to fund these new ventures. To improve his cash flow, he came up with a scheme to advertise out East. He offered the folks out East a chance to come here to California and buy into one of the small veins that splintered off his main vein with the chance of striking it rich. Each person or family would acquire a stake in a smaller vein near the main load and whatever gold was found would belong to them. Meanwhile, Stanton could take their cash and use it for further expansion and development in some of the promising areas just south of here. It would also expand his power and influence locally.

"Sounded good enough. The only problem was that it wasn't long before the large vein started to burn out. At the same time, several of the new prospectors were making lots of money on their stakes, and George didn't like it. He had spent most of his money exploring for new veins in nearby foothills. These efforts had gone bust, and his cash reserves were beginning to dwindle. He was becoming desperate for cash. So he came up with a plan to buy the miners out at double what they had paid for their claims, but nobody was biting. Many of them were in the process of getting rich, and naturally, they weren't about to sell. Their reluctance made George furious, and it wasn't long before some hired guns were beginning to show up in town. If someone refused to sell, he would soon get a visit from one of Stanton's new guns. It was getting ugly, and people were beginning to get frightened. And now he was offering them just fifty cents on the dollar."

Big Jon fell back in his chair and looked over at Cliff. "Are they threatening you?"

"Well, I had a visit the other evening from a gentleman named Dave Barton. Know the name?"

"Sure do. He's about the meanest snake this side of the Pecos River, and he won't hesitate a minute to gun you down if the money's right."

"Sounds like a great fellow." Cliff had a worrisome look on his face.

"One of the worst, and I have to say this, that George Stanton of yours didn't go halfway when he brought in Barton. He's one of the nastiest sons-a-guns I've ever known. He was the enforcer for a local cattle baron in Ellsworth, Kansas, back when I was ridin' shotgun on a local stagecoach line. A lot of small ranchers and squatters were starting to move into the area, and Barton's boss didn't like it. He turned Dave loose on the poor unsuspecting louts, and it got ugly. It wasn't long before several ranchers and squatters turned up dead. Everyone in town knew who did it, but because Barton's boss owned the local sheriff, nothin' was ever done about it. It will take a strong man to deal with a man like Barton. Is there anybody like that around here in law enforcement?"

"We have a county sheriff. But he was George's right hand man before he became sheriff."

"Well, I guess you can forget about him," Jon said. "Just for the record, Cliff, who is this fine sheriff?"

"Dan Cook. Not a bad fellow, but he is scared to death of George."

"Sounds like just about everyone around here is afraid of this Stanton fella," Jon replied as he downed another shot.

"Yeah. They are."

"Doesn't sound good, Cliff. Looks like you got a real problem on your hands."

Jon was trying to distance himself from the situation; he didn't want any part of this mess. With his reputation, the next thing he knew Cliff would be asking for his help. He had to call an early end to the evening before he got drawn into something.

"I hate to say it, Cliff, but I'm just plain tuckered out, and I better get me some rest. I gotta big day ahead of me tomorrow and need to get some serious shuteye."

Undeterred, Cliff pushed on. "Jon, me and the other prospectors could sure use a man like you around here. We're facing hired killers here, and most of the miners are just average folks—family people— just like those folks in Las Vegas. They have no idea how to deal with such people."

"Sorry to hear about your problems, Cliff, I truly am, but I can't help ya. I got enough problems of my own without borrowin' any. This saddle bum is heading on to Vinegar Bend in the morning to build a cabin and settle down. I wish you luck," he said as he pushed his chair back and stood to leave. "Evenin'," he said quietly, not able to look his cousin in the eye.

"Good night, Jon, and I understand what you're saying, partner. This is our fight. Don't blame ya a bit," Cliff said somberly, burnt a little by his lack of success.

Jon smiled, wheeled around and wove his way through the crowded saloon to the door. He felt troubled as he walked down the street to the hotel. He knew he had left dinner a little abruptly, but he just couldn't let himself fall into the same old trap. His friend and cousin was in trouble and needed help, and it tugged at him. The same thing happened at his last stop in Logan's Crossing, and a bloody orgy resulted with several people ending up dead. He couldn't let that happen again. Not if he could help it.

Chapter 6

Jon slept in the next morning; after a quick bath and a late breakfast at the local café, he hurried down to the stables.

The big wooden door at the stables squeaked as Jon pulled it open. "Anybody here?" he asked.

"Hold your britches on! I'll be right with ya," a voice shouted out from one of the stalls. "

As Jon walked over to Babe's stall and gently stroked her neck, he could hear the stablehand hurrying toward him. He stopped and looked at Jon, apparently annoyed that Jon had taken the liberty to enter Babe's stall.

"How's she doing, Mr.—?" Jon asked as he backed out of the stall.

"The name's Hank Clark, and she's doing just fine, but she's still a little tired. Another day's rest and grooming would do her a lot of good, Mr.—"

"Stoudenmire, Jon Stoudenmire. And you're the boss, Hank. Whatever you say. She was plenty tuckered when we got to town yesterday."

Hank nodded and watched as Jon ambled out of the stable area.

Jon tipped his hat to the wary hand and headed down Main Street to see about getting a few supplies. The weathered steps to the general store sunk a little as he stepped up. Suddenly he ducked to his left as a six gun blasted away nearby. Instinctively, he jumped down to the street, drew his six gun and spun to confront the fire. At the same time, the shooter turned toward Jon's menacing six gun. "Easy, partner, easy now, draw down, just shootin' an old nasty rattler here in the alley beside the store. Meant no harm." It was a familiar but unpleasant voice.

"No harm done, Barton, but something tells me it wasn't an accident." Jon eased his Colt slowly back into its holster.

"Oh it was, Jon. If I had wanted to kill you, we wouldn't be standing here talking about it. Just wanted to shoot this varmint before he harmed somebody." Barton leaned down, hooked the dead snake on his gun barrel and pointed it at Jon.

"Well, I guess we all owe you a debt of gratitude for saving our lives from this little critter," Jon said sarcastically. "What's a man like you doin' way out here in these parts anyway, Barton?"

"I was going to ask you the same thing, Jon. I hear you been spendin' a lot of time with Cliff Stone."

"Word gets around plenty fast."

"Yeah it does, Jon, and I'm listening real close to everything I hear lately," Barton said threateningly.

Jon's brow furrowed. "You're wasting your time with me, Barton. I'm just passin' through."

"That's good, Stoudenmire. That might save us both a little grief," the surly gunhand replied as he ambled over and tossed the snake out in the desert.

"What's goin' on in El Cabrera is none of your affair anyhow, Stoudenmire," he barked as he mounted up. "If you stick around, you'll have me to deal with." Before Jon could answer, he reined his steed around and rode quickly out of town.

Jon was furious as he watched Barton ride off on his painted sorrel. *That man could use a lesson or two,* he thought as he spit defiantly on the dusty street. But the truth was, as much as he despised him, Barton was a dangerous man. A stocky muscular man, he was quick and fearless with a gun and seemed to always be itching for a fight. Might be better to stick to his plan and let someone else deal with Dave Barton.

Chapter 7

The sun was getting intense as Jon stepped around the many potholes on the way to the Dead End Saloon for lunch. It was a typical day; gunfire could be heard out on the street, followed by the predictable whooping and hollering. This low mountain mining town attracted all sorts of bad actors, and he wanted no part of it. A short time later, he reached the saloon and pushed through the swinging doors. After a quick look around, he ambled over to the end of the bar and ordered a shot of Early Times. As Jake splashed whiskey in the thick glass, Jon's thoughts took him back to the first time he had laid eyes on his vineyard.

He'd never forget it. He was standing on a hillside looking down over the beautiful valley below. It was stunning, row after row of lush green vines being pulled downward by shiny bunches of deep purple grapes covered with dew and glistening in the morning sun. *What a paradise*, he thought. *I'll be there soon, Good Lord willin'*.

"Are you all right?" Lou Stanton's voice nudged Jon back to reality.

"Why, yes, I sure am, Lou. Just daydreamin' a little, I guess," a slightly red-faced Jon replied.

Lou laughed out loud. "I guess we all do that once in a while. Are you heading out today?"

"Well, I was plannin' on it, but I guess my horse needs another day of rest and grooming. I've been ridin' her pretty hard lately."

The dapper saloon owner smiled.

"Tell me something, Lou. Have you got any card players in this town? I got a whole bunch of time to kill, and I sure wouldn't mind a game of five card stud right now."

"Well, guess what Mr.—"

Jon interrupted. "It's Jon Stoudenmire, but call me Jon, please!"

"Well guess what, Jon, this may be your lucky day," Lou said. "Attorney Fred Smith, president of the town board, closes his office every day for a couple of hours just before lunch and deals a few hands. He always plays with the sheriff and two or three other board members. I'm sure he wouldn't mind if you joined them. They should be here any time."

"The president of the town board and Sheriff Cook, that's really somethin'," Jon said humbly. "Do they play stud?"

"Yes. Here they come now. Looks like there's…uh, just three of them," said Lou, standing on his tip toes so he could see over the batwing doors. "I'm sure they'll need a player now."

The three local leaders were talking and laughing as they entered the saloon for their daily game of stud.

"Good morning Fred," Lou said enthusiastically.

"Mornin', Lou! And how's the wealthiest saloon owner this side of the Rocky Mountains doing on this fine day?"

"Wealthy, my foot!" Lou chuckled.

Fred smiled and glanced over at Jon and nodded hello.

Lou noticed the acknowledgement and spoke up. "I would like you fellas to meet Jon Stoudenmire. He's just in from Arizona."

"How are you, Jon? Nice to meet you," Fred said as he reached forward for a shake. "This gentleman here is Dan Cook, our local sheriff. And this ugly critter over here is Bill Zollars. He's on the town board."

"Mornin', Fred, nice to meet ya. My pleasure, Sheriff Cook. How ya doin', Bill?" Jon said as he shook each man's hand.

"Jon here's looking for a game," said Lou.

"Oh, good, good, glad to have you. It would be a pleasure," Fred said sincerely. "We play at that table right over there." Fred pointed to a table in the corner of the room away from the other gaming tables. "It gives us a little privacy."

"Let's get started. I don't have long," the sheriff exclaimed as he glanced down at Jon's Colts.

"Do you fellas mind if I take the chair against the wall?" Jon asked as the men approached the table.

"You got somebody hot on your trail, Jon?" Sheriff Cook asked.

"Oh no, just habit I guess," said Jon as he moved around the table and sat down.

"No problem, Jon, but it's only ten o'clock. Most gunslingers I know don't get out of bed until noon.

You should be safe. Ain't that right, Fred?" the sheriff cackled.

"Well…uh, I guess so," Fred replied nervously.

Upset by the untimely gunslinger comment, Jon glared at the sheriff as he sat down across from Jon.

"Five card stud okay with you, Jon?" Fred inquired as he began to shuffle.

"Stud's the game. Deal 'em." Jon carefully slipped a cigar out of his inside vest pocket.

"Mind if I smoke, gentlemen?"

They all nodded their approval as Fred dealt high card for the deal. Sheriff Cook drew an ace right away. Fred slid the deck over the green velvet tabletop to the sheriff. He gathered them up, did a quick reshuffle and pushed them right for a cut. Bill tapped on the cards indicating no cut as Sheriff Cook hastily started the first deal.

Play was quiet at first, with nobody saying much. Jon had just won a pot when the sheriff spoke up.

"You the Jon Stoudenmire that gunned down all those men down Arizona way?" the sheriff asked. His eyes stayed on his cards, never making eye contact with Jon.

The other men fidgeted nervously in their seats, disarmed by the direct question from the sheriff. It wasn't polite to ask such a question of a stranger, especially in the middle of a friendly card game.

"The name's Stoudenmire all right, but I didn't gun anyone down. I was the sheriff, and I was enforcing the law against some very bad men. I'd think a man of the law like you would understand that." Jon glared at the sheriff. "We got us a friendly game goin' here, Sheriff. Let's keep it that way."

Sheriff Cook glanced over his cards at Jon. The two stared at each other for several seconds. The sheriff spoke. "We got us a peaceable town here, Mr. Stoudenmire, and we want it to stay that way."

Jon shot back, "Well, that's good, 'cause I'm probably the most peaceable man you'll ever know." Jon was staring daggers at him now, trying to keep his cool.

Unnerved by the intense stare from the famed gunman, the sheriff looked back at his cards.

"Hot damn!" Fred shouted as he dealt his up card. "I just hit an ace. Raise ya five!"

Jon collected himself and replied, "I know I'm crazy, but I'm gonna call that bet, Fred." He threw his gold piece in the pot.

Zollars grumbled something and threw in his cards.

"I'm afraid I'm going to have to fold also," Sheriff Cook exclaimed as he tossed his cards face down on the table. "And if you'll excuse me, gentlemen, I have to go back to my office and meet with some ranchers about some cattle rustling that's been going on out east of town." Sheriff Cook pushed his chair back and stood up; he nodded as he turned and walked toward the door.

Fred flipped over his hole card, revealing aces up. "Well, that's a heck of a note," Fred bellowed as he watched the sheriff walk away. "I just get hot, and the sheriff hightails it outa here."

"Beats my kings," Jon groused.

"How about a few more hands of hold 'em, gentlemen, and then we'll call it a day?" Fred asked as he raked in the pot.

"Sounds good to me," Jon replied.

"Me too," said Bill quietly.

Jon was still a little upset. His exchange with Sheriff Cook had not been a pleasant one. It was obvious to Jon that Stanton viewed him as a threat to his plans to take over the gold mines. The fine sheriff was sending him a message, but Jon wanted no part of this fight. As soon as Babe was rested, he was gonna saddle up and move on down the road.

The three men continued to play for a short time and then parted ways with a friendly handshake. Fred apologized to Jon for the sheriff's rudeness as the three men stepped out to the busy street. Fred turned toward Jon. "We're playing tomorrow, Jon. If you're still in town, you're welcome to join us."

"Thank ya, Fred, but I hope to be headin' out tomorrow."

"Travel safe," Fred said as he and Bill stepped off of the boardwalk and melted into the traffic on the busy street.

Suddenly, Jon heard two men shouting across the street near the bank. One of the men looked like Dave Barton. The other man was in the shadows of the overhang. There was a lot of shoving and finger pointing going on as a crowd began to gather. Jon jumped down from the wooden walkway and moved across the street for a better look. As Jon wove his way through the busy midday traffic, Barton yanked out his gun and clubbed the other man, knocking him to the ground.

As Jon drew closer, he saw that it was Cliff lying on the dusty road.

"This is my last offer. You got twenty-four hours to sell that property," Barton barked as he waved the six gun above the face of the fallen man.

Cliff, still groggy from the clubbing, staggered to get to his feet to confront his tormentor.

"You go to hell, Barton. I'm not selling!" he shouted defiantly.

"Just remember what I said, Stone—twenty-four hours!"

By now, quite a crowd had gathered, playing into Barton's hand. The more people who saw the clubbing and heard the threats, the fewer miners he would have to confront later. Barton turned to leave, almost bumping into Jon.

"You're a pretty tough hombre against an unarmed man." Jon pushed his chest forward, further blocking Barton's path.

"Got no fight with you, Stoudenmire. Just step aside and let me get on down the road."

"I'll think about it, Dave." Jon held still in the street. "Cliff and I go back a long way. You're pushin' your luck with me, Barton."

"Fine, consider me warned. But I can kill two men as easily as one," he said coldly as he stepped around Jon. "And I got plenty of help if necessary."

Incensed, Jon gritted his teeth. He wanted to kill Barton right on the spot, but he couldn't. It would only lead to more trouble and a longer stay in El Cabrera.

"Better watch your backside, Dave," Jon said as the gunman walked toward his horse.

"You heard me," Barton said as he mounted up and spurred his steed toward the edge of town. Jon was fuming, his hands hovering over his six guns as he watched the mouthy gunman ride away. He collected himself and hurried over to Cliff. "You okay?" he asked.

"Yeah…just a little embarrassed, I guess."

"You were never a fightin' man, Cliff, but you always stood up for yourself. What happened?"

"I'm not sure. I passed him on the way into town, and he must have circled around and followed me back in. He surprised me when I walked up to the bank. I didn't have time to get my wits about me. We had words, and the next thing I knew, he was clubbing me. Next time I'll be ready for him," Cliff said quietly, still shaken by the beating.

"That's good, give a varmint like him half a chance, and he'll put you in the ground."

Cliff frowned. "You're right, and I'm afraid he's got the whole town buffaloed. They all know he's a killer, and nobody wants to die. I'm afraid Stanton is winning this battle for the goldfields. Won't be too long before all the miners will have been chased off, and Stanton will control everything around here. All we'll have are busted dreams and thoughts of what could have been. It just ain't right, Jon!" The dust flew as Cliff smacked his hat hard against his leg. "A lot of innocent people are going to get hurt before this thing's over," Cliff said as he mounted up. He looked over at Jon without saying a word and rode out of town.

Cliff's comments really tore into Jon. How could he let his own flesh and blood down at a time like this? Cliff had come out here to start a new life and now these sidewinders were trying to take it away from him. Jon was the only one who could deal with these killers, and if he left, he would be leaving his cousin to their mercy. To leave now went against every instinct in his body. But he had to go. He had to stick to his plan to get out of town, or he might end up dead. And besides, this wasn't his fight. This was just a town he had stopped in on the way to his vineyard. He had to get a hold of himself and on his desire to put a bullet in the belly of Dave Barton and be on his way.

Jon was still upset as he gently pushed open the swinging doors at the Dead End. He made his way slowly to the end of the bar. He reached into his jeans pocket and tossed a five dollar coin on the bar. "Give me a bottle a whiskey, Jake," he muttered.

Jake slid a full bottle out of the rack, splashed the whiskey in a glass and set the bottle in front of Jon. He hurried back to the kitchen.

Upset, Jon gulped down the shot and quickly poured another. As he stood alone at the end of the bar getting more and more intoxicated, he felt himself becoming frightened as he began to ponder the events that were unfolding around him. He had no fear of Dave Barton or George Stanton or any of his henchmen. He had faced their type many times before and rather than fear them, he had only contempt for them. What frightened Jon was how he felt inside; his hatred of injustice was pushing him toward this fight, and he didn't like it.

Jon was shaken out of his thoughts by guns blasting out in the street. Suddenly the swinging doors burst open, and four men came charging in, laughing and shouting, guns still smoking. Table and chairs rattled as the folks quickly ducked out of the way of the aggressive intruders.

"What's the matter with everyone?" the lead man shouted. "Let's all drink up and have a good time."

Flames shot in the air as the swarthy little man fanned his six gun.

Jon immediately recognized the lead man as the raucous group made their way toward the bar. It was Injun Joe, a half-breed, part Apache and part white man—and one of the meanest and most wicked gunmen Jon had ever known. A veteran of the Lincoln County wars, he had made quite a reputation for himself by gunning down innocent cowboys. This must be George Stanton's latest hire, his most recent attempt to put the fear of God in the miners.

The breed was a rather small man with a large head and thin lips that seemed always to be twisted in a grotesque smile. His long black hair, square dark face, and black eyes with bushy eyebrows added to his ominous appearance. He had an ugly deep scar that started at his left temple and ended at the side of his mouth. Jon thought he had the look of pure evil.

Still shaken by his own inner demons, Jon knew that this was a very bad time for Injun Joe to show up. Jon was in a bad mood. One wrong move or misstep by Injun Joe, and he would get a free ticket to the happy hunting grounds.

It didn't take long for things to begin to happen. Joe glanced over and recognized Jon; his pace slowed noticeably as he made his way to the bar. Perspiring freely, he slid his guns back into his holster as he and the other men lined up at the bar. The sight of Big Jon seemed to unnerve him.

Jon felt hot, dirty, drunk and angry as he looked over at the nasty crew lined up along the bar. The tension in the room was so thick you could cut it with a knife.

Obviously intimidated by Jon, Injun Joe was stone quiet. Jon finally broke the ice.

"What brings you to town, Joe—lookin' for somebody to shoot in the back?" he said coolly.

Jon went on, not letting Joe answer. "I hope you're just passin' through, 'cause if you're workin' for George Stanton, you and I got a big problem, and I'm in no mood for problems right now!"

Sweat from Injun Joe's face dripped on the bar; his hands were trembling. The other men didn't move. They were more than likely just hired mine workers and would back off pretty quickly if trouble started. Jon knew if push came to shove, it would be him against Joe.

"Got no fight with you, Jon," Joe said nervously. "Best you leave matters to those people involved and get on down the road."

"Listen to me, you yellow-bellied son-of-a-bitch. Don't you ever try to tell me what to do. And I do have a dog in this fight," Jon said. Unable to control his anger any longer, he began to fill with rage. "My cousin is being forced out of his mine and I don't like it." Jon was almost shouting now; the liquor was taking effect.

Jon started moving slowly out from behind the end of the bar. As expected, the other three men backed away from the bar and hurried out the door. They obviously wanted no part in this fight. The door banged back and forth as other folks fled the saloon. Jake the bartender dropped onto the wood floor behind the bar.

"I wasn't trying to tell you what to do, Jon," Injun Joe said calmly. He continued to look straight ahead; any movement in either direction would cause Jon to draw, and he didn't want that. "We go back a long way,

Jon. I just wanted to be sure you knew what was coming down around here. No insult meant," Joe pleaded.

Just then the doors swung open, and Lou hurried in from a visit to the bank. He stopped dead in his tracks as he saw the looming confrontation between the two gunmen. Eyes wide, he scanned the room. He spoke very calmly, not wanting to rile anyone.

"What's going on here, Jon? Have we got a problem?"

Jon turned slightly toward Lou.

"Everything is—"

Suddenly, like a frightened animal, Injun Joe saw his chance to make his move. He jumped back from the bar, grabbled for his revolver and shot wildly in the direction of Jon. Watching the nasty bugger out of the corner of his eye, Jon drew and blasted away. The deafening sound of exploding gunpowder reverberated throughout the saloon as Jon poured three shots into Joe's midsection. His thick body reeled backward against the bar.

"I hope you burn in hell, Stoudenmire!" Joe screamed as his gun fired harmlessly into the floor of the saloon. He staggered around helplessly and then fell hard to the wood floor face down. With one last violent spasm, his body flipped over onto its back. The bad man had an ugly look on his dark face as he gurgled up blood and then fell silent.

Jon stood staring down at the fallen man. "Shoulda stayed in New Mexico, Joe." He whispered as he turned to walk away.

Badly shaken by the gory scene, Lou Stanton approached Jon.

"You know this isn't the end of this, don't you?" Lou said as he drew closer to Jon.

"Yeah, I'm sure it isn't. Your brother George is not going to be happy about me killin' one of his hired guns."

"I wasn't referring to my brother. I'm sure he's not—"

"Save your breath, Lou. When I accused Joe of working for George, he didn't deny it, so that's good enough for me."

"You best be certain, Jon. That's a strong accusation you're making."

"I know it is. Maybe you'd better start asking your brother a few questions."

Lou frowned as Jon excused himself and stepped outside.

The street was buzzing with activity. People were rushing toward the Dead End to see what was going on. One of the interested parties was Sheriff Dan Cook, just back from the rancher's meeting. The aggressive sheriff elbowed his way through the gathering crowd and confronted Jon as he was exiting the Dead End.

"Looks like we've had some trouble here, Mr. Stoudenmire," the sheriff said, blocking Jon's path.

"That's right, Sheriff! You'll find Injun Joe in there in a pool of blood. It was self defense. Lou Stanton and several others saw the whole thing."

"I don't know what happened in there, Jon, but it looks like you just killed a man, and I need to do an investigation. I want you in town for a day or so until I can get this thing sorted out."

"No problem, Dan. I'm startin' to kinda like this town. I was planning on stickin' around for a while anyway," Jon said calmly as he pushed by the sheriff and headed to the hotel.

Unnerved by the violent shootout, Jon avoided making eye contact with the curious townsfolk as he walked to Callahan's Boardinghouse. Exhausted, he stepped into the hotel and climbed the stairs to the second floor. He walked into his room, tossed his guns on the featherbed and dropped in the soft chair next to the bed.

There was a sudden knock on the door.

"Who is it?" he barked as he jumped up and grabbed his six gun.

"It's me, Cliff. Let me in."

Jon tossed his gun on the bed and hurried over to open the door. "Come on in."

Cliff looked concerned. "You all right?" he asked as he scanned Jon from head to toe.

"Yeah…yeah, I'm fine. Sit down." Jon offered Cliff a chair and sat down on the edge of the bed. "I thought you left town, Cliff."

"I did. But just a few miles out of town, I remembered that I hadn't finished my errands. I guess the knock on my head confused me a little. So I headed back to town. A short time later, I heard gunfire. I asked some cowpoke on the edge of town what was goin' on, and he told me a big stranger had just shot up the Dead End Saloon. I figured it might be you, so I hightailed down the street to the saloon. Someone in the crowd told me you were down at Callahan's, so here I am. What the heck happened down there?"

"Well, it wasn't pretty. After we parted ways, I moseyed on down to the Dead End for a drink. I'd just sat down when a heartless killer named Injun Joe came bustin' in the door, guns a blazin'. He's a mean nasty varmint from Lincoln County, New Mexico. After my run in with Barton, I was in a real foul mood, so he and I locked horns right away. I asked him if he was one of Stanton's hires, and he got quiet. That was good enough for me, so I called him out. He got nervous and went for his gun. I let him have it pretty good." Jon's voice was trailing off as he spoke of the gory scene. "Sheriff Cook showed up and ordered me to stay in town until he finishes his investigation. I gave Cook a piece of my mind and headed on down here."

"Hmmm—that's one way to get you to stay in town," Cliff joked lamely.

Jon smiled at his cousin. "I was planning on staying anyway. If ya got a minute, I'll tell you why."

"My errands can wait. Fire away."

"You remember that hot summer a long time ago when you and your pa came over to help us on the farm with the bailing?" Jon asked.

"Yeah. Your pa was down sick for a while and got behind. So we came over to help out. I remember that day well."

Jon scooted over and leaned against the wall next to the bed. "So do I, Cliff. I remember it like it was yesterday. You were eleven and I was thirteen, and it was hotter'n a firecracker that day. We were workin' a new field Pa had just bought from a neighbor the year before. It was way out, a long way from the farmhouse. We'd been bailing all day and were ready for a break. Your pa yelled over and told us to call it a day. He said we could take a dip in the river if we wanted before we headed back. He told us to water the mules before we left and not to dally too long. We threw down our pitchforks and hollered in delight. I swear our feet hit the ground before those pitchforks. We put our heads down and ran for that river, leaving a trail of clothes behind us. Naked as jaybirds, we dove head first into that old, muddy river. Remember how cold that water felt?"

"How could I forget?"

"It wasn't long before we were fightin' and splashin' and having a ball. That's when I spotted that big oak tree next to the river."

"Yep, you sure did."

"It wasn't long before I was clawin' my way up the muddy bank and shimmying up that big tree. I looked around and found a high, narrow limb that hung out over the stream. Hanging on for dear life, I scooted out to the end of the limb. You were laughin' and callin' me 'muscle butt.'"

"From where I was, it seemed like the thing to say," Cliff quipped.

"I guess so," Jon bawled. "I crawled clear out to the end of that limb."

"You sure did. You were crazy even then!"

"I grabbed a smaller limb just above my head. I pulled myself up to a standing position. That's when you told me to hurry up 'cause you saw some neighbor girls coming across the field! Remember?"

Cliff's face turned bright red.

"A bolt of fear shot up my spine. I covered my privates, took a couple of wobbly steps on that narrow limb and dove head first into that dark, muddy river. It seemed like forever before I hit that water. You know what happened next."

Cliff nodded, "I sure do."

"My head crashed into somethin' real hard, a rock or somethin'. A horrible pain shot clean up my spine—everything went black. When I came to, I was lyin' face down on the bank in a daze. You were pushing on my back and yellin', 'Don't die, Jonnie, please don't die!' You kept on pushin' and shoutin', pushin' and shoutin'."

Cliff chuckled nervously and shook his head.

"All of a sudden, a bunch of warm water came gushing out of my mouth. I rolled to my back and looked up at you. Your eyes were big as saucers."

"I was scared to death," Cliff laughed.

Jon's thick eyebrows furrowed; he leaned up on the corner of the bed. "You saved my life that day, cus, you sure enough did. I wouldn't be here today if it wasn't for you."

Cliff looked down at the floor. "Aw…hell, Jon, it wasn't nothin'. Besides, I shouldn't have lied about those girls."

"Lied! You mean there weren't any girls!" Jon hollered. "You no account sodbuster." Jon grabbed his pillow off the bed and began slapping Cliff on the head. Both men were roaring in laughter as Jon whacked the beaming Cliff a couple more times.

"We were pretty close back in those days, Jon." Cliff's eyes were moist as he glanced over at his big cousin.

"We sure enough were, partner." Jon gently ruffled Cliff's black curly hair and then stood and slowly walked over to the window. He looked down at the busy street and said, "I've been doing a lot of thinking, Cliff. Those God-fearin' folks down there in the street have been put upon by some very bad men. And like I said, I owe you big time, my friend. I'm more than ready to join you and the townsfolk in your fight against Stanton and his bunch of hired guns. But we'd better get at it. We got us a mess to clean up."

Cliff quickly stood, and a look of excitement spread over his face. "Welcome aboard!"

"Thank ya, Cliff." Jon smiled warmly. "I'm gonna take a ride out to the mines tomorrow and nose around a little bit. See what I can find out."

"Sounds good, Jon. I'll keep my ear to the ground here in town." Cliff turned for the door. "I best be goin'. The stores are going to close soon."

"Before you run off, where's a good place to get some grub around here?"

"Oh, that's an easy one. The Crown Restaurant's down at the north end of town. It's got the best food in town. The cook worked for Colonel Chivington during the war. Whaddya say I run my errands and meet ya down there in about an hour?"

"Sounds good, partner. See ya there."

Cliff slipped on his hat and hurried out the door.

Chapter 8

Jon gently tapped the top of the gold bell once again. A soft voice came out of the living quarters behind the front desk. "Just a moment. I'll be right there."

Jon could hear the clang of dishes and a cabinet door closing as he stood waiting patiently. He soon heard light footsteps and the swish of a gown across the floor. The oak door swung slowly open. A smiling Miss Callahan stepped out to greet him.

"Sorry, Mr. Stoudenmire, I was cleaning up a little. I didn't know you were out here." Maggie was blushing slightly.

"No problem at all, Miss—"

The pretty owner interrupted. "Oh! Maggie, please—everyone calls me Maggie."

"No problem, Maggie. I just needed to talk with you for a moment."

"Certainly. Go ahead."

"Somethin's come up, and I'm going to be sticking around for a while. Any chance I can rent my room a little longer?"

The unexpected request brought a smile to Maggie's face. "Why of course, Mr.—"

Jon quickly raised his eyebrows.

"Why of course, Jon. You can have the room for as long as necessary," Maggie said, the corner of her mouth curling up flirtatiously. "Our weekly rate is fifteen dollars, to be paid in advance. You already gave me five dollars for the first two nights, so you just owe me ten more to complete the week. We can continue on this basis for as long as you like."

"Well thank ya Maggie, I'm lookin' forward to it."

Maggie continued. "I saw you with Cliff Stone today. An old friend?"

Surprised by the question, Jon paused. "Cliff's my cousin. We grew up together back in Indiana," he said as he pulled two gold pieces from his pocket.

"Cousin, you say. How nice. I think a lot of Cliff. He's a good friend."

Eyebrows raised, Jon glanced up at the savvy Miss Callahan. "Just a friend, huh?"

"Yes, that's all, just friends."

Jon placed the coins in Maggie's open hand. She squeezed his hand gently as she accepted the coins, never losing eye contact with the surprised gunman. "Thank you, Jon," she said softly.

The unexpected squeeze startled Jon. He hesitated briefly. "I best be going," he said nervously. He smiled and backed awkwardly out of the front door.

"Where the hell did that come from?" Jon mumbled as he hurried down the dusty street to the Crown Restaurant.

After a short walk, Jon arrived at the restaurant, stepped inside, took off his brown felt hat and looked around. It was a fine restaurant with dark walnut trim around the doors and windows; cut-glass tabletops adorned with fine china filled the room. A lovely bouquet of fresh flowers sat atop each table. Cliff was waving at him from a table in the corner of the room. Jon hurried across the soft, red carpeting to his friend.

"Howdy, Cliff. Been here long?"

"Nope. Just got here."

"Nice place. I'm impressed." Jon dropped his hat on the table and sat down next to the wall.

"It just opened a few months ago, and they got the best darn food in town. Roast duck and scalloped corn is the special tonight with fresh-baked apple pie for desert."

"Sounds good, Cliff. Dinner's on me, and don't argue!"

"You got a way with words, sweet talker."

A dark-skinned waitress hurried over and carefully turned over the delicate cups. Smiling warmly, she filled them with steaming hot coffee.

"Thank you, Anita," said Cliff politely. "We'll have two specials please! And apple pie after dinner."

"Salad?" Anita asked.

Both men nodded.

"I bring you salad before dinner." She hurried off.

"Looks like things are goin' pretty good around here. Sure aren't any poor folk in here."

"Yeah, for the time being—as long as the folks are allowed to work their claims in peace. On the other hand, if Stanton gets control of all the mines, this town will dry up. A few people might stick around to work in nearby vineyards, but most of 'em would hightail it outta here. Things will be much different. He'll hire some Mexicans from nearby villages to work the claims, and they won't stick around town much. They'll just come in for supplies and then go back to their villages."

"What about his brother Lou? He'd be hurt also?"

"If George can control the gold around here, he will become a very wealthy man. Then he'll become a big shot in state politics. He's a very ambitious man, and I don't think he'll let anything stand in his way, not even his own flesh and blood." Cliff frowned.

"Where's this Stanton live?"

"He took over an abandoned Spanish Mission just outside of town, toward Vinegar Bend. He fixed it all up. It's a beautiful place, protected by a large adobe wall. The nuns used the wall to keep the kids in when it was a mission. Stanton added a locked metal gate and a few turrets on the corners of the wall to keep people out."

"Does he have a family?"

"Nope, he's never been married. He likes to play the field. A lot of women are impressed with his money. I guess he and Maggie have been seein' each other lately, and it looks like it might be getting serious."

"Well, at least he's got good taste. That Maggie's quite a girl."

Cliff shook his head. "I can't get a read on Maggie. Like I told ya, I've been out with her a couple of times. She's nice enough, but kind of hard to figure. I'm not sure what Maggie's after."

"Is she from around here?" Jon asked.

"Nope. She came here from Los Angeles about four years ago with her sister. They opened a nice women's clothing store down the street, but it never really got off the ground. I guess not enough miners wanted dresses," Cliff chuckled. "Her sister got fed up with the business and decided to go back to Los Angeles. Maggie sold the dress shop for about fifty cents on the dollar and bought the boardinghouse a couple of years ago. It's doing real well. She runs a nice business."

"Hmmm…a big city girl," Jon replied.

"Yeah, I guess so. Why all the interest in Maggie? You aren't gettin' any ideas, are you?" Cliff's eyebrows raised a little; he looked over at his nervous cousin.

"Oh no, just curious—that's all."

Cliff watched as the waitress carefully set the salads and dressing on the table. "Thank you, Anita." He said.

"Maggie best be careful with Stanton," Cliff remarked. "She's playin' with fire. He'll use her up and spit her out."

"I barely know the woman, but something tells me that she can take care of herself all right. Just a hunch or something." Jon grinned.

"I dunno, Jon. Stanton can be a real charmer if he wants to." Cliff set the cloth napkin on his lap. "Let's eat."

- - - - -

The fork clanged as Jon dropped it on the empty dessert dish, exclaiming, "Best darn apple pie I've had in a long time." Jon rubbed his full stomach, reached into his inside vest pocket and pulled out a cigar. He bit off the end and spit it into the spittoon next to the table. He sighed contentedly as he lit up.

"Smoke?" he asked as he pointed the cigar toward Cliff.

"No, thanks."

"You never told me, Cliff. How's your stake doin'?"

"Fair to middlin'," Cliff replied. "I have some good days and some bad days. I pulled three hundred dollars worth outta there one day last week. Biggest day I've had so far. But my average day is about twenty dollars a day."

"That explains the visit from Barton."

Cliff grimaced. "I think you're right. Several of the guys have been doin' okay in my area. Stanton's had his eye on our hill for quite a while."

"Kinda like a vulture soaring around waitin' for the kill," Jon snarled.

"Yeah, I guess so." Cliff glanced over at the front door and murmured, "Look who's here."

Jon glanced toward the door as Sheriff Cook and one of his deputies were just coming in the Crown; they were talking and laughing as they found a table and sat down. When the lawman looked over and saw Jon and Cliff, the smile dropped off his face. Jon and Cliff nodded at the surprised sheriff.

The men were interrupted by Anita's voice. "Anything else, gentlemen?"

"Naw, that'll be all," Jon said as she handed him the check.

"Thank you and pleeze come back."

"Thank you kindly, Anita. That was a wonderful dinner." Jon tossed a ten dollar gold piece on the table. "Keep the change," he said.

"Sí, señor, thank you very much!"

Jon led the way to the door, purposely walking past Cook's table. Jon smiled at the surly sheriff.

"Evenin', Sheriff. Good to see you again." Jon reached forward for a shake.

Sheriff Cook looked annoyed. He feigned a smile and extended his hand. "Hello, Jon," he said. "Didn't expect to see you here."

"You told me to stick around for a couple of days, so I may as well enjoy your little town while I'm here. No sense sittin' alone in my room."

The friendly bantering by Jon annoyed the sheriff. He looked hard at Jon and replied, "If you don't mind, my deputy and I got some business to discuss."

"No problem, Sheriff. You boys have a nice evening. Didn't mean to interrupt." Jon smiled as he and Cliff headed for the door. Cook quickly turned away and continued his conversation with his deputy, obviously irritated by the exchange with Jon.

"He needs to lighten up a little," Jon said as he and Cliff stepped out on the street.

"He's used to intimidating everyone, and you had him back on his heels, Jon. He's not used to that."

"I guess not," Jon laughed. "Tell me, what's the best way out to the mines?"

"Just past the livery stable there are two trails—one goes north and one goes west. Take the west trail and follow it all the way out to the mines. The miners got it pretty rutted out, so take it easy tomorrow."

"Sure will, Cliff. How about a little faro?"

"Naw, I got a lot to do out at the camp before it gets dark. I best be on my way." Cliff untied his black mare. "I have to go to the assayer's office tomorrow. If you're back in time, I'll meet you for lunch at the Crown around noon."

"Sounds good." Jon stood and watched Cliff ride off. As he turned and walked slowly toward the saloon, he thought about his exchange with Cook at the Crown.

The man's got an attitude, he thought as he pushed through the swinging doors and stepped into the smoky saloon for a night of gambling.

Chapter 9

Jon felt a cool breeze on his face as walked to the livery stable. The cock crowed as he hurried down the dusty street to pick up Babe and head out to the mining camps.

Jon had a lot to do today now that he was fully committed to fighting this battle. He was like a soldier who longs for the next encounter with the enemy. Killing Injun Joe and his run in with Sheriff Cook just whetted his appetite for the next fight to come. But he was no fool; Jon knew that he would need the support of the miners if he was to rid the town of George Stanton and his crew. It was time for a heart to heart with the miners.

Hank Clark looked up as Jon hurried toward the stables. "Looks like you need a horse, my friend."

"Sure do, Hank. How's she doing?"

"I put a dandy brush to her a little while ago. She's rarin' to go."

"Thank you for takin' such good care of her."

Hank smiled. "I'll throw a saddle on her and bring her right out."

The stable hand returned a couple of minutes later and handed the reins to Jon. He paused for a second. Looking up at Jon, he said, "I heard about your fight with Injun Joe yesterday."

Jon looked intently at the stable hand.

"I hope you don't mind if I stick my nose in your business a little bit."

Jon nodded.

"Rumors are flying around here that Stanton's real upset about Injun Joe. They say he's bringin' in more hired guns to take you out."

"Doesn't surprise me, Hank. Men like Stanton don't like to lose. Thanks for the tip." Jon quickly mounted up, spun Babe around and headed for the camps.

Jon's first stop would be at the campsite owned by Ned Sloan. Cliff had told Jon that Ned was one of the most respected men in the camps. He was a former colonel in the Confederate Army who had come out west to seek his fortune and start a new life. Getting a man like Ned Sloan on his side would help him form the kind of coalition he needed to defeat Stanton and company.

The sound of pounding hooves jarred Jon from his thoughts. He spun around to see Sheriff Cook fast approaching.

"I thought I asked you not to leave town, Jon," the sheriff said as he rode up.

"Oh, I'm not going anywhere, Dan. I just wanted to take a morning ride and give my horse here a little work. Besides, you should know enough about what happened at the Dead End by now to know that I'm innocent."

"Well, Lou did say it was self defense," Cook said begrudgingly. "But I still have other people to talk to who might have a different story."

"You better be careful there, Sheriff. I don't think that your Mr. Stanton would like to hear that you were tryin' to prove that his brother is a liar—even if you are tryin' to put me in jail." Jon grinned at the agitated sheriff.

"Just be sure that you're in town tomorrow, Stoudenmire."

"Oh, don't worry, Dan. I'm not goin' anywhere soon. I kinda like all of the attention I've been getting around here lately." He smiled broadly. "Now can I get on with my morning ride? My horse is getting a little antsy."

"Just be sure you're here in the morning," the sheriff said firmly as he reined around and headed back to town.

Dan Cook seemed angered by his meeting with Stoudenmire, but Jon knew that any further investigation would only besmirch the reputation of brother Lou and that George Stanton would not stand for that. Cook was damned if he did and damned if he didn't. More than likely, he would have to come up with another way to deal with Jon. Jon knew that he had to be ready for anything from the determined sheriff.

After the long ride through the lush countryside, Babe lurched up the final rocky hill toward the camps. Jon reined up at the top of the hill and looked down at the surprising scene below. The surrounding hills were a beehive of activity as scores of miners scurried about preparing for another long, hard day of prospecting.

Campfires flickered in the morning dew, steam rose from the many metal coffeepots sitting atop the hot flames, and the smell of bacon, grits, and biscuits filled the air. Men were standing in a nearby stream shouting and laughing; a few held up small pieces of broken mirror as they took their morning shave. Some were in the stream panning for the elusive gold nuggets, while the more fortunate prospectors sifted through the dirt in their long toms. On land, the surface miners and dry diggers were spread out over the hills as far as Jon could see. "Now I see what Stanton's after," he whispered as he spurred Babe forward and rode slowly into the busy camps. Just inside the entrance to the camp a man jumped out of his tent, hair a mess, and began to scurry around, looking for wood for a fire.

"Pardon me," Jon shouted.

The scraggly man spun around. "Yeah, what can I do for ya?"

"I'm looking for Ned Sloan's camp. Ya know where—"

"Yeah, yeah," the busy miner pointed. "He's up over that far knoll, down near the stream."

"Thank ya kindly," Jon replied as the busy miner went back to work.

As Jon approached Ned Sloan's campsite, he saw a very large man leaning over the campfire preparing breakfast. He was holding an iron skillet that smelled of bacon and grits over the hot coals of his campfire. Still a little hungry, Jon's stomach growled.

Ned Sloan looked warily up from the campfire.

"Howdy, stranger. What can I do for you?" The former military man was startled by Jon's sudden appearance.

"Well, uh, I believe you may be just the man I'm looking for," replied Jon. "Are you Ned Sloan?"

"Sure am. And I am not selling my claim, so if you are here on behalf of Mr. Stanton, turn that horse of yours around and go back where you came from." The big man spoke with authority as he grabbed hold of the Winchester rifle lying next to him. A stranger in camp right now could mean trouble for the miners, and Sloan wasn't taking any chances. "Don't make any quick moves, mister," he ordered.

Jon spoke calmly to the edgy miner. "Stoudenmire's my name. And I'm sure not here on behalf of Mr. Stanton. In fact, just the opposite. Cliff Stone's my cousin."

Slightly embarrassed, Ned sat the rifle down. "Oh, uh, Cliff told me all about you, Stoudenmire. I guess I didn't expect to see you up this way. Sorry for being so jumpy."

"No offense taken." Jon jumped down and shook Ned's outstretched hand.

"Welcome, Jon. Come on in."

"Thank ya, Ned. I'm just happy you didn't blow my head off," Jon chuckled.

Sloan's aggressive behavior showed Jon that he was a man of action. This was the kind of man he was looking for—someone tough enough to stand up to George Stanton and his hired guns.

A smile broke out on Ned's square face. "You just can't be too careful 'round here nowadays," he said. "Stanton and his boys are really putting the pressure on, and it could get ugly very quickly. Breakfast is just about ready—will you join me?"

"Thought you'd never ask." Jon tied Babe to a bush and sat down by the fire.

"Coffee?"

"Sounds good."

Ned lifted the pot; the hot liquid splashed into Jon's cup. While Ned was pouring, Jon took the opportunity to survey the campsite. He liked what he saw. It was very well organized. The fire wood was neatly stacked, his tent was perfectly pitched and everything was in its place. This was the camp of a former military man, a military officer. It was another example of a no-nonsense guy. But more than anything, Jon was impressed with the man himself. He was a huge man, over six feet tall and weighing well over two hundred pounds. His large frame and broad shoulders made him a very imposing figure for any adversary.

Sloan took a sip of coffee and looked straight at Jon. "Before I ask you what brings you up here, Jon, I want to tell you something."

Eyes wide, Jon looked intently at Sloan.

The former officer continued, "Cliff said you've got a reputation and that you recently shot down one of Stanton's men in the Dead End. That could be a problem. I'm not sure what the others miners are gonna think about our joining forces with a hired gun."

Jon winced at the hired gun comment. He calmed himself and then spoke. "Well, Ned, I know what you're saying, but let me assure you that there are no wanted posters out for me, and I'm no hired gun. The men I've killed were in the defense of myself or a friend."

"That's good, Jon, but I have to be perfectly honest. One of the miners told me that you've got a short fuse and when it goes off, people get hurt."

Jon's brow furrowed. "You seem like a decent sort, Ned, but you've insulted me twice." Jon stared hard at Sloan and spoke calmly. "I got a temper all right, but I use it to fight men like George Stanton and his hired guns. No innocent man need ever fear Jon Stoudenmire."

Ned was taken aback by the strong response. "I'm sorry, Jon. I didn't mean to offend you. I just heard some rumors, that's all. Then Cliff told me about the fight in the saloon, and I just—"

Jon interrupted. "No offense taken, I understand; but we best get started. These men are going to be damn hard to beat—especially with the local sheriff in their back pocket. We haven't got any time to waste."

"Let me apologize again, Jon, and tell you how glad I am that you're on board with us!"

"Don't mention it, my friend." Jon smiled at the genuinely contrite miner.

"I think the bacon is about done. How about some grub?" Ned tossed some grits and bacon on a plate and handed it to Jon.

"Thank you." Jon was impressed with Ned Sloan; the other miners respected him, and he was smart and tough.

- - - - -

"That was damn good grub." Jon set the empty plate on the ground. "I guess you military guys really know how to cook."

"Thank you, Jon, but it was my mama that taught me how to cook, not the military. Those military cooks will kill you," Ned laughed as he gathered up Jon's plate.

Jon lit a cigar. "Smoke?" he asked.

"Don't mind if I do." Ned scraped the scraps under a nearby cactus and threw the dirty dishes in a pan full of soapy water near the campfire.

Jon picked another cigar out of his pocket and handed it to the massive miner.

"Ned, I have one last request of you," Jon said as he leaned forward to light Ned's cigar.

"Fire away."

"I think a man like you can rally support from the miners all right, and that's good. But we're gonna need a couple of men who are willing to fight these varmints up close, man to man. Does anyone come to mind?"

The cigar smoke disappeared into the morning breeze as Jon waited for Ned's reply. He sat quiet for a while and then spoke up.

"Well, first of all, in case you hadn't figured it out, you can count me in."

Jon grinned. "I already had ya in, partner."

"As far as the other fellas, I think I know a couple who might fit the bill. Red Elliot and I served together in the Confederacy. He's a stand up guy. I think there is a chance he would jump in. And there's another fellow named Jack Malone. He's a former lawman from the Kansas territory—he's fearless and a crack shot."

"Tell me, Ned, would you be willin' to talk with these men and let me know what you find out?"

"Yeah, no problem, Jon. I'll be seeing those boys later today. I'll get back to you tomorrow evening."

"Sounds good. I have to be in town in the morning to meet with Dan Cook. Then I'll plan on ridin' out here tomorrow evenin' to see what ya found out." Jon dusted his chaps as he stood to leave. "By the way, when you're out in the camps today, if you would, stop by Cliff Stone's place and bring him up to speed."

"I was planning on it."

"It's been a pleasure." Jon mounted up and reined around toward town.

Ned gave a thumbs up as Babe reared and charged down the trail.

The hot desert sun was rising in the morning sky as Jon galloped back to town. He was encouraged by how well things had gone with Ned Sloan. He was sure Ned could get the miners to join in Jon's effort to stop Stanton and his gang of killers, and the help couldn't have come at a better time. But Jon knew that sooner or later, word of his visit would get back to Stanton. Several miners had ridden past Jon when he came into camp that morning. One of them might have recognized him and might then try to curry favor with Stanton by telling him of Jon's visit. Also, Ned's recruiting trip to the other campsites would also draw some attention. Jon had to make good use of the time available; he knew that he could be facing Dave Barton and Stanton's other hired guns soon enough.

- - - - -

Jon arrived in town and pulled up in front of Callahan's. As he pushed into the lobby, Maggie stuck her head out of her apartment door.

"Morning, Jon."

A surprised Jon quickly tipped his hat to the lovely Miss Callahan. "Mornin', Maggie. How are you?" he asked clumsily.

"Just fine, thank you. I'm sorry to interrupt your day, Jon, but I was wondering if you could give me a hand. I have an armoire I would like to move, and it's too heavy for me. Can you help a girl?"

"Why…uh, certainly, Maggie. But I…uh, just got in off the trail, and it's plenty hot out there. Maybe I should go up to my room and—"

Maggie interrupted. "Oh, don't worry about that, silly, you look fine to me. I grew up with four brothers, for heaven's sake."

"Well, okay Maggie, what have we got?" Jon skirted around the front desk toward her apartment. Maggie nudged the door open ever so slightly as Jon stepped in, forcing him to brush up against her. Clad only in a blue silk bathrobe, her long brown hair was hanging loosely on her shoulders. The scent of her expensive perfume filled the small boudoir. He saw a black floral bathtub in the corner, ready to be emptied.

"It's right over here, Jon." Maggie walked over near the armoire. "If you could just move it a few feet over next to the nightstand by my bed, I would appreciate it."

Jon smiled and stepped next to the large oak armoire. Maggie bent over to move the small nightstand out of the way. As she was leaning down, the silk belt on her robe came loose. The robe fell open, exposing her nude body. After an unavoidable glimpse at her shapely figure, Jon quickly looked away.

Maggie set the nightstand down, slowly pulled her robe together and retied the belt. "Darn robe," she said matter-of-factly. "It's always coming loose."

Jon was surprised by Maggie's lack of embarrassment. He wrapped his big hands around the base of the armoire, leaned down and pushed hard with his thighs. It begrudgingly slid over a few feet.

"Well, there you are, Maggie. Glad I could help." Slightly uncomfortable, Jon was in a hurry to leave, but Maggie was having no part of his quick exodus. She gently grabbed his arm, stopping his retreat. Her face was red and flushed as she spoke. "Thank you so much, Jon. It's awfully hard for a girl living alone. Sometimes a big strong man like you comes in handy." She smiled flirtatiously as she squeezed tighter on his arm. Her robe was slightly open at the top, revealing her delicious, well-shaped breasts. Strong emotions began to stir inside of Jon as he stared at her exposed cleavage; his knees started to shake. Certain of her motives at this point, he was finding her hard to resist.

Maggie's delicate fingers slid up the back of Jon's arm; she gently rubbed up and down on his bicep. His knees got weaker. "Won't you stay a while?" she pleaded as she slipped in front of him. Her robe fell open once again as she pulled him closer. Breathing hard, she forced her naked body up against him, pushing harder and harder. Jon could feel her firm breasts pressing against his chest. His mind was racing; he wanted her badly. It had been so long since he had been with a woman.

"Jon…Jon, I've been waiting so long for—"

Suddenly Jon put his hands on her shoulders and pushed her back. Embarrassed, she quickly pulled her robe together and crossed her arms in front of her. Her eyes went to the floor.

"I'm sorry, Maggie. You're one hell of a sexy lady, but somethin' tells me this is headin' for nothin' but trouble. You see, I got this little girl down Arizona way that I think's really somethin'. And you've been seeing Stanton and all. Little lady, I got enough trouble on my hands right now. I don't need any more. I best be goin' before it's too late." His hands dropped from her shoulders, and he walked quickly to the door.

- - - - -

The door clicked shut as Maggie yanked an onyx pin from her hair and tossed it across the room. "Damn!" she shouted as she plopped down on the bed. Humiliated, she punched angrily at the pillow lying next to her on the bed.

- - - - -

As Jon hurried out and closed the door, he was surprised to see a smallish, dark-skinned man standing in the corner of the lobby holding a bouquet of roses.

"Maggie home?" the surprised man asked.

"Why…uh, yes…uh, she's in there," an uneasy Jon replied as he walked over and started up the stairway. Jon looked down from the stairs as the man walked over and knocked on Maggie's door. The door opened quickly. *She thinks it's me,* Jon thought.

"Oh, you not dressed! So sorry, Miss Maggie! I come at a bad time!"

A nervous Maggie replied, "That's okay, Pedro. What can I do for you?"

"I have some roses from George."

"Damn it!" Jon groused as he reached the top of the stairs and stormed into his room.

Chapter 10

Late that evening, there was a loud knock on the door. Jon hurried over to answer it. "Yes?" he inquired, without opening the door.

"It's Cliff. Got a minute?"

Jon turned the brass knob and quickly opened the door at the familiar sound of Cliff's voice. "Hello, Cliff. How are ya? Please come in."

A look of concern clouded Cliff's face as he entered the room.

Jon slid a chair over to his cousin and sat down on the corner of the bed.

"We can talk now. Tell me what's on your mind."

"First, thanks again for staying on to help us with this mess," Cliff said sincerely.

"No problem, cus. I would like nothing better than to put Stanton, Barton, and the boys in the ground."

"You may have your chance before you know it. Things are heatin' up out at the camps. Curly Harmon, an old timer who was working a thick vein near the rim of the canyon, came up missing today."

The light filtering through the hotel window fell across Cliff's face. Jon could see the strain in his eyes as he told him about old Curly.

"Some of the miners talked to him last evening, and he said he'd been having some good luck lately. He told 'em he was going to get up early today and work his vein hard. When one of 'em went by his stake around noon, Curly was nowhere to be found. His donkey and tools were right where they had been the evening before."

"Looks like foul play," Jon surmised.

"Yeah, and the tension is really mounting. They think Stanton had Curly murdered so he could jump his claim. Curly was popular and well-liked—the miners are plenty angry and running scared right now."

"I'll bet they are," Jon said as he fell back on the bed. "I talked to Ned Sloan earlier about getting a few of the boys together out at the mines to help fight Stanton's group. With this miner coming up missing, it could help Ned's recruiting efforts."

"Yeah, I know. Ned stopped by my camp today and brought me up to snuff. He said Stanton got wind of your visit, later Barton showed up at his campsite. Barton told him he's comin' into town for a heart to heart with you tonight."

"Hmmm…doesn't surprise me," Jon said quietly, "but Barton's little showdown with me will have to wait. I need to know what Ned has put together out at the mines first." Jon jumped up from the bed. "Let's go back out to the camps and talk to Ned Sloan."

"Okay, Jon."

Jon spun the cylinders on his Colts to be sure they were fully loaded. He tossed his hat on and started toward the door. "No time to waste, Cliff. Let's get going."

The door slammed behind them as the two men hurried out.

Chapter 11

The sound of men's voices could be heard as Jon and Cliff approached the outskirts of the camps near Ned Sloan's place. Jon saw one of the men waving his arms and gesturing angrily as he barked at the others.

"If they will kill Curly, they will kill any of us!" he shouted.

"Yeah. They mean business—that's for sure," came the reply.

Just outside Ned's camp, Cliff's horse reared and whinnied as a snake slithered across the trail in front of her. The miners scrambled for their guns.

"Back off, boys," Ned admonished as the glow from the fire revealed the faces of Jon and Cliff. "It's Stone and Stoudenmire." The men drew down.

"Sorry, fellas. We got spooked back there," Jon said.

"No need for apologies, Jon. Come on in," Ned replied.

Jon and Cliff dismounted and stepped into the camp.

"Let me introduce you to these hombres who are thinking about joining the fight," Ned said.

Thinking about it? Jon was hoping that Ned had already convinced the other men to join in.

"This here ornery critter is Jack Malone. He's the former deputy sheriff from Ellsworth, Kansas, I told you about. Jack and his wife Nell came out here last year to work their claim. Since then, they have been doing quite well. Lately, they've been getting a lot of heat from Stanton and his boys."

"Howdy, Jack. I spent some time in Ellsworth. Rough town. I'm sure you're no stranger to trouble. Nice meetin' ya," Jon said as the two shook.

"This here fellow is Red Elliot. He and I were both officers under Jackson. Red got three commendations for bravery and was a fine officer."

"Pleased to meet ya. Maybe you should be runnin' this thing, Red," Jon laughed as he tipped his hat to the former officer.

"Howdy, Jon." Red chuckled nervously at the compliment.

"Can I get anyone a cup of coffee?" Ned lifted the pot off of the fire.

"Thought you'd never ask," Jon answered.

"How about you, Cliff?"

Cliff nodded.

"Jon, I'm sure that Cliff has told you that old man Harmon went missing last night."

"Yeah, he did, Ned. It's a shame. Heard any more about him?"

"Yes, unfortunately we have. One of the miners found his body today. It was partially buried under a pile of rocks about two hundred yards from his camp. It looks like when Curly arrived at his campsite this morning, someone was waiting on him. Poor bastard never had a chance. They shot him in the back of the head. Then they dragged his body to some nearby brush, dug a shallow grave and threw him in. They tossed rocks and dirt on the body and swept the tracks away. At first we couldn't find the body, but later on, a miner was riding by his camp and spotted some spots of blood leading toward the bushes. He dug into the brush and found Curly's body," Ned said sadly. "The miners have been in an uproar ever since. They're confused and frightened."

"Yep…that's just what Stanton and his boys want," Jon explained. "They want to scare the hell out of everyone so we'll turn tail and run. Nothin' would make them happier. But we can't run, because if we do, this town will be lost forever. Stanton will control this whole territory, and a man and his family won't be safe anywhere. It's time to ban together and beat these cowards. They shot old Curly in the back of the head— that shows how far they will go to get their way." Jon challenged the other men into action.

The men seemed moved by Jon's speech, but they had families to think about. Jack was married, and Red had two little boys at home. The two men were quiet as they pondered the situation.

Jon waited patiently; these were tough men, used to facing death and violence. He was pretty sure that they'd come around.

"Well, what is it, boys? Are we going to stick together and take these cowards out, or are we gonna have more good men shot in the back of the head?"

"You're right, Jon. Everything you said is right," Red said. "I've seen these kind before. They won't let up. I'm willing to fight—count me in."

All eyes turned to Malone. "I'm in," he said. "I never had any doubts. Curly was a friend of mine.   What's next?"

"Glad to have ya on board, men," Jon said quickly. "Now here's the plan. Ned, I want you to call for a meeting of all of the miners. When you get 'em all together, ask for several volunteers to act as lookouts. Then post these sentries at every entryway to the camp. If the sentries see any of Stanton's boys coming into the camp area, they need to tell you right away. Then all you boys need to ride out together and trail them at a safe distance, but close enough so they can see you. I want them to see you. This is important for two reasons. It will make them real nervous to know that we're watching them.   Also, they won't be shooting anybody in the head with the likes of you four behind them. I guarantee ya that."

"I'll get on it right away," Ned said.

Jon made eye contact with each man. "If they make a false move," he said gravely, "let 'em have it."

The men nodded.

Jon stood up to leave. "I have a date with Dave Barton. I best be goin'."

"Barton, huh? He's a bad apple," Malone said. "I had a run in with him in Ellsworth."

"Yeah, he's a real fine fella," Jon said quietly.

"I'll ride with ya, Jon." Cliff started to get up.

"No, Cliff. You're to help Ned for the time being. I can take care of Barton."

Cliff frowned and dropped back down next to the fire.

"Be careful with that hombre!" Ned shouted as Jon jumped on Babe, reined around and headed for town.

As he rode along, thoughts of Libby raced through Jon's mind. He could see her lovely face and feel her gentle touch as he moved toward yet another violent showdown. His Colts bounced at his side, the same Colts he promised her he would put away when he left Arizona. "Forgive me, darling," he whispered. "But these men need killin'."

As he approached the edge of town, Jon felt uneasy. He had a sense that something was very wrong. He reined up and pulled off to the side of the trail. He looked around and found a much less traveled route around and behind the buildings that fronted Main Street. He nudged Babe forward along the path, trying to keep out of the sight of people passing by on the road. Soon, the back of Hank's livery stable was in sight. He rode in carefully, dismounted, tied Babe to an abandoned shed and approached the back door of the stable.

"What the—!" a startled Hank exclaimed as he came out back to grab a bale of hay. Jon quickly put his finger to his lips. Hank recognized Jon. He motioned to a little room at the rear of the stable near the back entryway. As he and Jon ducked into the room, Hank grabbed a kerosene lamp off of a hook and lit it. He pushed the door shut, and the two men began to talk.

"Have you noticed anything unusual going on in town today?" Jon carefully grilled the old timer.

"Oh yes. Barton rode in a while ago and stopped at the Dead End. The town's real nervous. They think there's going to be a showdown between Barton and you for killing Injun Joe."

"Did ya see anything else?"

"I don't have the best angle to see the entire town here, but I can see the Dead End."

"What'd ya see?"

"Barton was talkin' to Lou Stanton out by the front door, and Lou was pointin' toward the edge of town to where George lives. Barton mounted up and headed toward Stanton's. Lou mounted up and rode the other way. He told me earlier he was leaving to spend some time with his lady friend down in Escondido. That's the last thing I saw. It was just a couple of minutes ago."

"I'm going to give Barton a little surprise party when he comes back to the Dead End," Jon said coolly. Thanks for the tip, Hank." Jon hurried out the back and untied Babe. He quickly walked past the remaining buildings to the end of town, brushed himself off, mounted up and rode slowly into town. The busy townsfolk hurried to get out of the way when they saw Jon coming. He stopped across the street from the Dead End and tied down. After looking around, he walked slowly across the dusty street to the saloon. Pausing briefly, he scanned the street one more time, then lowered his hat and pushed through the batwing doors. Once inside, he backed quickly to the left, pushing the swinging door up against the wall. Expecting a trap, he cased the room. His instincts told him a shooter was in the saloon. The nervous patrons got stone quiet—another tip off.

Jake the bartender saw Jon come in. Jon looked over at Jake; Jake raised his eyes up toward the landing. As Jon's eyes shot upward, he saw a dark figure moving in the shadows on the landing above the gambling tables.

Like a flash, he pulled both guns and cocked the hammers. Patrons screamed, chairs rattled, drinks spilled as the gamblers quickly ducked out of the way. The lantern light reflected off of his shiny six guns as he pointed them toward the landing.

"Come out here where I can see you, mister. Make it nice and easy, or I'll start shootin'," Jon shouted at the shadowy figure.

The figure paused on the landing. The crowd hunkered down even more, expecting a violent exchange to start at any second. Suddenly the man spoke up. "Don't shoot!" he pleaded. "I'm comin' out!"

The culprit moved out of the shadows, hands up. Jon began barking orders at the frightened gunman.

"Now take your left hand and very carefully unbuckle that gun belt and let it drop on the floor. If you make one false move, you'll be history!"

Jon motioned for a man at the bottom of the stairs to go up and retrieve the guns. The man hurried up the stairs. He looked nervously up at the shaken gunman as he cautiously reached for the fallen guns. He grabbed them and quickly scampered back down the stairs.

"Now, move over to those stairs, and come on down nice and slow." Jon dropped one gun in the holster and moved over to the bar. "When ya get down, come over here where I can get a good look at ya!"

The man moved nervously down the oak stairs. Eyes wide and sweating profusely, he reached the bottom of the stairs and walked to where Jon was standing. Jon wrapped his fingers around the man's collar, spun him around and slammed him up against the bar. Jon could feel the terrified man's heart pounding as he tightened the grip.

"Now, damn you! Tell me what you were doin' up there in those shadows with a gun belt on—and this better be good!"

"I'm just a hired hand, mister, doin' my job, that's all."

"Start talkin'!" Jon tightened the grip and shoved him higher on the bar. The frightened man was gasping for breath as he squeezed even tighter.

The red-faced man strained to get the words out. "Uh…uh…o…okay, okay, I was waitin' on ya, all right. I…I was…uh, supposed to shoot you if Barton didn't get the job done."

"Who hired ya?"

The man hesitated, afraid to answer. Jon pushed the cold barrel of his six gun against his neck.

"Stanton," the man said almost inaudibly.

"That's what I thought. It's that son-of-a-bitch Stanton," Jon barked as he let the man slide slowly down the bar. He loosened the grip on his neck, stared at him for a minute, yanked him around and shoved him toward the door. He pulled his gold watch out of his vest pocket and quickly checked the time. "Go find Barton and tell him I'll meet him in an hour, at six o'clock. Out on the street," Jon shouted, as the surprised man stumbled out the door. Jon stared at the swinging doors for a second and turned around. "Gimme a shot Jake."

Jake set a shot glass on the bar as he spoke to the crowd. "It's okay, everybody. The trouble is over. Let's get back to whatever you were doing." He motioned for the piano player to start playing again. Sounds of the old favorite "Tumbling Tumbleweeds" soon filled the room.

Jon watched the whiskey flow in the glass. "Thanks for the tip, Jake."

"No problem. I don't like Stanton and his gang any more than you do, Jon."

Jon leaned back as he downed the shot. He set the empty glass on the bar and reached in his pocket.

"No," said Jake. "This one's on me."

Jon smiled at the friendly barkeep. "See ya at six. If you need me for anything, I'll be down at Callahan's. Keep it under your hat," Jon said quietly.

Jake nodded as Jon turned and left the saloon.

- - - - -

Things were frantic down at Stanton's mansion. The sentry had just arrived with Jon's message. Stanton had gathered his boys together for a quick meeting; he was pacing in front of his huge stone fireplace smacking a buggy whip on the palm of his hand.

"What the hell went wrong?" George shouted. "I thought you had a plan, Barton, and now this!"

Barton's eyes shot toward Stanton. "We had a plan, damn it! One of the boys saw Stoudenmire out at the camps just before I left. I thought we had plenty of time, but he got to town sooner than I expected. It doesn't make any difference, anyhow—he's a dead man either way!"

"Calm down, Dave," Stanton replied, anxious to calm his vicious gun.

"I wouldn't take this Stoudenmire too lightly." Buck Johnson, Stanton's right hand man, jumped into the conversation.

"Just what do you know about him, Buck?" Stanton asked.

Buck replied, "He's a drifter, gambler and good with a gun. One of the boys out at the mines is from Dodge City. He knew Stoudenmire when he was a younger man, just startin' out. Says he has a real bad temper when someone messes with his friends. He's a dead shot and not afraid of anything."

"Uhmm! And isn't Cliff Stone his cousin or something?" George's brow furrowed.

"They grew up together back in Indiana. They go way back."

"You're one of the best, Dave, but this man's already killed Injun Joe, and now he wants to try and kill you. I think we should hold off, not fall into his trap."

"Hell, I'm not afraid—"

Stanton interrupted. "I know you're not afraid of him, but I can't chance getting you killed right now. We'll take care of this Stoudenmire when the time is right." Stanton scribbled a note on a piece of paper and ordered one of the men to deliver it to Jake at the Dead End.

Barton frowned and spit on the floor. "You better know what you're doin', Stanton, 'cause you're makin' me look real bad. I'll be out back shootin' if anyone needs me." He stormed angrily out of the house to the courtyard.

A disgruntled Stanton watched the gunman leave. "Where in the hell is Sheriff Cook when we need him?" he barked, trying to quickly change the subject. "Go find him and tell him to figure out a way to run this Stoudenmire fella out of town. That'll save a hell of a lot of trouble."

"Sure enough, boss," Buck said as he hurried out the door.

Suddenly, the shy Pedro stepped forward and grabbed Stanton's arm. "Got a minute, boss?"

"Why yes, uh...yes, Pedro. What is it?"

"It's about yesterday when I went to deliver the flowers to Miss Callahan. I think we should talk in private, in your office."

"Certainly, Pedro. Come right in." Stanton's head nodded toward his office. He turned to the others. "Meeting's over, boys. Stick close in case something comes up." The boys dispersed as he and Pedro stepped into the den.

Chapter 12

Jon sat on the corner of his featherbed at Callahan's loading his six gun as someone began pounding on the door. He snapped the cylinder shut and moved over next to the door.

"Who is it?"

"Sheriff Cook. Open up, Jon. I need to talk to you right away."

"Are you alone?" Jon demanded.

"Yes. Open up."

"All right, Cook, but listen to what I'm tellin' you. I am going to open the door, and I want you to show me your hands first and then come in very slowly. Any quick moves, and I'll blow your damn head off. You understand?"

"Calm down," Cook replied as he reached for the handle.

"Don't get smart, Cook. Just do what I say!" Jon snarled as he leaned back against the wall.

The sheriff came through the doorway hands first. Jon looked through the crack in the door and out to the hallway. There was no one else out in the hall.

"Come on in," he ordered.

The cautious sheriff came slowly in the room nervously looking around for Jon. Jon poked him in the side with his gun. "Move over a little," he ordered as he quickly closed and locked the door. The sheriff took a couple of steps toward the center of the room.

"And to what do I owe the pleasure of this visit, Sheriff? With all the trouble that's brewin' around here, I thought maybe you found a reason to leave town or somethin'," Jon said sarcastically.

Cook scowled. "You've already killed one man, Stoudenmire. We don't need any more killins' around here. The folks are gettin' nervous."

"No more killins', huh? Why don't you tell that to that sidewinder that was waiting upstairs at the Dead End a little while ago?" Jon said angrily. "I guess it's only murder around here when people try to defend themselves. Anything involving George Stanton never seems to be outside of the law around your little hellhole."

Cook glared at Jon. "You're trouble, Stoudenmire," he growled. "You shot a man in cold blood at the Dead End Saloon. People are nervous. Seems like our town's been turned upside down ever since you arrived. We don't need your kind in El Cabrera, Jon. I'll be keeping an eye on you, partner."

"Go right ahead, Sheriff. I shot Injun Joe in self defense, and everyone knows it."

"Just watch your step," Cook barked.

Jon grinned at the pompous sheriff as he unlocked the door and ushered him out of the room. Jon knew that deep down the sheriff realized that he was in over his head with this situation. This visit was just to impress Stanton. When push came to shove, Cook would stay out of the way.

Jon splashed water on his face from the white porcelain pan next to his bed and patted dry. Now that Cook knew where he was, he was afraid he might get a surprise visit from Stanton's boys; he wanted to be out of the room.

He stepped out and peeked over the railing; Maggie wasn't there. He felt relieved as he hurried down the stairs.

Suddenly a head popped up from behind the counter. "Why, good evening, Jon. Looks like you're in a big hurry."

Startled, Jon's pace slowed dramatically. "Oh...uh, why hello, Maggie. Didn't see ya over there. How are you today?" Maggie looked lovely as usual—her yellow calico dress left little to the imagination as she leaned over the counter.

She smiled warmly at Jon. "Please be careful. I hear things are getting a little dangerous out there."

"Well thank ya, ma'am. A fella just can't be too careful." Jon tipped his hat as he stepped out the door. *Sure wish there was a back door to this place,* he thought as he hurried out to the street.

It was a warm clear day in El Cabrera. The soft breezes from the nearby ocean felt good on Jon's face as he ambled toward the Dead End. There were smiles and nods from the townsfolk; Jon could feel the town coalescing behind him in this fight. The steps creaked as he hopped up to the boardwalk and walked in the Dead End to kill a little time. The earlier visit from Sheriff Cook had upset him. He was ready for Barton. The sooner the better.

"Back so soon?" Jake joked.

"I got a visit from our fine sheriff a while ago. He knows where I'm stayin'. I thought it best I get out of there."

Jake looked at Jon. "I just got a visitor myself," he said.

"Oh yeah?"

"It was one of Stanton's boys. He told me to give you a message from George. Barton won't be coming down to face you—they think it's a setup. He said he'll deal with you in his own time, on his own terms."

"What?" Jon slammed his fist on the bar; his face contorted with rage. "That no good bastard's got another thing comin'!"

"What are you gonna do?"

"I know Barton didn't buy into Stanton's little plan—his reputation is at stake. I need to get a message directly to Barton. I think I can goad him into a fight."

Jake poured Jon another shot.

"I need a favor, Jake. I need you to go down to Stanton's and tell Barton to quit hidin' and come out and fight me like a man. Be sure Barton hears the message. He's a lot of things, but he's no coward."

"Will you pay to bury me?" Jake asked half-jokingly.

"It's me they want—they won't hurt you. Besides, everybody likes you, Jake." The corner of Jon's mouth pushed up to a grin as he lifted the small glass, sloshed the whiskey around and downed the shot.

Jake quickly untied his apron and hung it on the hook behind the bar as he prepared to go down to Stanton's place and deliver Jon's message.

"Take it easy on 'em Jake," Jon grinned at the anxious tender.

Jake sneered at Jon, "See you in a few," he said as he stepped out from behind the bar.

- - - - -

Jake was having second thoughts as he walked toward Stanton's place. These were violent men. What if they didn't like what he had to say and took it out on him? *How do I get myself in these messes?* he thought.

The guard at the front gate shouted at him as Jake approached Stanton's compound. "What ya need, Jake?"

"I got a message for Barton."

The guard jumped down and pushed the heavy metal gate open. He grabbed Jake firmly by the arm and escorted him up to the porch. "Wait here. He's out back shootin'. I'll see if I can get him," he said gruffly.

The front door swung open suddenly as Pedro hurried out. When he saw Jake, his pace slowed. "Uh...hello, Señor Jake," he said, tipping his sombrero.

Jake nodded at the friendly Pedro as he watched him hop off of the porch and push through the gate.

Jake glanced to his left as Barton and the sentry walked out from behind a large avocado tree at the corner of the house. Barton, wearing blue denim and a black vest, looked thick and strong as he stepped up to the porch. Jake had seen him a few times around town, but never up close. Dark, empty eyes and a perpetual smirk caused by a small scar on the corner of his mouth made him look very daunting. He was agitated as he walked up to Jake.

"Let's have it, Jake. What's this big message from my friend, Jon Stoudenmire?"

Jake hesitated, taken aback by Barton's powerful presence.

"I ain't got all night." The surly gunslinger grew impatient.

"Okay, Dave, here's what the man said. He said that you should quit hidin' and come out in the street and fight him like a man." Jake winced as he waited for Barton's response.

"So he wants me to quit hidin', huh?" Barton said angrily. "Well, tell your friend Mr. Stoudenmire that I know a trick when I see one! He's tryin' to bait me into chargin' down there so he can gun me down," Barton said spitefully. "It ain't gonna work, Jake! You tell him that—it ain't gonna work!"

Barton was talking big, but Jake sensed that he didn't like what he was doing either. Jake could tell that he would much rather fight Jon face to face out in the street. Stanton's plan was making him look like a fool.

Suddenly the anxious Jake did something he hadn't planned on. It was just a hunch, but he felt it was right; he took a chance and called the bad man out.

"Dave, I know it's not like you to hide from a fight." Jake scanned his face, an inquisitive stare was his only reaction. Jake went on, "That's not your style. I know you want this fight. You're the best. You're just trying to keep George happy."

Barton got quiet and stared at the ground, flipping his shoestring tie over and over again with his finger. Jake knew that he had struck a chord with the bad man. Barton was one tough hombre, and he didn't like people thinking he was running from a fight.

Finally he spoke. "You're right, this ain't my style. You go tell Jon that I'll be out in the street straight away. And be sure and tell him that he didn't trick me—I knew what he was tryin' to do. I'm just tired of his big mouth. Tell him he'll get his fight."

Suddenly, the front door burst open, almost knocking Jake down. An angry Stanton charged out of the house. "What the hell's going on?" he screamed.

Barton's eyes shot toward Stanton. "I'll tell ya what's goin' on out here, George! Stoudenmire just called me out, and I'm goin' down to face him straight away. And don't try to stop me!" The surly gunman spit on the ground.

Surprisingly, Stanton paused for a minute and then smiled at the gunman. "That's fine, Dave," he said. "You're right—I think it's time we dealt with this Stoudenmire fella. Just be sure you get the job done. I want him dead." His broad face broke into a malicious smile.

Barton turned toward Jake. "Go give Stoudenmire my message."

George turned and nodded at the sentry, who hurried over and opened the gate. Jake pushed past the unfriendly guard and walked rapidly down the street toward the Dead End.

When he arrived at the saloon, Jon was leaning on the end of the bar talking to one of the girls. Slightly out of breath, Jake hurried over to Jon to deliver Barton's message. The bar girl smiled at Jon and walked away.

"Just calm down here, partner, and tell me what you found out," Jon said, a little surprised by Jake's rapid entry.

"I...uh gave Barton your message, and at first, he was angry because he said you were trying to trick him into coming out into the open. Then we talked for a while, and I convinced him to come out and fight you face to face."

"Ya convinced him, huh? Well I'll be, that's really something!" Jon said, slapping the friendly barkeep on the back. "Good for you!"

Suddenly Jon's expression darkened. "When's the low-life comin'?"

"Straight away. He said he was coming down straight away!"

"Good."

"You got what you wanted, Jon, a showdown."

Jon could feel his mood changing; the fight would soon be on. And now it would all be out in the open where Jon had a chance. Stanton would probably send backup with Barton—Jon had to be ready for that. He could feel the darkness coming. He downed the shot and set the glass calmly on the bar.

"One more," he said.

Jake poured the drink. "Godspeed, my friend," he said quietly.

- - - - -

The bartender's visit was actually a relief to Dave Barton. He had hated every minute of waiting at Stanton's house; he felt like a coward. Now he was relishing the opportunity to do what he did best—kill someone. He couldn't wait to tie his guns down and head out to the street to face Jon one on one. He looked over at George. "I'm glad you changed your mind, Stanton, or I might have had to kill two men today instead of one. Why the change of heart? It ain't like you."

"I got my reasons, Barton—just get the job done," the mogul grunted.

"Don't worry, George. This will be easy."

"I wouldn't be so sure about that. I hear the man's one tough son-of-a-bitch. Injun Joe didn't last very long, so you better not underestimate him."

"Joe was a coward. He was no match for Stoudenmire. He was out of his league." Barton glared at Stanton as he hopped off of the porch and headed for town.

- - - - -

Jon spun the cylinders on his six guns; they were fully loaded. He straightened his tie, tipped his hat down and stepped out onto the street. Steely calm, his senses were on high alert. He felt no fear, only contempt for Dave Barton. A tortured childhood had prepared him well for this fight. The thought of losing never entered his mind. He loved the horror of these violent exchanges and relished the fact that he had been put in this position. When the lead started flying and the smell of gun smoke filled the air, he would be at his very best. Jon pushed the swinging doors open and surveyed the scene outside. He jumped off of the wooden boardwalk and stepped out to the street. He was calm, nerves steady as he waited for yet another bloody battle to begin.

- - - - -

Barton squinted into the setting sun as he stepped out of Stanton's courtyard and began walking toward town. Up ahead, people were scurrying to find a good place to watch the coming clash. They were looking for storefronts to enter or alleyways to duck into. Within a matter of minutes, the folks had settled in, and the street fell silent. A few birds chirping and loose boards clapping in the wind were the only sounds to be heard. As he reached the outskirts of town, Barton was unaware that two of Stanton's boys had fallen in behind him. He stopped and scanned the street ahead; his eyes narrowed when he located Jon standing outside of the Dead End Saloon.

- - - - -

Jon zeroed in on the location of the trailing henchmen. He spit on the ground as he stepped out to confront Barton. After a few steps, he turned to face his adversary, careful not to make any unnecessary moves that might spook the cold-hearted gunman before he had his say. He pulled up and spoke calmly. "Evenin', Dave."

Barton sneered, unfazed by the big gunman's friendly address. "You shoulda left town when you had the chance, Jon. You could've avoided all this."

"I appreciate your concern, Dave, but I wouldn't have missed this for anything."

Beads of sweat were forming on Barton's forehead. "You're a stupid man, Jon. You got no dog in this fight, and now you're going to die. It's a shame."

Jon looked into Barton's cruel empty eyes. "A while back I watched you kill a snake in the alley by the hardware store, Dave," he snarled. "Now it's my turn to kill a snake." Jon grinned at the nasty gunman.

The snake comment infuriated Barton. He couldn't control himself any longer; he went for his gun.

Jon drew with lightning speed and began firing, yellow flames shot from the barrel. Barton's body blew backwards as the hot lead blasted into his midsection. There were loud groans and screams from the bystanders. Barton's gun fired harmlessly into the air.

"You got me, you son-of-a-bitch drifter!" Barton groaned as his muscular body bounced backwards on the hard street. His back arched, and then his body fell motionless on the ground. Smoke drifted up from the bullet holes in his chest as blood poured onto the dusty street.

Certain of the kill, Jon scanned the street for the other men. The man to his left had vanished; the man on the right was running toward a water trough, gun drawn.

A sudden breeze blew away the thick smoke from his earlier gunfire, giving him an unexpected clear shot. He cocked and fired. The man screamed and grabbed his chest, staggered forward, and braced himself against the trough. Jon, filled with rage, approached quickly through the smoke. The man tried to right himself for a shot; there were two more blasts from Jon's guns. Red spread through the water in the trough as he flew backward into his watery grave.

Jon stood in the center of the street. His smoking six guns hung at his side as he surveyed the bloody scene. Another war, another fight was over; two men had died, and once again he was still standing. His heart beat rapidly. He felt isolated and alone. He heard a distant "hiya," and turned to see an angry Stanton taking the whip to his helpless charger as he hastened back to his fortress. A door opened at Callahan's. Maggie stepped out on the boardwalk and stared unflinchingly at Jon. Tears welled in the warrior's eyes; his heart was heavy, his soul diminished by yet another dance with death.

Chapter 13

"Take it easy!" Jon yelped as a bucket of steaming water splashed into the metal tub.

The bathhouse owner smiled as he hurried out to refill the bucket. Jon slid down in the tub, hoping somehow the water would wash away the pain and sorrow he felt after the bloody battle earlier in the day. He breathed deeply as he stared at the dancing flames in the nearby fireplace. The look of horror on Barton's face as the lead blasted into his gut rushed through his mind. He felt the numbness that such violence brings. Horribly conflicted, he thought of Libby and his broken promises to her. *Is there room for love in a heart like this?* he wondered. In agony, he forced himself to wash up; he couldn't dally any longer. He had to meet Cliff and Ned Sloan at the Crown Restaurant at seven o'clock.

"Won't be needin' that—got to be goin'," Jon barked as the owner hurried over with another bucket. He stood up, grabbed a towel off of a nearby hook, dried off and quickly dressed. He slapped on some cologne from a nearby shelf and flipped a gold piece to the owner. "Thank you kindly," he said.

The happy owner smiled.

Jon hurried out of the bathhouse, jumped down onto the rutted street and hustled down to the Crown.

Cliff and Ned were already inside waiting as he hurried in.

"Evenin', fellas."

"Evenin', Jon," the two men said in unison.

"Coffee?" Anita asked as she approached.

"Thought you'd never ask. Thank you." Hot steam rose as the waitress filled his cup and topped off the others'.

"The other boys are having the special. Veal parmesan. Is that all right with you? It's very good tonight."

"Okay, fine with me. I just hope these varmints aren't steering me wrong." Jon grinned as Anita rushed away.

"Cliff tells me you had quite a time out in the street today," Ned said.

"Yeah, I guess so," Jon replied. "The man needed killing. It had to be done."

"I couldn't agree more, Jon. The miners wanted me to thank you personally for taking him out."

Jon nodded at the former confederate officer.

"I ran into Sheriff Cook a little while ago at the Dead End," Cliff said.

Jon's eyebrows raised.

"He says there's been nothing but trouble ever since you came to town. He said when a man like you goes around killing people, it can stir the emotions of people in the community. He said it was hard to say what some folks might do. He thought for your own safety you ought to leave town."

"Yeah, he told me that earlier," Jon said.

"He said to tell you that you better watch your backside. Then he finished his beer and walked out."

"I guess what he's saying is that Stanton is probably gonna kill me, and if he does, Cook ain't going to do a damn thing about it.   That's what I'm hearin'," Jon chuckled.

Cliff fought back the laughter. "That Co…Cook's quite the sheriff, a real man of the law!" he howled. The men all roared.

"I've never felt so safe," Ned shouted.

Stern stares from nearby diners soon quieted the men down. Jon grinned at the other men—the tension-relieving laughter felt good to him.

Ned fiddled with his fork as he became serious. "I think the fine sheriff is right in one regard," he said. "We best be ready for Stanton's revenge. He's gonna be plenty mad now with both Barton and Injun Joe dead."

"He's not going to give up, that's for sure. He'll be hiring more guns. With the law in his back pocket, he's got nothing to lose," Cliff grimaced.

"You're right, Cliff. He'll be back," said his older cousin. "It's all about power for men like George. He'll die to get his power, and he'll never give up. Right now he'd love to kill me. I've seen his type a hundred times. Their pride won't let them quit. He's goin' to find every available gun within five hundred miles of here. The fight's just beginning. And ya know what?" Jon made eye contact with both men. "We'll be ready for him."

"What do we do next?" Ned asked.

"Are Malone and the boys watchin' the camps?"

"Sure are. We've got sentries posted at each entry."

"Good. Keep it up, Ned. It's going to take Stanton a while to arm up. Cliff, can you see Stanton's headquarters from your claim?"

"Yep, I sure can. I'm only about two hundred feet away."

"Does he know you're there?"

"Nope, I'm up over a hill on the back side looking down at the building, and there's a whole bunch of us working that area. With my big straw hat on, he'd never pick me out of the crowd."

"Good. Keep an eye on things. Watch for new men showing up and so on. He'll make his move soon. We've got to be ready for him."

"Sounds like we got a war coming." Cliff scowled.

"Think so."

"One more thing, Jon," Ned said. "Just lately some of the men down at my end are complaining that their claims are burning out. They've tried several methods, and they've dug awful deep, but there's not much there."

Cliff jumped in. "I hear it's gettin' slow in the stream, too."

"Hmmm…I wonder if Stanton knows that."

Both men shook their heads.

"Well, that's sure something to ponder," Jon said quietly. "By the way, boys, while Stanton's arming up, I may ride out and visit Carlos at my vineyard tomorrow. He probably thinks I died or something."

The men nodded.

"Dinner is served!" Anita announced. "Veal parmesan, scalloped potatoes and corn." Two young boys set the men's dinners on the table as the coffee cups were filled. Conversation and chuckles ensued as the men dined quietly.

- - - - -

Jon spurred Babe forward to a full gallop as he rode through a clump of juniper trees; his anticipation grew as he neared the vineyard he so longed to see. He passed the small village of Vinegar Bend, comprised of just a few dozen adobe huts and a dusty street. A Mexican woman chased her small child, playfully touching him with a switch, while he giggled in delight. The other women toiled at their daily chores while the men worked in the nearby vineyards. Jon wondered if his winery would look the same as when he left it so long ago. He trusted his manager Carlos, but time can change many things. Brimming with anticipation, he crested the final hill and pulled up for a look. His heart was full as he surveyed the lush green vineyards below. It was spring, and the grapes were just starting to grow. In the corner of the valley he could see Carlos's white sombrero as he barked orders at the hired hands. Jon rode quickly down the path to the valley, anxious to see his old friend. The vines of the Muscatine grapes looked strong and healthy as Jon rode around the side of the vineyard toward Carlos. Carlos didn't see Jon approach.

"Hello, my friend," Jon shouted.

Busy talking with the men and adjusting a trellis, Carlos didn't hear the greeting. One of the other workers heard him and poked Carlos in the side. He pulled up from the vine, and his dark, weathered face broke into a huge smile when he saw his old friend.

"Hola, Jon! Hola!"

Jon jumped off Babe. The two men embraced. "So good to see you, my friend," Jon said as his hands gripped Carlos tightly by the shoulders.

"I thought you'd never come, Jon. My heart is full! Let's go to the hut where we can talk!"

Jon nodded and followed Carlos to a nearby hut that served as a makeshift office and tool shed. The wooden door creaked open; Carlos cleared some junk off a small table in the corner near a window. Dust flew as he smacked the seats on the wooden chairs with his sombrero.

"Seet down, Jon," he ordered. "I have a treat for you." Carlos opened a nearby cupboard, removed a wooden box and gently laid it on the table. He took a key from under the desk and opened the box. Inside were six delicate wine glasses, each sitting in its own compartment lined with red velvet. Carlos carefully removed two of the long-stemmed glasses and set them on the table. The silver etchings on the crystal glasses displayed the picturesque vineyards and rolling hills of the nearby areas.

"Be right back." Carlos hurried out the door. A few seconds later, Jon looked through the back window and saw him running toward a small door in the side of a nearby knoll. He emerged a couple of minutes later carrying a dark green bottle with a white label.

Carlos hurried in and set the bottle on the table; he reached into a desk drawer and pulled out a corkscrew. He handed it to Jon. "Please, señor!"

Jon grabbed the corkscrew from Carlos as he pulled the bottle closer. He turned the bottle so he could read the black print on the beautiful white label:

J S WINERY—VINEGAR BEND, CALIFORNIA. He looked affectionately at Carlos as he pushed the screw into the top of the bottle, twisted it several times and carefully popped the cork. Anxious for a taste, he quickly filled both glasses with the ruby liquid. Without saying a word, each man tipped his glass to the other and sipped the wine.

"It tastes wonderful, my friend. I can see you have given your heart to my vineyard. I bless you for this," Jon said sincerely.

"It my pleasure, Jon. Your generosity has given me a good life. I owe you much."

"Compadre," said Jon, raising his glass once more.

"Compadre." Carlos's glass rose high.

Jon carefully set his glass on the table. "I just came out for the day, Carlos. I have business in El Cabrera I must take care of."

"And what business could be more important than your wonderful vineyard, señor?" Carlos asked with a smile.

"Good question, my friend. On my way here to the vineyard, I unexpectedly reunited with my cousin in El Cabrera. I discovered that he and the other gold miners in the area are being threatened by a local man named George Stanton."

"Oh yes, yes, I know of George Stanton. He has sent his men out to the vineyards a couple of times. They ask a lot of questions about the wine business. They say they would like to buy us out."

"Hmmm…that's interesting. George must have his sights on the wine business also."

"Yes, his man Buck say that he would make us a good offer for our land. I told him that I was not interested. He told me to think about it, and he would be back. He say the wine business is good because it never run out like gold. He say Mr. Stanton would pay us all very well for our land, and we could all stay and work for them at good pay. He rode off to talk to the other owners."

"That snake!" Jon said angrily. "He knows the veins are burning out, but he still needs that gold. He can mine the remaining gold for the next few years and then use it to try and buy the wineries. If the owners refuse, he will force them out or kill them—just like at the goldfields. If he succeeds, he will control the entire valley and have a source of great wealth for as long as he lives—and a base of power to fund his political ambitions."

"It don't look good, Jon."

"Tell me, Carlos, do they know who owns J S?"

"No, amigo. He asked me if I owned it, and I say no, a man out East own it. Then they all laugh real loud and say it must be some rich uh…I think they say…a high pockets, yes that's it, some rich high pockets must own it. They all think that was funny."

"Did any of the others sell out?"

"No. There are three other vineyards in the valley, and none of them sell out. They all worried, though. Pablo owns the vineyard next to us. He is very old and doesn't always understand. We are afraid that Stanton might trick him into selling. That would be a shame because he promised to give it to his son Domingo when he dies."

"I'm staying at the Callahan Boardinghouse. Please come right away and tell me if Stanton or his men come out here again. And don't tell them that I own J S

under any circumstances. Please be careful, Carlos—
these are dangerous men who are after power and
wealth, and they will kill to get it."

"I know. My friend Manuel owns the other vineyard
near here, and he tells me there was a killing in the
goldfields. I worry about you also, my friend. Even
way out here in California I hear of your courage and
bravery—please be careful. You just got back to
Vinegar Bend. I don't want to lose you again." Carlos
looked intently at his employer.

"Thank you, Carlos. Your concern means much to
me, and your friend is right—an old man was gunned
down in the goldfields recently. And Stanton has already
called me out in an attempt to kill me."

"What happened, señor?"

"It backfired, and I sent two of them to the
heavens." Jon looked over at Carlos. "I appreciate your
concern, but I have made a covenant with my cousin to
clean out that rat's nest, and I must honor it. Especially
after the news you gave me today. It will take some
time, and it will be dangerous, but I have no other
choice."

"You are a man of great honor. I must respect your
decision to fight for your cousin and to protect your
vineyard. I will say no more."

Jon nodded and smiled at his old friend. "This wine
is wonderful, Carlos, and my glass is empty. Shall we
have another?"

"Ah-ha! Wonderful, mi amigo, more wine it is."
Carlos quickly filled their glasses. Jon tossed his brown
felt hat on the table as his chair fell gently against the
wall. He slid two Havanas out of his vest pocket and
gave one to Carlos. Carlos quickly struck a match on his

boot and lit the cigars; smoke filled the air as the two men settled in for a long evening. Lively conversation soon filled the small hut nestled on the edge of the lush vineyard.

Chapter 14

The light from the quarter moon illuminated the well-worn trail as Jon made his way back to El Cabrera. The wonderful hospitality of his old friend Carlos had caused him to stay at the vineyard well into the night. He was feeling no pain, humming one of his favorite tunes, "Old Dan Tucker," as he rode along the moonlit path. It was near midnight when he arrived in town. The street was empty except for several horses tied to the hitching post in front of the Dead End. Jon spurred Babe forward past the popular haunt. Light from the lanterns inside threw yellow squares across the street. Jon glanced inside; a bargirl gently laid her arm on the shoulder of one of the many gamblers. The diehards were still up testing lady luck. Tempted to stop and play a while, he rode on instead.

The street turned dark and quiet after Jon passed the saloon and rode toward Callahan's; he looked into the shadows and noticed Stanton's fancy buggy sitting in front of the popular boardinghouse. He pulled up to the hitching post, dismounted and tied down. The front door was partially open—someone had entered in a hurry. Jon could hear voices coming from Maggie's room as he carefully pushed the door open and gently closed it behind him. Trying not to disturb the late night lovers, Jon walked quietly toward the stairs to his room. His pace slowed when he heard Maggie whimpering and sobbing. Concerned, Jon stopped to listen.

"You damn whore!" Stanton shouted angrily. "You've made me look like a fool!"

Suddenly Jon's mind cleared. His senses went on full alert.

"I'll teach you, you dirty—"

"No, George, no! Not again! Please!" Maggie's voice was full of terror. Jon heard what sounded like a buggy whip hitting flesh as Maggie screamed in pain.

Anger shot through Jon like a bolt of lightning as he leaped over the front desk. He grabbed the door handle. It wouldn't budge—the door was locked. He leaned back, raised his leg and kicked. The door flew open. Jon burst into the room, fists doubled. He was sickened by what he saw. Maggie's nightgown was down to her waist, and she was kneeling face down on her bed. Blood oozed from several wounds on her bare back as the muscular Stanton, buggy whip in hand, spun toward Jon.

"What the hell…" the surprised mogul bellowed.

Jon rushed over, yanked the buggy whip out of Stanton' s hand and threw it across the room.

"How 'bout tryin' me on for size, George?" Jon's fist blasted into Stanton's gut.

His eyes went wide with shock. "Oh Gawd!" he screamed as he folded over in pain.

Maggie leaned up and slid her calico nightgown up over her bare breasts. She scooted over on her knees and cowered near the end of the bed as Jon's brutal beating continued. Jon grabbed Stanton by his ears and slammed his knee into the brute's forehead, knocking him backward against the wall. George bounced off the wall and began staggering around and looking for a weapon, he saw a cast iron stoker by the fireplace. He stumbled over and jerked it out of the stand. Lifting it above his head, he charged toward Jon. Jon ducked to the side as the heavy stoker slammed into the wood floor and stuck straight up. Jon slammed the dazed man with the back of his hand, knocking him hard to the floor. Jon bent over and lifted him up, he drove his fist into Stanton's midsection again and again until he fell back to the floor. Jon leaped on top of him. Grabbing him by his collar and the seat of his pants, he dragged him moaning and kicking across the room and out the door. With a mighty effort, Jon lifted the bulky man up and tossed him across the front desk. George crashed headfirst onto the wooden floor in the lobby. "Damn," he moaned, holding his head.

Jon jumped over the desk and yanked the whimpering brute to his feet, he looked him straight in the eye as he pulled tight on his collar. "Only a sniffling coward like you would beat a woman, George!" he snarled. Full of rage, he smacked Stanton across the face several times with the back of his hand.

"Stop! Stop! I've had enough!" George pleaded.

"That's what Maggie said just before you buggy whipped her!" Jon's fist once again blasted into Stanton's gut. He folded over as Jon pulled the front door open and dragged him outside. Jon strained as he lifted the heavy man and tossed him on the leather seat of his buggy. Stanton held his stomach and groaned; his white silk shirt was stained with blood. Jon grabbed the reins of Stanton's nervous steed and pointed her toward the mansion.

"You ever get within a hundred feet of Maggie again, I'll kill ya!" Jon screamed as he yanked his hat off and smacked the hindquarters of the prancing steed. The horse leapt forward toward the edge of town. George bounced on the seat. "You bastard!" he moaned as the buggy rolled away.

Jon hurried back inside to Maggie's room; she was sitting on the edge of the bed sobbing. Her face buried in her hands, her back covered with blood.

"I'll get the doc." Jon turned to leave.

"No! No! Please don't, Jon!"

"But you have to—"

Sobbing louder, Maggie interrupted. "I'm a proud woman, Jon. I don't want the town to know what that monster did to me. I should have never taken up with a man like him in the first place. I would be humiliated if people found out."

"Stanton might let it out."

"Do you really think George Stanton wants the town to know that Jon Stoudenmire beat him senseless?"

Jon hesitated. "We have to do something, Maggie. Your back is a mess."

"My housekeeper Katie stays in room 101. She's a good friend. I can trust her. She was a nurse during the war and has a bag of supplies she uses when we have cuts and bruises around here. She'll take good care of me—would you get her, please?"

"Right away." Jon hurried out the door and through the lobby to room 101. Several doors cracked open as nervous patrons peeked out to see what the commotion was all about.

Jon paused for a second. "It's all right, folks. A drunk staggered in, fell and cracked his head on the floor. We're taking care of it. Everything is okay—just go back to sleep." There were grumbles as the doors clicked shut one by one. Jon reached Katie's room and knocked. A short time later, the door creaked open. A sleepy Katie was standing before him holding a small lantern.

"What's going on?"

"It's Maggie. She's been hurt and she needs you," Jon pleaded.

"Oh, no! What happened?"

"She took a beatin' and she's cut up pretty bad, but I think she'll be okay."

"I'll grab my bag and be right down." Her door clicked shut as Jon hurried back to Maggie's room.

"Katie's on her way," Jon barked as he hurried into Maggie's room.

Maggie managed a weak smile. "I don't know how to thank you, Jon. The ma....man was terrifying! I've never been through anything like that in my life. I thought he was going to kill me." She covered her face and began to sob uncontrollably.

Jon rushed over and knelt down beside her, gently stroking her hair. "Just hold on, darlin'. Katie's on her way."

She grabbed his hand firmly; her terrified eyes looked up at him. "Please don't tell anyone, Jon. Please!"

"I won't, Maggie. I won't tell a soul. And don't worry about George. I told him if he ever comes near you again, I'll kill him. I don't think he'll be back."

"Thank you so much, Jon," she said quietly as Katie hurried into the room with a pan of hot water. Her leather medicine bag hung over her arm.

"Oh my God, Maggie, you poor thing!" Katie gasped as she set the pan on the night table and snapped open the leather bag. She dipped a clean cloth in the warm water and gently dabbed Maggie's wounds.

With things under control, Jon stood and walked slowly toward the door. He heard Maggie admonish her friend.

"Katie, you must keep this to yourself. No one must know!" Maggie said firmly.

"All right, Maggie, but what kind of animal would do this?" she replied.

Jon paused and looked down at the broken lock. Katie glanced over. "Don't worry. I was born on a farm with three younger sisters and no brothers," she said. "Soon as I get Maggie bandaged, I'll fix that lock in a jiffy."

Jon smiled at the spirited Katie and left the room.

Chapter 15

The grayish light of the moon shone through the black clouds as the bright flames of the campfire lit up the dark night. Huddled near the fire for warmth on the cool spring evening, the rough men boasted of recent conquests.

"The gringo was stingy at first. He did not want to share his gold, but you convinced him to be very generous. You are a persuasive man, Paco Delgado." An evil smile broke out on the dark man's face as he spoke to his leader.

"Thank you, Arturo. I tried hard to convince him. It was not easy," Paco replied as he reached inside his poncho.

"Why does a man need five fingers anyway, mi amigo?" Laughter broke out among the men as Paco pulled a man's index finger from his bright red poncho and displayed it to the others.

Suddenly the laughter subsided as one of the banditos raised his hand and reached for his rifle. "Shhh! I hear a horse approaching."

"Go see who it is, pronto!" Paco commanded. Several of the banditos grabbed their guns and hurried to the edge of the camp to confront the intruder.

A voice shot out from the darkened pathway. "Don't shoot. It's Pedro Rubios. I need to talk to Paco."

"Hold your fire!" Paco jumped up. "That is indeed the voice of Pedro Rubios."

The men soon surrounded their unexpected guest and led him into camp.

"Pedro, I did not expect to see you so far from home." Paco approached the visitor as Rubios dismounted, and the two men quickly embraced. "Come in and sit down," Paco ordered as he pointed toward the campfire.

Pedro approached the group cautiously and took a seat by the fire. Soon the others were finding their places around the dancing flames. Rubios looked warily at the motley crew.

Paco spoke to his men. "This man and I ride together many years ago—he is fearless and a good shot." He smiled at Pedro.

Pedro smiled nervously.

"A glass of rum, my friend?"

"Gracias. Sounds good, mi amigo."

The leader gestured for one of the men to get a cup of rum as he returned to his spot by the campfire. "What brings a man like you down to the border? It's a long ride from El Cabrera." The bandito handed him a cup of rum.

"I come to see you at the orders of my boss—"

The bandito interrupted. "Señor Stanton?"

"Yes."

"And how is Señor Stanton?"

"He's not so good right now. He had too much to drink the other night and fell out of his buggy onto some rocks. He's pretty messed up."

"Hmmm...is he going to be okay?"

"Yeah. He's a pretty tough hombre."

Paco grinned.

"But his injuries are the least of his worries, mi amigo. The miners have organized and turned his goldfields near El Cabrera into an armed camp. With the help of a man named Jon Stoudenmire, they are attempting to steal the mines away from Señor Stanton and deprive him of what is rightfully his. As you may know, Mr. Stanton has very grandiose plans for the future. These men want to ruin these plans."

"What does your Señor Stanton want from me? Surely a little old Mexican boy like me can be of little help to a man of his stature," Paco said coyly.

"He thinks you can, Paco. Two of his best men have been shot down by Stoudenmire just in the past week. He needs fresh guns, and he needs a man who is not afraid to fight Stoudenmire. You are that man, Paco. He's willing to pay you a hundred dollars a week and your men fifty a week if you bring your guns to El Cabrera."

Paco grimaced. "Hmmm...you get right to the point, amigo. And I must be honest, your offer has taken me a little bit by surprise."

Pedro pushed on. "You and I go back a long way, Paco. We rode together when I was just a pup. I come to you now because I need your help. Mr. Stanton feels it is important that Jon Stoudenmire be killed."

The dark bandito paused and thought for a minute. "The heat has been on pretty good around here lately.

The rangers have been sent to the border by the governor to take me out. Several of my men have been killed or quit in the past year. We number only five now, and we have to…what you say? 'Look over our shoulder' all the time. A temporary change of scenery might be nice right now, but what you ask is risky, amigo, very risky. I have heard of Señor Stoudenmire— he is a very dangerous man."

Pedro squinted through the smoke of the campfire. "Señor Stanton wants to be governor of all of California one day, but Stoudenmire and his men stand in his way. If you help out and Mr. Stanton becomes governor, he will see to it that all charges pending against you are dropped, and you will be free to conduct your business in peace. There would be no rangers to bother you—the border would be yours."

"All charges—that's a lot!" Arturo shouted as laughter filled the camp.

Paco raised his hand for quiet. "No rangers, drop charges, that's good." He rubbed the thick stubble on his chin as he paced in front of the fire.

"I will come for two hundred a week and one hundred for my men." He paused. His black eyes looked hard at Pedro. "And when I kill Señor Stoudenmire, I want five hundred more."

"Five hundred!" Pedro exclaimed.

"Like I say, amigo, he is a very dangerous man."

"So are you, Paco. People cower in fear at the mention of your name."

The evil bandito's face broke into a smile. "My final offer."

Pedro frowned as he slowly stood and stared at Paco. Raising his cup of rum, his face broke into a grin. "It's a deal."

"Gracias," Paco replied as the two men touched cups and sipped the rum.

"We have unfinished business to take care of here. Tell Señor Stanton the five of us will be there on the first of the month. And tell him that we want pay for the first week in advance as soon as we arrive."

Pedro nodded.

"I hope you will sleep with us tonight, mi amigo."

Pedro nodded again.

Paco raised his cup. "Now let us celebrate our new partnership." His pocked face broke into an evil smile as the two men touched cups again. "Long live Pedro Rubios!" he shouted.

"Long live Pedro Rubios!" the other men shouted in unison. Laughter and conversation filled the air as the happy banditos and Stanton's messenger emptied their tin cups and took their places by the warm fire once again. The cold, dark night settled around the isolated camp as the men celebrated their unholy union well into the night.

- - - - -

Pedro said his goodbyes to Paco and his men early the next morning and hurried off on his journey back to El Cabrera. He was excited to tell George of his success in obtaining the services of the fearsome bandito and his men. Although forced to pay more, George had given him leeway to up the ante to two hundred a week. The five hundred for killing Stoudenmire was not discussed with George and would not be well received by him. He dreaded telling him.

- - - - -

His long ride over, Pedro arrived at Stanton's fortress. "Open up!" he shouted. "It's me, Rubios." A man ran out to greet him; the iron gates creaked open as Pedro spurred his horse toward the hitching post by the front door. He dropped off of his steed and quickly tied down. "George here?" he asked.

"Yes. He's out back on the veranda. He said he wanted to see you as soon as you got back."

Pedro hurried around back, anxious to tell his boss the news. He found Stanton sitting alone, staring out at his garden.

"George!" he shouted.

Stanton glanced up at the returning envoy. "Yes...yes, Pedro. Glad you're back safely. Sit down, please." Stanton pointed to a wooden chair across from his own as he slowly sat up; he was obviously still in some pain.

"How are you doing, boss?" Pedro asked as he plopped in the chair.

"Oh fine...fine. My ribs are still a little sore. But I'll live."

"Glad to—"

He was interrupted by Stanton. "Enough about me. Go on, did you find Paco?"

"Sí, I did, George. He was still using one of the old hideouts he used when I rode with him years ago."

"Good. What did he say, man? Go ahead!"

"Things are not good for him right now along the border. The Governor of California has the rangers after him. He's really feeling the heat."

"And..." an impatient George replied.

"So sorry, señor. He agreed to ride with us, but he wants two hundred a week and a hundred for his men." Pedro looked nervously at George.

"That son-of-a-bitch!" George bawled. "He knows he has me over a barrel, and he's squeezing me for more money." George grabbed his side and grimaced as he stood up and began pacing the veranda. "But I told you that you could go to two hundred. So I'll have to live with it," he mumbled. "What else did he say?" George continued to pace as he stared down at the clay tiles on the veranda floor.

A very nervous Pedro replied, "Well, uh...I...uh, told him about Stoudenmire."

"Yes...and?"

"He's heard of Stoudenmire."

"Okay, man, what the hell did he say about Stoudenmire?"

"He said he's a very dangerous man."

"Yes, yes, we all know that. Did you tell him that I would like to have Stoudenmire killed?"

"Yes...I...uh, told him." Pedro frowned and looked down at the ground.

"And...!" an incredulous Stanton shouted.

"He said he wanted five hundred dollars to kill him." Pedro closed his eyes as he awaited George's response.

"Five hundred! Why, that no account outlaw. I hope you said no!" George screamed.

Pedro fiddled nervously with the gold ring on his little finger as he stood and walked to the edge of the veranda, his back to Stanton. "We need him badly, señor. There's no other way with Stoudenmire and the others against us. We have to have his help!" he murmured.

"My God, have we all gone crazy around here? Five hundred dollars!" George winced in pain as he kicked a wooden chair off the porch. He clasped his hands behind his back and began pacing gingerly back and forth. "Suppose you told him I'd pardon him also?" The stocky leader shot a hard look at his loyal friend.

Pedro stared at the ground.

"That's what I figured," George mumbled.

George stopped pacing and spoke quietly. "You're right, my old friend. Things are getting out of hand, and we need the bastard. But I don't like it one bit. And he better deliver, or he won't get a dime."

Pedro was speechless.

"When's he coming, Pedro?"

"Uh…he…uh, said he had a few loose ends to tie down near the border. He said that he and his men will be here on the first of the month, and he said he want his first week pay in advance." Pedro's eyes squeezed shut in anticipation of George's answer.

"In advance? Why that…!" George shouted. "I may kill the bastard before he has a chance to kill Stoudenmire." He walked over and dropped carefully in his chair.

"You make good decisions, boss. He will be mucho help to us. We lucky he is coming."

George spit on the ground. "I guess sometimes you have to deal with people like him to get what you want," he grumbled. "And you're right, Stoudenmire has to be stopped. I will give Paco what he wants. I will deal with your old friend."

Pedro smiled and turned toward George.

"Hungry?" George asked.

"Si senor."

"Estela!" George turned toward the house and shouted.

A small, brown-skinned woman hurried to the veranda. "Yes, Señor Stanton, what can I do for you?"

"Please set two places with my finest china in the dining room for me and my friend Pedro, and tell Alonso to prepare two of my best t-bone steaks for dinner. Announce to us when dinner is ready. In the meantime, my friend and I will enjoy some brandy."

Estela hurried off and returned shortly with two snifters and a bottle of brandy. She carefully placed a glass in front of each man and filled them.

George lifted his snifter and pointed it toward Pedro. "To you, my friend!"

Pedro smiled broadly as he lifted the delicate goblet and gently touched it against George's. "To our future governor!"

Stanton's square face broke out in a big smile. "Our future does look bright, my friend, very bright." Born a poor kid and raised on the mean streets of New York City, George learned early on the power of intimidation. After the death of his father, the two-fisted youngster moved west to find his fortune. Coming from such meager beginnings, the thought of becoming the Governor of California intoxicated him. The two men drank brandy and talked quietly of their plans of conquest as the orange sun sank slowly behind the distant landscape.

Chapter 16

The aroma of freshly brewed coffee smelled great as Jon sat alone in the corner of the Dead End Saloon. Jake set down a cup and splashed it full. "Waitin' on someone?" he asked.

"Yeah, Cliff and Ned Sloan should be here shortly. Thanks again, Jake, for helpin' me out with Barton the other day."

"No problem, Jon."

"Lou still out of town?"

"Yeah. I got a wire today from Escondido. Seems the love bug has struck the boss. Said he was going to take a little trip to Los Angeles with his lady friend. Won't be back for a couple of weeks."

"Couple a weeks. Sounds serious." Jon blew on the hot coffee; the steam scattered above his cup.

"Yeah, weddin' bells will probably be ringing before long."

"You'd better have a talk with him," Jon laughed.

"Maybe so," Jake chuckled as he went back to the kitchen.

Jon was alone with his thoughts as he sat in the dark

corner of the nearly empty saloon. Morning was a slow
time at the Dead End. The late night gamblers were
getting a little shuteye and wouldn't show again until late
afternoon or evening, and the noontime gamblers
hadn't arrived yet. Jon felt his anger growing at George
Stanton. The usually friendly Maggie was not at her
check-in counter again this morning when he left
Callahan's. Jon figured she was still recovering from the
beating she'd received from Stanton and was spending
more time in her quarters. A gentleman by nature, the
beating of a woman was a hard thing for Jon to
reconcile. The whipping he gave Stanton wasn't enough
in Jon's eyes. The man was trying to bust the dreams of
all the miners and wine growers in the area for his own
personal gain. Jon detested men like him, especially
women beaters. He wanted to put George Stanton in his
grave in the worst way. Suddenly the batwing doors
burst open; Cliff and Ned hustled in.

Jake stepped out of the kitchen and pointed them
toward the corner. The men hurried over to Jon's table.

"Sit down, boys. We got plenty to talk about," Jon
said quietly.

The men circled the table and sat down.

"What's up?" Cliff asked.

"Seems as though Stanton's got his eye on some
bigger fish."

"The wineries?" Ned asked.

Jon frowned and nodded. "'Fraid so," he replied.

Chapter 17

"Why we ride so fast, Paco?"

"We have some business to take care of near the border, Arturo. Then we will stop at Rios and visit our loved ones before we make the long ride to El Cabrera," the deadly bandito shouted over the horses' pounding hooves.

"What business?" Arturo yelled.

"Señor Jim Johnson and Señor Will Collins."

"Ah, the ones who gunned down Ambrosio and Carmela."

Paco reined hard to a stop; his white quarter horse pranced nervously in the dusty road as the other men surrounded him.

"Yes, Arturo, we must say goodbye to mis amigos before we leave for El Cabrera. If they find we're gone, they may try to visit our families." The evil man spit on the ground and spurred his horse forward; the others closed in behind.

- - - - -

Return of the Gun

"You sure you want to go through with this, Will?" Ranger Johnson tossed another log on the fire. Night was falling; a cool breeze blew through the young rangers' camp.

Rubbing his arms, Will scooted nearer to the fire. "Go through with what?"

"Marryin' that little filly over there in San Diego."

"Well, I reckon I better. Her folks sure been doin' one heck of a lot of plannin'."

"What's the date?"

"The first Saturday of next month." The shy Will snatched a small stick from the ground and scribbled nervously in the dirt by the fire.

"I'm glad our stint's up this month, or you'd have an awful lot of disappointed people up there in San Diego," Johnson laughed.

Will playfully tossed the stick at his good friend. "Well guess what, Jim."

"What?" Jim ducked. The stick bounced off of his shoulder.

"I actually knew that. I actually knew I'd be finished this month." Will grinned and shook his head.

"You did?" Jim exclaimed. "You're actually smarter'n I thought ya—" he suddenly stopped in mid-sentence; his eyes went wide. "Did you hear that click, Will?"

"Sure enough did, partner."

Suddenly, loud gunshots rang out from the dark night.

"Ahhh!" Will murmured as his body slumped over and fell onto the cold ground. Another bullet ricocheted off of the metal coffeepot atop the fire. A small dark circle of blood quickly spread across the back of Will's tan shirt as he lay on the ground.

"Will!" Jim screamed.

- - - - -

"Good shot, boss," Arturo barked as he and the men charged into the camp and quickly surrounded the two rangers. Paco elbowed the men out of the way; the flames illuminated his square, dark face as he stopped by the fire.

"Your eyes are wide with fear, mi amigo," he growled.

Jim scanned the evil man's face. Moments earlier he had been talking of pleasant things with his close friend Will, and now he was facing a brutal killer while his friend lay dying on the ground.

"I wonder if you were this frightened when you gunned down my friends Ambrosio and Carmela in the valley near San Bonito, señor?" Paco lifted his rifle and slammed the butt against the young man's head; he fell hard to the ground. Blood began to spill from his ear.

Jim looked over at Will lying next to him on the ground. Will whimpered as he tried to raise his head.

"Finish him," the cruel Delgado ordered.

Arturo cocked his six gun, aimed it point blank at Will's head and pulled the trigger. The hot lead blasted into the young man. His head bounced violently off of the ground and fell still.

"Bury him where he won't be found, and cover the grave. Then tie the other one to that tree over there where we can see him." Paco pointed to a nearby oak tree. "Our young amigo may want to talk with us as we enjoy the warm fire."

Two men dragged the limp body of Will Collins away from the camp toward a nearby stream to bury him. Arturo lifted young Jim to his feet and lugged him over to the large oak tree. He pushed him up against the trunk as another man wound a rope around him several times. A dark stain of urine showed on the front of his jeans as he dangled near the fire.

"Look like he wet himself, boss. I wonder if Ambrosio wet himself before this coward shot him." Arturo laughed as he spit on the ground.

"I don't think so, amigo. Ambrosio was a brave man."

"It was a fair fight," Jim murmured. "He came at me first."

Suddenly, there was a blast from Paco's six gun.

"Ughh!" the young lawman exclaimed as the bullet splintered his lower leg. Blood began to show through his jeans; he writhed in pain.

Paco glared at the suffering ranger. "Fix some coffee, Felipe. We need to relax and enjoy the evening. How about if you make us something to eat? That sounds good. We can have dinner and enjoy our new friend here."

Felipe hurried to the back horse and pulled out a bag of coffee, flour and beans. Soon the coffee was brewing over the fire, and the flour was sizzling in a frying pan.

"In the mañana, after we say goodbye to our young friend here, we will need to stop at our village and spend a little time with our families before we leave for El Cabrera," Paco said calmly.

"Good idea, boss. I miss my family very much. I hope they miss me also," Arturo replied.

"I'm not so sure, Arturo. Your wife always looks so happy when we leave," one of the men shouted. The other banditos howled in delight.

"We are not being very polite, mis amigos. We are leaving the young señor out of our family discussions. I'm sure he have a family also. Pour him a cup of coffee, and we will talk of his family," Paco ordered.

Felipe lifted the metal pot off of the hot flames and poured the steaming hot coffee in a tin cup.

"Thank you, Felipe." Paco grabbed the cup, stood and walked over to the tree where Jim was tied. The young man's head was battered and swollen from the crushing blow from the rifle butt; his jeans were stained dark from the bullet wound that shattered his lower leg. His narrow eyes were glazed over with terror.

"Tell me about your family, señor. I'll bet you have a fine family. My friends and I would like to know a little about your family."

The ranger tried to collect himself. "M…My m…mother owns a laundry. My f…father found work at a r…ranch up north. I have t…t…two brothers and a sister."

"What a nice family you have, señor. Let me tell you about my family. I had a nice family once also—a wonderful father and a mother, three brothers and four sisters. Unfortunately, I lost my parents at a very tender age. It was very, what you gringos say?

"Traumatic," one of the men shouted.

"Yes, yes, a very traumatic experience." His bushy eyebrows raised. "It seems men came to our house uninvited late one night while my family was sleeping.

One of them climbed quietly through a small window in the pantry. Unfortunately, my padre was sleeping very soundly and did not hear the intruder. He was a very proud man. There would have been several dead men if he had heard them. The man who climbed in the window unlatched the front door. The other men rushed into our home and before my poor padre could react, they clubbed him senseless and cut his throat. Then two men held mi madre on her bed and ripped off her night clothes, exposing her naked body. The other men raped her time and time again while we little ones watched in horror through the bedroom door."

Paco scowled and spit on the ground. "Then the men rode off leaving us children to fend for ourselves. I was the oldest, so I led the children into town to the constable's house. He had no choice but to send us off to an orphanage in Mexico City. The orphanage was controlled by a brutal headmaster." He grimaced. "He beat us daily."

Paco stepped over closer to the young officer; their faces were only inches apart. "I found out later that the men who attacked our home were rangers, just like yourself, mi amigo." Paco glowered at the terrified victim. "That is the wonderful story of my family—did you enjoy?"

The battered ranger raised his head and stared blankly at his tormentor.

The cruel highwayman reached over and grabbed the young man by the top of his shirt. He ripped the cotton shirt open, fully exposing his bare chest. He pushed the young man's chin up with his index finger and lifted the still steaming coffee up to the wounded man's lips. "Here is your coffee, señor. I almost forgot. So sorry."

The vicious man tipped the cup back slightly and let the still steaming hot coffee drain down the front of the ranger's bare chest as he screamed in pain.

"Stop! Please stop!" Young Jim begged the horrid brute to stop. Red welts popped up on his chest, but the bad man showed no feeling.

"Oh my," Paco said as he stared into the cup. "There is a little left, forgive me," his thin lips turned up in a cruel smile as the dark, hot coffee splashed square in the middle of the face of the tortured man.

"My eyes! Oh my God, my eyes are on fire!" The badly injured prey screamed in agony for several minutes and then started to moan. His eyes and forehead were an ugly mess; his eyes began swelling shut almost immediately from the terrible trauma. He was suffering horribly; it was more than he could bear. Suddenly, his head dropped on his chin and his battered body fell still. His limp body dangled from the ropes facing the nasty banditos.

"That very rude," Paco barked. "He fell asleep during our party." The nasty man bellowed in laughter. After a brief pause, Arturo and the other men joined in on the cruel laughter.

"How's the food coming, Felipe?"

"The beans are ready and I have made a few tortillas. Are you hungry, Paco?'

"Yes, but first we must serve our guest. It is only polite."

Felipe scooped the warm beans from the iron pot and dumped them in the flour tortilla. He folded it over and handed it to his master. Paco took the tortilla over to the unconscious ranger, grabbed him by his hair and yanked his head back, causing his mouth to fall open.

Next, he crammed the warm tortilla full of beans into the ranger's mouth. "Enjoy your dinner, señor. If you want seconds, just let me know." He dropped the youngster's head and laughed hysterically. Beans dribbled down the young ranger's swollen chest and fell to the ground; the flour tortilla still hung from his mouth. Paco rejoined his sinister gang of thugs as the smell of death filled their vile campsite.

- - - - -

Fingers of smoke drifted up from the dying embers in the campfire as the yellow sun rose in the morning sky. An early riser, Paco walked to the nearby stream with the metal coffeepot. He dipped it into the flowing stream and walked back to the campsite. He grabbed a long stick with his free hand and stirred the grayish coals in the fire pit; small flames ignited. He tossed several small limbs on the fire, and the flames grew. He set the metal pot on the hot coals. "Wake up, men," he barked. "It's time to get up and ride."

The men slowly sat up, rubbing their crusty eyes. Arturo, a deep sleeper, was snoring away. Paco kicked his foot. "Get up, Arturo. Your woman is waiting to see you. It time to go." Reluctantly, the bandito sat up; his thin fingers ran through his black hair.

"Why we up so early? We got all day to ride," he complained. The smallish man's arms reached for the sky.

"You say that every day, Arturo. You sleep too much," Paco chided his old friend.

"Quiet—I hear something!" One of the men exclaimed. "It is our friend."

The young ranger was semi-conscious; he was moaning, but otherwise not moving. Paco looked over at the pathetic sight. His face was a horrible mess; his eyes were oozing slits of puss. The huge blisters on his chest had turned an ugly bluish-black color. Red ants from a huge nearby anthill covered his lower leg, eating away at him. Lines of ants were moving up and down his body; his chest and face were slowly being covered by the swarming insects. It was a horrid, macabre scene.

Paco sneered at the dying man. His face showed no sympathy. "Take him to the stream, and clean the ants off him and bury him. Be sure to cover the grave with leaves and twigs. We don't want the authorities to find him."

"But Paco, he is still alive," one of the men yelled.

"Bury him," Paco said coldly as he poured hot coffee into a tin cup.

"But Paco!"

"Bury him!"

- - - - -

"It will be good to get home, mis amigos!" Paco shouted as the gang of marauders rode down the narrow trail toward the small village of Rios, just over the border in Mexico. The trail took a sharp turn to the right and led the men through a grove of orange trees. Then it dropped down into a lush, grassy valley near a small lake. Several adobe huts became visible as the men raced to their homes in the hot noonday sun.

The women were washing clothes by the lake, and small children were playing in the streets as the men approached. One of the women looked up from her washing. "Muchachos! Muchachos!" she shrieked as she ran toward the fast approaching gang. The other women stopped what they were doing and followed suit. The children screamed and began jumping up and down as the men rode in.

Paco's white quarter horse danced in front of the group; he smiled broadly, leaned down and touched the hands of several children as the women arrived and surrounded them. Paco searched the crowd for his wife and son but could not see them.

"Your Maria is at the house doing her mending," one of the women shouted.

Paco tipped his sombrero to the lady and spurred his horse forward to his large adobe home on the edge of town as the shouts of joy continued. Paco pulled up quickly in front of his home, jumped off of his horse and rushed through a small wooden gate. His Maria was just coming out of the front door. Tears were brimming in her eyes as she ran toward her man. They fell into each other's arms, hugging and kissing. A bad and evil man at times, Paco loved his Maria more than anything in the world. His heart was full.

"Oh, Paco," she murmured, "I miss you so. You'll never know how much I miss you when you go away from me. It's so wonderful to see you again."

Tears rolled down the famous bandit's cheeks as he looked at his beautiful wife. Her dark, lovely face was adorned with gorgeous chocolate eyes, and her pretty mouth seemed always to be in the shape of a smile.

"How do I leave such a beautiful girl as you?" he asked joyfully. "I must be crazy." His thick fingers moved gently through her long, black hair.

"Let's go inside," she said with a flirtatious grin. "We have some catching up to do."

"Where is Lope?"

"Your loyal son and some of the other boys are fishing at a distant lake. They won't be back for several hours. We have time before he returns."

Paco smiled mischievously. "I love my Lope, but his absence comes at a very good time." He gently lifted his wife up in his arms and stepped up to the wood plank porch. The boards creaked as he walked through the door and into their home. Maria kicked her legs up and down and kissed him repeatedly on the neck. They hurried through the living room filled with pottery and beautiful oil paintings to their bedroom at the back of the house. Paco bumped the door open and then kicked it shut with the back of his foot as they hurried toward the bed in the corner of the room. Paco bit down on Maria's dress strap and pulled with his teeth; it fell to her waist as the two lovers jumped onto the soft featherbed.

"I think of this often when I am on the trail, my Maria, and now it is happening," Paco murmured.

"I live for these moments, Paco. I love you so!"

Window shutters banged in the breeze as the two passionate lovers made love and whiled away the afternoon in each other's arms.

- - - - -

Later that afternoon, Maria sat sipping tea on the long front porch. She smiled as her son Lope and his father wrestled around in the front yard, kicking, grabbing, and screaming in laughter. Growing into manhood, the young Lope was anxious to test his famous father.

"You only sixteen, but you fight like a man," a panting Paco shouted as both combatants suddenly stopped their aggressive play and rolled flat on the ground, chests heaving.

"You're lucky, Paco—he took it easy on you," Maria shouted in delight from the porch.

"Oh no, mama, I didn't take it easy. Papa strong as a bull. He could have taken me at any time. He was easy on me," Lope replied as he sat up. Yellow strands of grass covered his dark, wavy hair.

Paco stood, his chest still heaving, and reached down for his son. "You flatter me, my respectful son," he said. The two friendly warriors clasped hands. Paco pulled his son to his feet, and they warmly embraced.

"I love you, papa," Lope said softly.

"And I love you also, my son." Tears welled in the eyes of the hardened bandito as they embraced. "You make me very proud."

"Thank you, papa," Lope said politely as he began looking for his sombrero. "With your permission, I must go now. Several of the steers got loose today. The other boys and I must round them up."

"Of course, my son. I will be here until the morning. Do your manly duty and round up steers." He smiled proudly as his son jumped over the rail fence and hurried down the dirt street. Several boys appeared from nearby huts to join him.

Paco stood and watched as his handsome son and the others raced to the stables. Maria walked over and nestled in next to him. She looked longingly at her man as the two sat down on the long, wooden chair. "He look up to you. He thinks there is nobody like his papa."

"He's a good boy," Paco replied softly.

"But he know not what you do, my Paco. All of the young boys here in the village believe their papas work for the Mexican government as mercenaries to help protect all of us from the awful gringos."

"And is that not what I do, my Maria?"

Maria frowned. She gently laid her hand on her husband's arm. "The gringos have not attacked us for many years, Paco," she said. "You have gringos who are friends of yours. At first you were so angry about what the rangers did to your parents that you hated everybody north of the border, and you went after them with a vengeance. But now I see a man who not only robs innocent gringos, but his own people as—"

Irritated, Paco interrupted. "That's enough, Maria. I don't want to talk about it. I do what I have to do to provide for our family. You should be happy—you have the finest home in the village."

"But what if Lope find out what you really do, what then?" Maria was distressed as she pushed on, ignoring her powerful husband.

Paco got to his feet and paced back and forth. "Why, when I come home for a short visit, do you have to bring up such things? Can this not wait?"

"Wait til when, Paco? We always just have short visits. If I wait til we have a long visit, I will be an old lady, and our son will be gone. We must talk now." She looked directly at him.

An angry Paco spun toward his wife. "Are you ashamed of me? My wonderful wife is ashamed of her

Paco—a man of great respect among his people. Is that what you are saying to me?"

Maria looked down, away from his hard stare. "I love you, Paco, with all my heart. I still remember that dashing, handsome young man who swept me off of my feet so many years ago. And I see all of the good in you, Paco. You are always kind and gentle to me. It breaks my heart to say these things to you, but I hear the stories and I used not to believe them. But there have been too many. I know now, Paco, that you can be a very bad man at times." Tears began to pour from her eyes at her own revelations. "My heart is breaking, Paco! Lope looks up to you like no other son, but he is starting to ask questions. And I don't know what to tell him! I am tortured by it all."

"What questions?" Paco bellowed. "What questions does he ask?"

"He has heard the stories too. The whole village has heard the stories."

"I ask you, what he say?" Paco's face was red with anger.

Tears continued to pour from Maria's eyes; her face was full of pain. "He ask me, my love, if…if…"

"If what?"

"If you are a murderer," she cried out as she fell on her knees and began hugging his legs. "I'm so sorry to tell you this. I'm so sorry, Paco." She was sobbing uncontrollably.

The anger faded from the face of the legendary bad man as he looked down at his beloved Maria, sobbing and begging his forgiveness. He reached down and gently pulled her arms from his legs and lifted her up.

He pulled her to his chest; his muscular arms went around her shoulders as he embraced her warmly.

They hugged and sobbed for several minutes, and then Paco spoke quietly. "I made a promise to an old amigo of mine, my dearest Maria, and I am, if nothing else, a man of my word. I must honor this commitment, so I will be leaving in the mañana to ride to El Cabrera. But I promise you this, my love, with all of my heart. It will be the last time that Paco Delgado ever ride. The pain in your eyes is more than I can bear. I will come home and farm this valley and fish with my son. I will ride no more."

Maria's red, swollen eyes were full of joy as she looked at her man. "Paco, I am so happy! I always know you love me, but now I know how much you love me and Lope. It will be wonderful to have you home!" she said as she hugged him tightly.

"What you say today stunned me, but I know it's from the heart. I saw my parents murdered and raped by the heartless rangers. I vowed to get even, and I have. But now I have a son who is growing up and needs a father who does more than just rob and kill. I will spend time with my son, and I will tell him that I fought for the honor of my family and have no regrets. But I will tell him that I will fight no more and that I have done some things that I am ashamed of. I will tell him I want better for him."

"Oh Paco, I love you so!"

Paco lifted his lovely wife up in his arms, carried her over and sat down in the rocking chair. Not another word was said as the two rocked together in the chair; her thin arms hung around his neck, her face lay on his chest. They closed their eyes and quietly rocked for over an hour as Paco whispered softly in her ear.

Arturo rode up later that afternoon. "Sorry to interrupt you lovebirds," he shouted as he rode up to the front of the house, "but the boys caught many fish today. My Bonita and I would like to invite you to enjoy the fish with us this evening at our place. The whole village is invited. We hope you will join us, boss."

Maria looked up and smiled at her man. "It's okay. I would like to go."

"When, Arturo?"

"Just before sunset. We will build a big bonfire and fellowship together."

"We will be there!" Paco replied.

Arturo waved his sombrero in the air and rode quickly away.

- - - - -

The light from the flames shone brightly on the happy faces as the celebration began that evening. Paco stood near the fire, his arm firmly around Maria's waist. The tequila was flowing freely, and much laughter could be heard.

"You throw a good party, mi amigo. I have never seen my people so happy, Arturo," Paco shouted.

"Thank you, boss. Felipe has been hard at work preparing the fish, our dinner should be ready soon. We will celebrate into the wee hours!" He raised his cup of tequila to Paco; several others around the fire joined in. "I prepare a toast to the great Paco Delgado, a hero to us all!" he shouted.

"To Paco! To Paco!" the others shouted to their leader.

Paco smiled nervously and nodded at the chanting crowd. Maria looked up at her man and smiled politely, bravely hiding her feelings. Paco's expression changed as he looked down at his Maria. He slid his arm off her waist and took a step toward the fire. He took a sip of his tequila. Flames shot skyward as he emptied his cup in the fire. The folks screamed their approval at the antics of their dashing leader. Paco raised his hand to quiet them down as the light from the fire shone brightly on his square, weathered face.

"My friends, I have something to say to you that will come as a surprise. I want you to hear me out, for I will not say it again." He lifted his sombrero off and held it in his hands. "As I look around our village, I see our children growing. Many of our young boys are growing into manhood—my son Lope is one of them. The old men and women in the village are growing older. Many have passed away. More rangers are coming, and more will continue to come. People are moving here in great numbers. It is getting harder and harder to do our job. We have lost several good men lately, and we will lose more. The people of California still fear us, but times are changing. Maria and I have talked, and I have decided that it is time to settle down. I will ride no—"

"No! No!" the men shouted over him.

"We must not give up!" one of them yelled.

Paco raised his sombrero above his head for quiet once again. "Look around at the women and children, my brothers. Look at their eyes, and look into their hearts. They are not yelling for us to go. They worry for us. They need us here to help farm the land and fish the lakes in this beautiful valley. No, my friends, our families want us here."

The men grumbled, but with less gusto as they looked into the sullen eyes of their wives and children.

"But Paco, you make a promise to Pedro Rubios, and you always keep your promises," a disappointed Arturo barked.

"Yes, you are right, Arturo. I did make a promise to ride to El Cabrera, and I am a man of my word. We will ride to El Cabrera in the morning."

The men cheered and raised their cups. "Long live—"

Paco interrupted the men. "But this will be the last trip. When we return from El Cabrera, I will ride no more."

There were grumblings in the crowd; the men had long faces as they mumbled their disapproval. They could not believe what they were hearing. Maria moved over and put her arm around Paco's waist.

A smile broke out on Paco's face as he looked back at the crowd. "We have fought the good fight, mis amigos. But there comes a time to fight no more. We have much to be thankful for. Our cups are full. We must continue to celebrate—this night belongs to us. We will leave tomorrow for our long ride to El Cabrera. Then we will return home and reunite with our families. And please don't fret, my friends, for the Mexican people will always remember Paco Delgado and his brave band of freedom fighters!"

It was quiet for a moment as the men absorbed Paco's words. After a short pause, one of them shouted, "Hey! Hey! Long live Paco!"

The men smiled as they hugged their women and children. They raised their cups and began chanting "Long live Paco Delgado! Long live Paco Delgado!" Some of the old folks began to dance by the fire as the raucous celebration resumed and carried well into the early morning hours.

Chapter 18

Jon locked the door to his room and dropped the key in his vest pocket. He tossed his felt hat on the bed and sat down at a small desk in the corner. He slid the desk drawer open and pulled out some parchment, laying it on the table. Carefully removing the black pen from its holder, he dipped it in the glass ink bottle and began to write.

My dearest Elizabeth:

Arrived safely and unexpectedly met up with cousin Cliff Stone in El Cabrera, a few miles from winery. Cliff asked me to stay and help with a business matter. Will be at the vineyard soon.

I am of good health, my dearest. I miss you sorely. You are in my dreams often. I long to hold you in my arms again!

Your faithful lover,

Jon

Jon's eyes glistened as he carefully placed the pen back in its holder and folded the letter in half. He picked up his hat, hurried out of the room and quickly locked the door behind him. He jumped down the stairs past an empty front desk and went out the front door to the street.

Main Street was buzzing with activity as Jon wove his way between the many wagons and buggies in the bustling mining town. He hurried down the dusty street, leapt up on the boardwalk and pushed the door open to the telegraph office. The aging operator looked out from under his black visor as the bell on the top of the door jingled, announcing Jon's arrival.

"Can you get me a line to Logan's Crossing up Arizona way?" the anxious Jon blurted out.

"Just hold on there, young feller," the aging operator barked. "I'm in the middle of one right now. I'll be right with ya."

Jon grinned at the old timer as he plopped down in a wooden chair next to the operator's desk. He was surprised at how quick and nimble the old cuss was as he tapped out the message on the sounder.

Suddenly the clicking stopped, the old man ripped off the tape for that message, quickly rolled it up and set it on the desk. He turned toward Jon. "Okay, feller, what can I do fer ya today?"

"I need to send a wire down Arizona way."

"Arizona way, huh?" The old man rubbed his chin. "Been havin' a little trouble getting through to some places in Arizona lately. Seems like the Comanche down there are madder'n hornets about somethin', and they keep cuttin' the lines. What town are ya aimin' for?"

"Logan's Crossing," Jon replied, eyebrows raised.

"Hmmm...Logan's Crossing. I'll send 'em a test and see what happens." The old timer clicked the sounder several times as Jon waited in great anticipation.

"Hmmm...well, I'll be," the man mumbled.

"Well, what is it? Can ya get through or not?" Jon asked impatiently.

"Looks like it's your lucky day. They got my signal. Ya better give me that message 'fore somethin' goes wrong."

Jon quickly unfolded his letter to Elizabeth and handed it to the old codger. "It's, uh...to, uh...Miss Elizabeth Thompson," Jon murmured, slightly embarrassed to give the intimate letter to the gnarly old operator.

"Well, give it here!" the old man hollered. "Ya think I ain't never seen a love letter before?" A grin broke out on his wrinkly face as a red-faced Jon handed him the letter.

The old man's bony fingers maneuvered the keys with great skill as Jon sat watching. Suddenly, he stopped and leaned back in his chair. "Well, that's it. I can't go no further." He frowned as tobacco juices dribbled down his chin.

Wide-eyed, Jon jumped up out of his seat. "That's it?" he shouted. "What happened?"

"I can't go no further."

"Why not?" a frustrated Jon demanded.

The old timer leaned to his left and hocked one in the metal spittoon on the floor. Smiling from ear to ear, he looked up at Jon. "'Cause I'm all done. Your letter's in Logan's Crossin' just the way you wrote it."

"Why, you old geezer, I oughta whup you a good one!" Jon laughed out loud. "You really got me!" Jon threw a five dollar gold piece on the desk. "Keep the change," he shouted as he walked out of the office, still chuckling at the old timer's gag.

"Hey, Jon!" Jon turned quickly at the sound of his name as he stepped down from the boardwalk in front of the telegraph office. He saw Cliff approaching. "Morning, Cliff. What are you doing in town this time of day?"

"I need to talk to you, Jon, right away. There's been some goings on out at the camp this morning," Cliff said fretfully.

"Okay, cus. Let's go down to the Crown and have a cup a coffee. The breakfast crowd is probably out of there by now, so we'll have some privacy."

"I have to stop at the bank for a minute, and then I'll be down pronto."

"Sounds good," Jon replied as Cliff reined his horse around and headed for the bank.

- - - - -

Cliff entered the Crown and smiled as he spotted Jon in the corner. He carefully maneuvered between the empty tables, pulled a chair out and sat down across from Jon. Anita hurried over and poured him a hot cup of coffee.

"Thank you," Cliff said.

"What's up?" Jon asked, anxious to get on with it.

"Stanton had some visitors this morning." Cliff carefully took a sip of coffee.

"Anybody I know?"

"Not sure. Ever heard the name Paco Delgado?"

"Who hasn't?" Jon grimaced. "He's a cold-blooded killer if there ever was one."

"Yep, he sure is. He rode up to Stanton's office out at the mines earlier this morning. I could tell it was him from a mile away with his famous white sombrero, red poncho and beautiful white quarter horse. He stands out like a sore thumb. It's like he's invitin' someone to take a shot at him or somethin'."

"Could ya hear anything?"

"I stopped diggin' and listened real close. Like I told you, I'm workin' the ridge right above Stanton's office, so I could hear some of the convesation."

"What'd they say?" Jon asked.

"They didn't say much. They just shook hands and stuff, but I did hear one thing that set me back a little."

"What was that?"

"As they were walking to George's office, I heard Paco laugh out loud and shout, 'Don't worry, George— you cut off the head, and the snake will die.'"

"Really!"

"Yes, so be careful, Jon."

"How many men were with him?"

"Four."

"Hmmm…," Jon mused. "This is costing George a little money. He'll want me dead for sure."

"Looks that way." Cliff stared down at his coffee. "Jon, I did a lot of thinkin' on the way into town and—"

Jon interrupted. "That's somethin' new and different?"

"Just shut up and listen, smart aleck."

Jon grinned.

"I've known of a lot of bad hombres in my day, but this Delgado is a horse of a different color. He's pure evil. When I asked you to help out, Jon, I didn't know this thing would end up like this. You been duckin' lead ever since ya got here, and now Delgado's got you in his sights. I wouldn't blame ya a bit if you just—"

"Just what?" Jon quickly interrupted. "Rolled on down the road and left my good cousin and the good people of El Cabrera to fight these nasty hombres alone?" Jon sat up in his chair. "This thing's personal for me now, Cliff. I've seen too much. This ole saddle bum ain't goin' anywhere til Stanton, Delgado, and the rest of his gang are cold and in the ground. You understand, bucko?"

Cliff smiled. "Sure enough do, cus."

Jon sank back in his chair. "I 'preciate the thought, though, I really do, but we got us a job to do, partner."

Cliff nodded. "What's our next move?"

"We can't wait, Cliff—we gotta hit them before they hit us. I want you to ride out to the mines in the morning and round up Sloan and Malone for a meeting. Have Red stay and guard the camps. On your way out, check out Stanton's place and see if Delgado and the boys are there. There should be fresh tracks. I'm sure they just met up out at the mines, but they got plenty of planning to do. My guess is they rode to Stanton's place—it's more private. They're probably gonna hang out there in some of those empty bunkhouses in the back of the compound and wait for their chance to take me out."

"Where do you want to meet me and the boys?"

"This is your town, Cliff. Where's a good place?"

"There's an old abandoned cabin a few miles north of town. Just follow the trail until you pass the second bend in the road. You'll see a crack in some big rocks to your left. It looks a little tight, but your horse will fit through okay. After ya clear the rocks, you'll drop down a steep hill into an opening by a little pond. The cabin's on the other side. An old man and his wife lived there for years. She up and died of consumption a few years ago, and it was more than the old man could handle. One night he stuck his six gun in his mouth and pulled the trigger. Ain't nobody lived there since the poor old bastard shot himself."

Jon stood up and slid his hand in his front jeans pocket; he tossed a silver dollar on the table. "I best be goin', I'll see ya at that old cabin tomorrow afternoon."

"Sure thing."

"I'm gonna make a quick trip out to the winery in the morning and warn Carlos and the others of the pending trouble. Hard tellin' where this fight's gonna end up. They need to be ready." Jon stood to leave.

"Just one more thing, Jon."

"Yes, Cliff—what is it?"

"If you get to the cabin first, sit still and listen close. The old man's ghost likes to talk to his guests. It gets downright spooky at times."

"Is that right?" Jon replied, wide-eyed.

"Yep, that's what I've heard."

"Hmmm…that's scary all right, but ya know what?"

"What?" a grinning Cliff asked.

"He'll probably be the smartest hombre I'll talk to all day."

"Damn, I thought I had ya there for a minute," Cliff groaned as they left the cafe.

- - - - -

Stanton and Delgado and his gang were sitting on the veranda at Stanton's compound. Their horses were safely tucked away in stables out back. The new arrivals had made homes in several of the empty cabins near the stables. George had invited them to join him and Buck Johnson for a drink.

"The finest tequila in California, my friends," George bragged as Estela filled the porcelain cups for the gnarly banditos. She gingerly maneuvered around the table as several of the ruffians tried to pinch her backside. George grinned at the antics of the men.

George tipped his cup to Paco and the others. "Welcome to El Cabrera, my friends."

"Thank you, Señor Stanton," Delgado replied as he and the others raised their cups and sipped the tequila. "It is very good, señor." Paco's evil face broke into a smile.

"I trust you had a safe journey," George said.

"Oh yes, señor. The journey was long, but very good." Paco smiled and took another sip of tequila.

George leaned forward and dropped his elbows on the long oak table. "If I may have your attention for a moment, gentlemen, I would like to tell you why I have brought you here."

He waited patiently for the men to stop giggling and groping at Estela's backside. Annoyed, George motioned her away. She hurried off; soon all eyes were on him as he spoke. "I have controlled the goldfields in this area for some time now, gentlemen, but unfortunately, there has been a recent attempt by some of the local miners to take the fields away from me. Their leader is a new man in town name Jon Stoudenmire. He rode into town last week and met up with his miner cousin Cliff Stone. Stone talked him into staying here and helping them with their dastardly deed of forcing me out of the mine fields. A hardened gunman, Mr. Stoudenmire has already shot to death two of my best men. Your job will—"

Paco interrupted. "Yes, yes, with all due respect, Señor Stanton, we know all of this. Pedro tell us—you need not continue. We will kill your Mister Stoudenmire and the others. That's no problem. But money is a problem. I tell Pedro we want our first week up front or no deal."

An angry George sat up in his chair. "You'll get your money, Delgado."

"I want it now," he shot back. "We are just poor boys from Mexico. We have no money, señor. We must be paid." He and the others chuckled.

George's face flushed with anger. "You'll get your money when I'm damned good—"

Buck Johnson quickly interrupted his volatile boss. "Uh…pardon me, George, but why don't we just pay the gentlemen as Pedro agreed so we can go ahead with our plans?" Buck smiled nervously at his angry boss.

George was incensed, his eyes wide, but he also realized that he needed these men very badly. This was no time to blow the deal. He controlled himself and spoke. "Excuse me," he said as he stood slowly, "I will be right back." His face still flushed with anger, George rose and walked deliberately to the den. Pushing the door closed behind him, he knelt down in front of the safe. After a couple of deep breaths, he reached in, pulled out a canvas bag and counted out six hundred dollars. He tossed the bag back in the safe, slammed the door shut, stood and walked back to the dining room. Still fuming, he dropped the money on the table in front of Delgado.

"There's your damn money."

Delgado nodded, counted the money and stuffed it in the leather bag on his waist sash.

George sat down. "You seem to know so much, Delgado. What's your plan?"

Paco fiddled playfully with the string on his sombrero. "Like I tell you out at the goldfields, Señor Stanton, if we cut off the head, the snake will die. Señor Stoudenmire is giving them more courage than they would have otherwise. After I keel him and he is dead and in the ground, the other men will fight with less gusto. Most of them will quit. A few might fight. If so, we will clean up the scraps, and your problem will be over."

"Sounds like a cozy little plan, Delgado, but what if most of them don't quit?"

An ugly smile broke out on the man's dark face. "If it doesn't work, then we go to plan B."

"Which is?"

"We kill all of them," Paco sneered as he and his men broke out in laughter.

George seemed intrigued as he watched Paco and his banditos celebrate the ugly thought.

"You are indeed a wicked man, my friend, but I like your plan. Shall we drink?" he raised his cup to the vicious killer.

Delgado did the same. "Here's to you, Governor," he roared.

Stanton's expression suddenly changed. He knew what Paco meant; it sobered him to think that he might have to appease this horrid man if he someday became governor. He grimaced at the thought as he drank his tequila.

Paco set his cup on the table. "May I explain my plan further?"

George looked intently at Delgado. "Go ahead."

"We have to be very careful how we keel Señor Stoudenmire," Paco laughed nervously. "You want him dead, but you don't want us to be, how you say?"

"Careless," Stanton barked.

"Yes, that's it. You do not want to be careless. Is that right, señor?"

"Why yes, yes, of course. We have to be careful," Stanton replied.

"Well then, señor, on the day we keel him, we need to be sure that you and your men have a good alibi. You need to be somewhere in town where everybody can see you. That way no one suspect you."

"Hmmm...good point, Delgado. Where could we be that day? Let me think," George mused as he rubbed his chin. "Ah yes, that will be easy."

Paco's eyebrows raised.

"Most Saturday nights me and the boys go into town for dinner. My brother Lou owns the Dead End Saloon, and he stuck a big table in the corner that's more or less reserved for us. We gather there, have dinner, and get all roostered up. The whores love it— we're big spenders."

"Very good, very good, amigo," Paco replied. "Everyone will see you at the saloon. So we will plan to keel your Señor Stoudenmire while you and your men are in town playing with those little whores." Paco and the men roared once again.

Annoyed, Stanton laughed halfheartedly.

Paco stopped laughing and continued, "Mi muchachos and I will come up with a plan to get Stoudenmire alone that night. It will be easier if we get him alone so nobody see him get keeled. After we take care of him, we will put the body someplace where nobody will ever find it. Stoudenmire will be dead, and then we can wait and see what happens with the others. If they continue to fight, we will keel more. If the resistance ends, you will pay us, and we will ride out of town and return to our families."

"Hmmm…sounds like a good enough plan. But don't be surprised if the other boys fight on," George exclaimed. "They're no pushovers. They are plenty tough men in their own right." He glanced over at Delgado.

"We shall see, amigo, but first we must take care of Señor Stoudenmire."

"Well, we can talk more at breakfast in the morning," George replied. "I must be going."

"Sí, we will talk again in the morning," Paco replied as he stood and grabbed a full bottle of tequila off of the table. He raised the green bottle above his head. "Mañana!" he shouted to the other men.

"Mañana!" the men shouted. They pushed behind their leader as he waved the bottle in the air and hustled from the room.

George winced at the gall of the Mexican bandito for taking his tequila. "That arrogant son-of-a-bitch," he murmured.

Chapter 19

"Hola, Jon!" Carlos shouted. He stepped back slightly as Jon jerked to a stop in front of him. Jon jumped off Babe and tied down.

"Let's go inside, Carlos. We need to talk."

Carlos turned to shout some orders at a nearby worker. "Take over, Ignacio. I need to talk with Señor Stoudenmire."

Carlos waved his hand toward the cabin. Jon followed him inside.

"Glass of wine?" Carlos asked as he hurried in.

"No thanks, Carlos. I can't stay long."

"If you don't mind, señor, before you say why you come, I must tell you something. You may need to know this before you say what you have to say." Pedro smiled nervously, hesitant to interrupt his boss.

Jon's eyebrows rose. "That's okay, my friend. Fire away," he replied as the two men sat down at the table.

"Remember the other day when you were here, and I told you that Buck Johnson and his men had been out to see us?"

Jon nodded.

"Well, I just find out that one of the owners may have sold out to Stanton that very day. His name is Harter, and he had been losing a lot of money gambling in Vinegar Bend. We think he needed the money, and so he sold out to Señor Stanton. Not sure, but we think so. Harter's men are still working the vineyard, but their leader has been replaced by a new man—one of Stanton's men."

"Damn, that's not good at all." Jon was concerned. "I'll check the court records when I get back to town and see if it's true—if it is, we've got big problems."

"How so?" Carlos asked. "It is only one small vineyard."

"You're right, but it will be much easier for Stanton now. This gives him a foothold in the wine country as well as in the goldfields. He will be able to watch the goings on around here more closely. He will sniff out the weak sisters, and his hired guns will move in and force 'em out. He will gain more and more control and have greater influence over the wine fields. He has to be stopped!"

"I see, señor," Carlos replied.

"I'm afraid I have some bad news of my own." Jon's eyes narrowed.

"Oh?"

"After the loss of Injun Joe and Dave Barton, Stanton has brought in some new guns. They just arrived in town."

"New guns?"

"Yes, and deadly ones—Paco Delgado and his gang."

"Oh my, mi amigo! He is a legend in Mexico and a very, very bad man. I would be careful with him—he play very rough."

"Sounds like you know of him."

"Oh yes. All of my people know of Paco Delgado."

"Tell me, what do you know, Carlos?"

"I will do my best." Carlos hesitated and then went on, "Many years ago, some renegade rangers began riding into small villages and terrorizing my people near the border. They were ruthless and cruel. One of the families they attacked was that of Paco Delgado. He was just a boy at the time. They shot his father while he lay sleeping and then they rape and kill his mother in front of the children. Then they burnt his house to the ground. They were very bad men. Paco vowed to get revenge. After a few years in an orphanage, he left and formed a gang of his own to pay back the gringos."

"Why did the rangers attack the villagers?"

"They say that Santa Anna sent some soldiers over the border to raid the gold mines in California. They say Santa Anna needed the gold for his fight with Texas. There was no proof of that, but that's what they say. They said the Mexican soldiers killed many innocent people, and the rangers were getting revenge."

"Hmmm...so Paco has been at it ever since?"

"Yes, and he is still a hero with the Mexican people because he stood up to the gringos. But the gringos quit fighting many years ago, and Paco has continued to rape and murder near the border. Now he steal from everyone—his own people as well as the gringos. He has become an evil man."

"That's quite a story, Carlos. Better keep your guard up, my friend. I don't know where this thing is going. Do you have a weapon out here?"

"Oh yes. My rifle is in the cabinet." Carlos nodded toward a tall cabinet in the corner of the room.

"Good. Keep it loaded. Also, warn your men that there might be trouble coming." Jon turned to leave.

Carlos grabbed his arm. "One more thing, Jon."

"Yes, Carlos?" Jon looked back at his friend.

"Hate does not die easy, mi amigo. My people know that Paco does many bad things, but they still remember what the rangers did to their families."

"And?"

"I will warn my workers, and I will ride out and tell all of the other owners in this area about the possible trouble. But I want you to know that in a fight with Paco Delgado, I am not sure what they will do."

"I understand, Carlos. Let's hope the fight doesn't come here," Jon replied. He hurried out and mounted up as Carlos was stepping out of the cabin. "Keep safe," he shouted.

"Gracias, mi amigo."

Jon spurred Babe to a gallop and started back to El Cabrera for his meeting with the miners at the dead man's cabin. Jon rode quickly and was soon on the outskirts of town. He dropped down the final incline and rode into town. He glanced to his left and saw Buck Johnson sitting on his horse and talking to one of his men as the man chucked supplies into the back of a wagon.

"Mornin', Buck," Jon called out to Stanton's loyal foreman.

A surprised Buck glimpsed over at Jon, said nothing and looked back at his men.

Jon pulled up and tied down in front of the assayer's office next to the small courthouse in the center of town. He glanced back to be sure Buck wasn't looking and hurried into the courthouse. The wooden steps creaked as he jumped up onto the boardwalk. He pushed the door open and stepped inside. A sign reading "Recorder's Office" hung above one of the doorways. He walked over to the doorway and looked through the smoked glass window; he could see someone moving around behind the counter inside. Removing his hat, he hurried in.

"Howdy," Jon said to the well-dressed clerk.

"Hello to you, sir, and what can I do for you on this fine day?"

Slightly uncomfortable in front of the business-like clerk, Jon was ill at ease. "Well…uh, I…uh, own a winery out by Vinegar Bend, and I heard there'd been a recent sale of land in that area. As you can see, I have a vested interest in the goings on around there, so I was wondering if that information was available to the public."

"I believe I do remember a recent sale out that way, and yes, my dear man, any sale of land is of public record," the clerk lectured. Small round glasses on a thin gold chain dangled around his neck. He lifted them and set them carefully on the end of his nose, strolled over to a large drawer in the counter and pulled it open. He began thumbing through the long files.

"Here it is," he said to himself. His thin fingers pinched the file as he pulled it from the drawer. Looking satisfied, he walked over and set the file on the counter.

He flipped the file open, his bony finger pointed toward the entry. Jon leaned forward and read:

Claude A. Harter and wife Constance Harter did willfully and without duress convey a warranty deed of trust to George S. Stanton for the considerations of $2,000.00 on April 10, 1881, recorded April 22, 1881. Thirty-seven acres more or less in the plat of Section #30 in Township #28 North of Range #7 East, as copied from Page 365, of Surveyor's Record #2, of Santa Cruz County, California.

Jon frowned as the impatient clerk fiddled nervously with his pocket watch. "Thank you, sir. That's what I needed to know." As Jon hurried to leave, he glanced through the clear glass panes on the front door and saw Buck Johnson riding by with a wagon full of supplies. *Stocking up for his new guests,* Jon thought as he stepped out onto the street and mounted up. He spun around and headed out of town for his meeting with the men.

- - - - -

"He shoulda been here by now." Cliff was concerned as he pushed his wooden chair back and walked over to the front window. Through the broken panes, he saw a dark figure moving in the rocks near the road.

"Think he's coming," Cliff shouted.

Jack Malone jumped up from the table and stepped over for a look. Ned Sloan leaned forward on the table.

"Yeah, it's him," Malone announced. "Ain't another palomino like that one around here."

Cliff hurried over and pulled the rusty lever up on the front door; it creaked open. He watched as Jon approached and dismounted. "We're all here, Jon. Come on in."

"Thanks, Cliff. I'd been here a little sooner, but I had to stop by the courthouse and check somethin' out," he said as his cousin motioned him in.

Jon ambled in and plopped down in an empty chair next to the table.

Ned Sloan's eyes narrowed as he looked over at Jon. "Cliff tells me we got some unexpected visitors down at Stanton's place."

"Yeah. Looks like he means business."

"You're right, Jon. That Delgado's as bad as they come," Ned replied. "His name sends chills up my spine, but he's always stayed down around the border. Never been much of a problem around here. Til now, I guess."

"My hunch is Stanton paid him a pretty penny to get him up here. And if we ever had any doubts about how far Stanton would go to take over your claims, we know now," Jon replied.

The men grumbled and shook their heads.

"There's more, fellas. I stopped at the courthouse a while ago for a reason. When I was out at the vineyard today, Carlos told me that he and some of the owners had suspicions that Stanton might have bought one of the nearby vineyards. So I stopped at the recorder's office in the courthouse to check it out."

"And?" Ned asked.

"Carlos's fears were warranted. It was all recorded there in the courthouse, bigger than life. On April 10, a plot of land in that area was deeded over to Stanton. It was recorded on April 22. Now he has a foothold in the wine country. Once he gets control of the goldfields, he'll try to strong arm the other vineyard owners into selling. If the owners refuse, he'll threaten them—if they still refuse, he'll kill them. If he's not stopped, it won't be long before he controls all of the vineyards along with the goldfields. It's not good."

"What can we do?" Malone asked.

"Things are heating up fast around here, so we need to stick around town and keep an eye on Stanton and Delgado. I want you boys to ride back to the camps and get somebody to work your claims for a couple of days and then hightail it back into town first thing in the morning. When the trouble starts, we need to be ready to move in fast—that's the only way to deal with these men."

"Okay, Jon," Sloan replied. "Let's get going."

"Let's not leave together. Might tip 'em off," Jon said.

"Malone and I will take the back way to the camps so nobody will see us," Sloan replied.

"Sounds good. Cliff and I will take the main road, and then he can head on out to the camps later. See ya in the morning." The men shared a quick handshake and left.

Chapter 20

"Come in, Paco." Stanton smiled and pointed to a chair in front of his desk.

Delgado walked over and sank into the large leather chair; the brown handles of his long guns protruded from his sash. "Good afternoon, señor."

"Tomorrow is Saturday, my friend. We need to come up with a plan to get our friend Stoudenmire alone. Do you have any ideas?"

"Sí, señor, I think we do. It kind of happened by accident."

George's eyebrows lifted as he glanced over at the wily bandit.

"Last night Arturo and I sipped our tequila and talked into the wee hours, and we both remembered we had an old friend who works near El Cabrera at a winery. We thought he might join us in the fight. He's good with a gun, and he knows us well. He would also know a lot about the local area."

"Yes, yes, man—go ahead," Stanton replied.

"Arturo rode out there early this morning when the dew was still on the grass and spoke with him." Paco paused for a moment.

"And?"

"Arturo found our old friend working at a nearby vineyard, just like we thought."

George gave an impatient snort as he shuffled through the papers on his desk.

"Well, it looks like we hit the, uh…how you say?"

"Jackpot?" George barked, looking up.

"Sí…sí, the jackpot, that's the word. It seems our old friend does work at J S Winery."

"J S, yes, I've heard of that one," Stanton mumbled and returned to his work.

"I think you know the owner of J S Winery, Señor Stanton."

"I do?" George replied, still somewhat preoccupied with his paperwork.

"I think so." The corners of Paco's mouth turned up into a grin.

"Okay, okay, who the hell is it?"

"Jon Stoudenmire." A wide-eyed Paco waited for Stanton's reaction.

Stanton's mouth dropped open. "What?" he exclaimed. "J S Winery is owned by who?"

"You heard me right, señor." Paco seemed delighted by the shocked look on the wealthy mogul's face.

"Why that son-of-a-bitch. I guess I never put two and two together. J S, yes…yes," George laughed out loud. "And I thought he was just passing through."

Delgado smiled broadly. "Ignacio said that a man named Carlos run the winery for Jon. He say that Carlos and Jon are very close and have been friends for years. He say that Jon own the vineyard for many years."

"Well, I'll be damned!" Stanton stood and pushed back from his desk. He paced the floor as he attempted to fully absorb the startling news.

Paco paused for a moment and went on. "Arturo and Ignacio put their heads together and came up with a plan. Ignacio will ride into town tomorrow just before sundown with a message for Mr. Stoudenmire. He will tell him there has been some trouble out at the vineyard and that Carlos needs Jon to come out right away. On his way out of town, we will set a trap and kill him."

Stanton stopped pacing and looked directly at the wily bandit. "Hmmm…good, good. Anything else?"

"Sí. I had a surprise visitor a little while ago."

Stanton looked puzzled.

"Señor Johnson stopped by my room and said when we come up with a plan he would like to help us. He said he know the area very well and will be a big help."

"Yes…Buck asked me about that yesterday. I told him to talk to you. What did you decide?"

"I said okay. Then I told him about our plan and ask him if he can help us find a good place to kill him."

"What did he say?" Stanton was acting somewhat disinterested, but in actuality, he was very glad that Johnson had brought the idea up to him. He didn't trust Delgado. The thought of having Johnson along suited him just fine.

Paco continued. "Señor Johnson thought for a minute and then he said yes. He say there is a secret trail behind the compound that leads to a clump of trees next to the stream. The trail to the vineyard goes right through those trees. He say it would be a perfect place to take Stoudenmire out. After we kill him, we can take the body to Señor Johnson's cabin in the woods until the smoke clears. He say nobody knows where the cabin is."

"Hmmm...good plan. And yes, even I don't even know where the hell that cabin is. He's real closed mouth about it."

"You and the boys will be at the saloon having a good time with the whores. Nobody will suspect you." A sly grin broke out on the killer's pocked face.

Stanton grinned. "And after the killing of Stoudenmire, I'll put Sheriff Cook on the case. He'll make sure that none of us are implicated. And be damned sure you get the job done," Stanton barked. "This Stoudenmire fella is one tough SOB."

"You insult me, señor! If I say the man will be keeled, he will be keeled." An angry Paco glared at Stanton.

"All right, all right," Stanton murmured.

Paco's glare subsided. "Me and the boys are getting tired of sitting around here doing nothing. We are going into town for a drink."

"Okay, but be careful. We don't want any trouble. We've got a job to do."

"There will be no trouble, señor. We just a little thirsty, that's all."

"If you will excuse me, Paco, I have some work to do." George dropped back in his chair and fingered through a stack of papers.

"Good day, señor," Paco said.

"Goodbye and no trouble," George groused.

Paco nodded and hurried out the door to gather up his men for their foray into town.

- - - - -

"Look over there, Cliff." Jon nodded toward the front of the saloon as they rode into town.

"I think we got some visitors at the Dead End," Cliff replied. "Never seen those ponies before."

"They're pretty colorful all right, what with all those shiny sequins on the saddles and bright blankets. Looks like south of the border ponies to me," Jon said, brow furrowed. "Paco's in town."

"Looks like it."

I'm kinda thirsty—how about you?" Jon asked.

"Yeah, I could use a drink."

"I'd like to look these boys over a little bit." Jon reined Babe over to the hitching post in front of the saloon. The two men quickly dismounted, tied down and hopped up on the boardwalk. The batwing doors swung open as they walked into the rowdy saloon. It was getting on toward evening, and the faro tables and blackjack games were at full throttle. A smile covered the face of the red-vested piano player as he pounded on the ivory keys. Lively music filled the air.

Jon saw Paco's white sombrero at the end of the bar; his men were spread out next to him. His pulse quickened as he and Cliff walked slowly across the room. He could feel his anger growing as he approached the end of the bar and slid in next to Delgado.

"Usual?" Jake asked.

"Sounds good," Jon said as he and Cliff leaned against the bar. Busy drinking and laughing, Delgado and his men didn't notice their arrival.

"Howdy, boys!" Jon barked over the music.

Paco spun around, his hand on his six gun. The smile fell slowly from his face as he looked up at Jon.

He stared hard. His wide, pocked face was dark, his eyes black and menacing. Strands of deep black hair hung loosely on his forehead atop his broad, muscular shoulders.

"Jon Stoudenmire," Jon barked as he reached forward for a shake.

The corner of Paco's wide mouth turned up in an ugly grin; his hand fell off of his six gun. "Paco Delgado. Pleasure to meet you, señor," he replied as the two men shook.

"Set these fellas up," Jon shouted at Jake. The bartender hurried over; the tequila splashed into their glasses.

"Thank you, señor," Paco replied. "Mi amigo Pedro tell me all about you." Paco smiled as he turned and looked down the bar at Pedro. Pedro smiled nervously.

"Is that right?" Jon replied calmly.

"Yes, he tell me that you are one bad hombre, that you shoot two men dead in El Cabrera. We came to visit our friend Pedro here for a couple of days, then we be on our way. We very friendly, we are not looking for any trouble, are we boys?" He looked down the line as the other men shook their heads.

Jon grinned at the nasty varmint and raised his glass of whiskey. "That's good, Paco, 'cause we don't like troublemakers around here. Not one damned bit!" Jon downed his shot and set it on the bar. He glanced over at Cliff and tipped his head toward the door.

"Have a good day, gentlemen," he said as he and Cliff pushed back from the bar and ambled toward the door.

Surprised by the sudden departure, Paco and his men wheeled around to watch them leave. "He big!"

Jon heard one of the men exclaim as he and Cliff pushed through the swinging doors.

Cliff smiled at Jon. "He's sure an ugly varmint."

"Yeah, he sure enough is."

"Bet ya wanted to let 'im have it."

"Yep, I wanted to blow 'im away in the worst way, but this isn't the time. We gotta tie him to Stanton. Right now we can't do that—he hasn't done anything. We have to wait til Stanton plays his cards, and then I'll deal with that killer. I just wanted to get in his face a little bit, let 'im know I'm around." Jon grinned.

"I think ya got his attention."

"Hope so," Jon replied. "I'm headin' down to the room to wash up. How 'bout dinner later on?"

"Okay, but first I gotta take some ore to the assayer's office and get a haircut. I'll give ya a knock when I'm finished."

Jon nodded as he turned and headed down the dirt street toward Callahan's. As he approached the boardinghouse, his heart was heavy. Thoughts of Maggie's awful beating flooded through his mind—the screams, the pain, the terror in her eyes. It angered Jon. She'd never been the same since that awful night; she seldom came out of her room. On the few occasions she did come out, that big smile was gone from her face.

Jon hopped up on the boardwalk and peered through the smoked glass windows on the door. The front desk was vacant. Jon pushed the door open and stepped inside.

Unexpectedly, the door to Maggie's room opened. Maggie stepped out toward the front desk; she winced when she saw Jon. Her eyes darted away. She composed herself and looked back at him. "Why, uh…hello, Jon," she said nervously.

"Afternoon, Maggie." Jon watched as she fidgeted nervously with some keys on the counter. She looked lovely as usual. Her long brown hair fell over her bare shoulders; her pink calico dress fit snugly, accentuating her well-formed bosom. Gold earrings dangled from her ears. Her gorgeous brown eyes glanced toward him as he started toward the stairs.

"Jon," she said quietly.

Jon turned. "Yes, Maggie?"

"Got a minute?"

"Sure do." Jon stepped over and laid his hands on the counter.

"How are you, Jon?" She smiled hesitantly.

"Just fine, thank you. And you?"

"Oh…I'm okay, I guess."

"Don't sound too sure."

"Well it's…uh, been a little rough for me since that, uh…"

"I know," said Jon. "It's okay."

She looked directly at Jon; their eyes met. "I've been meaning to talk with you, Jon."

Jon looked intently at her.

"I've really been struggling lately. I've been having a tough time."

"I'll bet," Jon replied. "I've missed seein' those nice smiles when I come and go."

"I'm sorry, I've just been kind of staying to myself lately. Oh, friends stop over once in a while, but I haven't been out much." She paused, collecting her thoughts. "I…guess I…uh, never thought anything like that could ever happen to me. I thought I could take care of myself out here in this rough ole west, but I'd never met a man like George Stanton before." Her eyes started to well up. "Thank God you came along that night, Jon, or I don't know what would have happened." The tears began to stream down her face. She slid her hand in the bodice of her dress, pulled out a hanky and dabbed the tears away.

Jon frowned; his heart ached for her.

"I'm leaving, Jon. I'm getting on the stage tomorrow and going back to Los Angeles to live with my sister. My friend Katie's going to buy the business. There's nothing here for me anymore. I should have never taken up with that man. I should have known better. But a girl gets lonely, and he was kind to me and bought me fancy clothes and all. I guess like an idiot I fell for it. I made an awful—"

Jon interrupted. "We all do things we're sorry for, Maggie. Please don't blame yourself. It wasn't your fault." Jon was crestfallen, shocked by her decision to leave town.

Maggie smiled and nodded. "Thanks, Jon. It's just such a shame. I loved it here. I loved running this little boardinghouse. For once in my life, I owned something. It was all mine, and I was so proud of myself. But then he came along. Now all I can think about is the pain of that buggy whip ripping into my back, his fists bashing my arms." She threw her hands up to her face and began sobbing. Jon moved closer and gently laid his hands on her shoulders.

"It's okay, Maggie," Jon said softly. "That will never happen again."

She looked longingly at the muscular gunman. "You're so brave. I just don't know how to thank you for what you did that night." Her red eyes looked directly at Jon. "I've never met a man like you before, Jon—so strong, so brave." She hesitated and then said very softly, "and so sensitive and caring." She laid her shaking hand on his and squeezed it gently. "You stir feelings inside of me I've never felt before!" Trembling, her eyes darted up and down Jon's face searching for signs of a reaction.

But Jon was silent; a nervous smile was all she saw. Embarrassed, she quickly looked away and jerked her hand back. "Why is it every time I'm around you, I make a damn fool of myself, Jon? I'm so sorry."

"You're no fool, Maggie. You're a wonderful girl. You've been through a hell of a lot. You got nothin' to be ashamed of." He smiled tenderly.

"That's one lucky girl down Arizona way. She oughta get down on her hands and knees and thank the heavens above. I envy her." A distraught and red-faced Maggie dropped the keys in a drawer and turned to leave.

"Maggie," Jon said quickly. She stopped, her back to him.

Jon paused as he looked at the red welts still visible on her back. He spoke softly. "I don't know if what I'm gonna say will matter or not, but I don't think less of you, Maggie, not one little bit. You were just followin' your heart. There's no sin in that."

She turned toward him, tears streaming down her cheeks. "I'll never forget you, Jon!" She reached up, kissed his cheek and then quickly ducked in her room. The door clicked shut.

Jon stood staring at the closed door, his heart pounding. His arms dropped to his side as he turned and walked toward the stairs. A strong feeling of melancholy filled him as he mounted the final step and hurried down the hall. He pulled out his room key and stuck it in the lock. The door fell open. He walked into the room and tossed the key on the end table. *That lousy son-of-a-bitch*, he thought as he leaned down and stuck his hands in the pan of water next to the bed and splashed his face. He dabbed his face dry and angrily tossed the towel on the floor. "He's a dead man," Jon whispered as he dropped on the bed.

- - - - -

The town was busy as Jon and Cliff headed for the Crown.

"Let's cross here," Jon said as the two men hopped down on the street.

"Over there, Jon." Cliff nodded toward the other side of the road.

Jon grinned. "Looks like our fine Sheriff Cook and Councilman Zollars are headin' down to the Crown. Let's say hi."

The two men hurried over and stepped up on the boardwalk in front of Cook and Zollars as they approached the eatery.

"Evenin', Sheriff. Evenin', Bill." Jon reached forward; the men quickly shook. "Got a minute, Sheriff?" Jon asked.

"Well, Bill and I are having our weekly meeting with the other councilmen. I really must—"

Jon interrupted. "Won't take long."

Cook grimaced and stood still.

"I'll go on in," Zollars said. "Nice seeing you, fellas." He tipped his hat to Jon and Cliff.

"Nice seein' ya, Bill," Jon said as the councilman hurried inside.

"Go ahead, Jon. I ain't got all night," Cook barked.

"Seems like we got some visitors in town."

"Oh?"

"Yeah. It seems one of George's men is friends with Paco Delgado. He's in town and stayin' down at Stanton's compound. Cliff and I ran into him yesterday at the Dead End, and he says he's just visiting his old friend Pedro, but I know better."

"Well, I don't. A man has a right to visit whomever he likes. That's none of my affair," the agitated sheriff replied. "Now, if that's all you want, I've got to be going." He turned for the door.

Jon grabbed his arm firmly. "Listen close, Cook. I hear Delgado's one of the nastiest varmints you'll ever see in your tormented little life. Folks tell me he likes to torture people and slit throats and things like that. I hear he's murdered dozens of men. He's a long way from the border, and he brought four men with him. He's not here visiting anybody—he's here to take me out, Sheriff, and you know it."

"You can't prove that."

Jon's eyes narrowed; he squeezed harder. "It's gonna get ugly around here real quick, Cook. A whole lot of people could die. There's gonna be a bloodbath like you've never seen. And you better hope and pray Stanton comes out on top. 'Cause if he doesn't, I'm personally coming after you, Cook—you can count on it."

Cook pulled away. "Is that a threat, Jon?"

"Take it however you want. Just remember, if Stanton goes down, you better start lookin' over your shoulder. Your crooked little world is about to blow apart, Sheriff."

Red-faced, Cook jerked loose from Jon's firm grip and hurried into the restaurant.

"I just lost my appetite, Cliff. Let's go to the Dead End and get a drink," Jon said as he stared angrily at the departing Cook.

"Sounds good, Jon. I'll get the first round."

Chapter 21

Jon stretched his arms to the ceiling as he sat up in bed late the next day. Shading his eyes from the late afternoon sun, he leaned across the bed and looked down at the hectic street scene below. Derby hats and bonnets bobbed as the folks went about their daily routines. A horse whinnied as a frustrated driver cracked his whip above the head of the anxious steed. A little boy in suspenders ran out of the drugstore waving a bag of jelly beans above his head, his blond hair blowing in the breeze. His parents beamed in delight.

After another quick stretch, Jon tossed his covers back, sat on the edge of the bed, and ran his fingers through his thick black hair as he stared at the wooden floor.

There was a hard knock on the door. Jon went for his gun.

"It's Cliff, Jon. Open up."

Jon stumbled over to the door, turned the lock and pushed it open. Cliff hurried in.

"Afternoon, bright eyes," Cliff joked.

"Afternoon, cus," Jon replied. "How late did you keep me out last night?"

"We played stud all night, my friend. Afterward, we grabbed a bite. Then I rode on out to the camps, and you wandered back to your room. How ya feelin'? You don't look too good."

"Not worth a damn, thank you." Jon frowned. "How 'bout you?"

"I'm rarin' to go!"

"You make me sick." Jon shook his head.

"You all right? You look a little down."

"Yeah. I just been thinkin' a little, I guess," Jon replied.

"About the girl back in Arizona?"

"Yeah, I guess so."

"About that promise?"

Jon grimaced. "I told her never again. And now here I am right in the middle of somethin'. I could have ridden on down the road to Vinegar Bend, but I didn't." Jon wrung his hands; his eyes went to the floor. "I guess I love the fight too much to give it up. It kind of bothers me."

Cliff laid his hand on Jon's shoulder. "Things are gettin' ugly around here, Jon. I wouldn't blame ya if you just rode on outta here."

"There's one problem with that, partner," Jon sighed.

Cliff's eyes widened.

"I got nowhere to go. That snake Stanton's got his foot planted right in the middle of that wine country. Can't go there—he'd just be waitin' on me. I guess I'm just gonna have to kill that bastard right here," Jon growled.

Cliff looked at his tough friend. "What about Elizabeth?"

"Well, I ain't no good to her dead, and the best way to stay alive is to hit these varmints head on." He paused. "Sorry for the whining, Cliff."

"Don't think nothin' about it. Hell, I been in love before. It kinda puts stars in your eyes."

"Yeah, I guess it does." Jon grinned. "Now get outta here so I can clean up a little."

"Okay, partner, but there's one more thing."

"Yeah, what is it?"

"I saw Stanton's black quarter horse along with several others lined up in front of the Dead End a few minutes ago. Looks like the boys are in town for a little fun."

"Hmmm…ya don't say. Hard tellin' what they're up to. Where are Ned and Malone?"

"I swung by Ned's camp on the way into town. He said he was waitin' on Malone and that they'd be in town shortly."

"Good. I'll meet you guys down at that café on the edge of town in half an hour. What's it called?"

"Digger's."

"Yeah, I'll meet ya at Digger's."

"Sounds good, Jon." The door slammed as Cliff hurried out.

- - - - -

"Whoa! Whoa!" the smallish driver shouted as he leaned back and pulled hard on the leather reins. Dust flew as the Wells Fargo stage pulled to a stop. The metal brake squeaked as the stage ground to a standstill.

The driver jumped down and began tossing bags up to his partner on top.

Jon stepped off of the boardwalk in front of Callahan's. Hand above his eyes, he squinted toward the stage. Maggie came out of the shadows; she reached forward for the driver. She paused briefly, turned and looked over at Jon and then stepped up and disappeared into the cabin. The driver quickly closed the cabin door and hopped back to his seat. The whip cracked; the four steeds jumped forward as the stage rolled swiftly out of town.

Jon's heart was heavy as he watched the stage disappear. He angrily kicked a tin can to the side of the road as he walked quickly toward Digger's.

Digger's was a small café in a rickety clapboard building on the edge of town. It was the favorite of the miners, vineyard workers, late night gamblers and occasional vaqueros who rode into town. The food was good, and Digger kept it open all night. The smell of steak and potatoes filled the air as Jon neared the busy eatery.

Suddenly, a horse rode up from behind. Startled, Jon jumped to the side to avoid the big steed as the rider pulled up. "Sorry to alarm you, Señor Stoudenmire, but you must come to the vineyard right away!"

Jon recognized the dark-skinned man from his trips to the vineyard. "What is it, Ignacio?"

"There is trouble, señor! Some men threatened Carlos at gunpoint. They say they are taking over the vineyards. He says they mean business—he need you to come out right away."

"Damn them!" Jon shouted. "Tell Carlos I'll be there pronto!"

"Sí, señor." Ignacio spun in the street and charged out of town.

Jon pushed through the wobbly door at Digger's, rushed inside and quickly scanned the room. Cliff and the boys were sitting at a table by the cash register talking to Digger. Jon hurried over.

"Sorry, men, I gotta go. There's trouble out at the vineyard."

"I'll go with ya!" Cliff shouted.

"Thanks, partner, but you boys better stay here and keep an eye on Stanton and his gang. This is my problem." Jon turned and hurried out the front door. Anger rose up inside of him as he ran to the nearby livery to pick up Babe for his unexpected trip to J S Winery. *Probably Delgado and his men,* he thought as he approached the stables.

- - - - -

Cliff's eyes narrowed as he glanced over at the other men. "Somethin' don't smell right, boys."

"Yeah, I agree," Ned replied. "Let's get after him."

"Hold the steaks, Digger. We'll be back later on," Cliff shouted.

"I'll bet," the friendly owner replied. "Oh well, the boys from the Triple X will be in 'fore long. They'll eat 'em."

The three men pushed back from the table and headed for the cash register as the sound of Babe's powerful hooves went thundering past.

"Coffee's on me!" Digger shouted. "Get after him!"

Cliff tipped his hat as the men hurried out, mounted up and raced after Jon.

- - - - -

"Here come Ignacio!" Paco exclaimed as he stepped out to the trail. "The gringo won't be too far behind."

Ignacio's horse pranced on the trail as he pulled up and spoke to Paco. "I tell him. He should be here any minute, Paco. He seem very upset."

"Muchas gracias, amigo!" a smiling Delgado replied.

Ignacio nodded as he spurred his horse forward and raced down the trail to the J S Winery.

Paco jumped back behind the large oak tree and cocked his rifle. "We must be still, boys. He be here soon."

Paco glanced at Arturo, a crack shot and just a few yards to his right. "You ready, Arturo?"

"Sí. I have a clear shot from here." The nasty bandito spit on the ground as he glared at the well-traveled path some hundred yards away. The path wound between some large rocks before dropping into the wooded area bordering the stream.

"You the best," Paco barked at Arturo.

"Oh, you flatter me, mi amigo." Arturo grinned at his brutal boss.

The savvy leader glanced behind the tree to his right at Buck Johnson; he looked across the trail as his other two men found hiding places in the thick brush.

Suddenly Johnson raised his hand. "Quiet! I hear something!" He quickly leveled his rifle for a shot.

Paco looked ahead as a rider appeared on the horizon; dust flew as his charger bounded down the trail toward the woods and the waiting ambush.

"Hold fire until he close enough," Paco mumbled as the rider drew near.

"Palomino!" Arturo exclaimed as he jerked his rifle to shoulder level and took dead aim. "It's him!" He squeezed the trigger; a powerful blast echoed through the woods.

Several more rifle shots rang out. The deafening sounds reverberated through the trees. The palomino reared up as the hot lead blew into the rider's body, blasting him off of the frightened steed. He dropped behind some nearby rocks and disappeared. The shooters watched anxiously and waited. After a few seconds, the body rolled slowly back to the rutted trail. The rider's arms dropped to his side; his head fell still. Yellow flames shot from Paco's rifle as he took a final shot. The lifeless body jerked.

"He look dead," Paco shouted. "Let's go finish him off, just in case!" Paco jumped out from behind the tree and raced down the path toward the body. He stopped suddenly and raised his hand. "I hear horses," he cried. Running close behind, the other men stopped.

Three dark figures on horseback rode over the horizon. One of them was huge.

As they raced closer, Johnson shouted out, "That's Stone's painted sorrel, and the big man must be Ned Sloan! Let's get outta here—those boys can shoot!"

Several loud rifle shots rang out from the rapidly approaching riders as the men scurried back to the woods for cover. Flying lead whizzed by their heads; a small limb snapped above Paco's head. "Asshole!" he mumbled. Nearby, one of the men screamed and dropped to the ground. He rolled to his back and fell still, blood oozing from his chest. Johnson dropped down, cradled the man in his arms and lifted him. Dodging bullets, he carried the body over and laid it across the man's horse. He grabbed the reins and quickly wound the leather around his saddle horn and mounted up.

"They trying to keel all of us!" Paco bellowed as he leapt on his steed.

"Let's get to the stream and ride to my place!" Johnson yelled.

"Sí, amigo! Lead the way!" Paco shouted as he ducked under a large limb.

"Uhggg!" one of the men screamed as he slumped in the saddle; his steed ran on with the rider's head bobbing from side to side.

"They hit Diego!" Arturo screamed. He slowed up and frantically grabbed the reins of the wounded man's horse. Ducking bullets, he led him into the stream.

- - - - -

Cliff saw the body lying next to the trail, reined up and quickly dismounted. "My God, it's Jon, and he's been hit!" he cried as he hopped down on the rocky path. His knee hit the ground next to Jon's still body.

"How is he?" Malone yelled as he rode up, rifle smoking.

"Don't know." Cliff slid his hand under Jon's head. The front of his shirt was soaked red; a puddle of blood had formed in his ear from a head wound. Cliff gently lifted his motionless body. "Jon! Jon!" he shouted. Tears welled in the hard man's eyes.

Returning after giving a brief chase, Sloan shouted out, "They went into the stream, I lost—" He stopped

mid-sentence as he glanced down at Jon's crumbled body. "What the hell!" he exclaimed. "He looks….uh."
Malone interrupted. "Dead! Those bastards killed him!"

- - - - -

Paco, Buck Johnson and the banditos struggled up the muddy bank of the stream. "This way," Buck shouted as they spurred their steeds forward toward the secret hideaway. They raced ahead, winding through several miles of narrow trails and thick woods. Suddenly, Buck's hand shot up as he reined up on the edge of a clearing. A small, grassy valley opened up below. The men pulled alongside him and gazed down at the tranquil scene. Eyes wide, they looked at the rustic log cabin nestled against a knoll on the far side of the vale; a stack of freshly chopped wood lay against the side of the cabin. Nearby, two goats grazed lazily on the valley's grassy floor. A milking cow in a nearby fenced area stared quietly at the men. Light reflected off of a small pond behind the cabin and filtered through a stand of tall birch trees.

"We're here," Buck announced. He spurred his horse gently forward. The others followed as he dropped down the steep, narrow trail into the valley. The horses' hooves sank into the muddy ground as the men reached the basin's floor and rode toward the cabin.

"I been watching Diego. He die on the way." A somber Arturo frowned as the men reached the cabin and dismounted.

Paco glanced over at the dead man's body dangling over the horse's neck. "Poor Diego," he said quietly. "Take him and our friend Alejo and bury them on the hill on the other side of that pond. Dig deep so the animals can't dig them up and eat them," he ordered.

Johnson dismounted and stepped over to a nearby shed. He reached inside, grabbed a shovel and tossed it to Arturo.   A surprised Arturo snatched the shovel from the air and sneered at Buck. His expression slowly calmed as he led the dead men's horses down the path to the pond.

"Come in," Buck said as he walked over and pushed the front door open. Paco's large white sombrero bumped the side of the door as he followed Stanton's right hand man inside. The cabin's main room was neat and well kept. A large stone fireplace filled the south end of the room. A wooden table surrounded by six chairs sat in the middle, and several large oranges filled a clay bowl on top. Two closed doors at the far end of the room piqued Paco's curiosity.

"Bedrooms," an observant Buck announced.

Paco nodded. "Nice casa, señor. Why you keep your beautiful place such a secret?"

Buck's eyes narrowed at the probing question. "There's a reason. How about a drink and I'll tell ya about it?" he replied.

"You have a way with words, mi amigo," Paco laughed as he slid a wooden chair out and plopped down.

The metal cups clanked as Buck set them on the table. "Whiskey okay?" he asked as he pulled open the door to a small cabinet.

"Sí, Señor Johnson. Whiskey is fine."

Buck pulled a large brown bottle from the cabinet, bit down on the cork and yanked it free. Reaching forward, he poured the brown liquid in the cups. Lifting his cup, he took a sip and reluctantly began to answer Paco's personal question about the cabin. "George and I thought it might be a good idea to have a place to go if things ever got too hot in town. So he asked me to find a secluded place, and I did. I bought this spread from a retired army colonel a couple of years ago. Even George hasn't been out here."

"So...nobody know where you live?"

"Not a soul. Most folks think I live at Stanton's compound. I stay there so often, they don't know the difference." Buck's head tipped back as he emptied the tin cup and quickly filled it again.

"Nice little plan you boys have," Paco said as his thin lips turned up in a nasty grin.

All of a sudden, a weak, almost inaudible voice could be heard coming from one of the bedrooms. The words were slurred and hard to understand.

"Someone here?" a startled Paco asked.

"Yes...just a minute," Buck answered as he hurried over, yanked the ladle off of the hook and quickly dipped it into a bucket of water. The water splashed over the sides of the ladle as he rushed to the bedroom. After several minutes, Buck stepped out and shut the door. He looked over at a bewildered Paco.

"It's my son. He's been terribly injured; I need to take him to the hospital in Santa Cruz, but his treatments will cost nearly a grand, and I don't have it."

"What happen to him?" Paco asked.

Buck winced at the direct question, once again taken aback by the aggressive bandito. He gritted his teeth and answered, "Some cowards jumped him out on the trail, they beat him senseless and left him for dead. Some Pauma Indians found him and took him to a nearby trading post. An old friend brought him here. If it weren't for those Injuns, he'd be dead."

"That not good." Paco took a sip of his whiskey. "How old your son?"

"Twenty-two."

"He talk kind of funny, it kind of sad." Paco chuckled nervously.

Buck glared at the heartless man. He gulped down another cup of whiskey and refilled it. "More?" He lifted the bottle toward Paco.

"No, gracias."

Buck stepped over near the door, cracked it open and looked out toward the pond. "The boys should be finishin' up soon," he said calmly.

"I think so," Paco replied. "I have a son also, señor. I very proud of him," he continued.

"I'll bet you are." Buck's head tipped back as he drank the cup dry; dust flew as he set it on a nearby windowsill. He grabbed a leather strap from a hook on the back of the door and turned toward the table. Paco's white sombrero hung down his back.

"I'm very proud of my son also, Paco."

"That good that you proud of your son. Hope he live."

Buck wound the leather strap around his hands and moved toward the table. "I think you may know my son," he said softly.

"Oh no, I don't think so, señor!" Paco replied quickly. "How would I ever know your son?"

"Oh, I think you do, my friend! He's a ranger from down your way. Jim Johnson's his name—ring a bell?"

A wide-eyed Paco tried to jump up as he grabbed for his six gun.

Buck's hands flew over the back of Delgado's head; the leather snapped tight and locked on the frantic man's thick neck before he could rise. Buck twisted the noose tight and yanked with all his strength. The leather dug into the nasty man's neck as he yanked him side to side. Paco groaned, fighting for all he was worth. Buck pulled harder on the leather strap, lifting the gagging bandito off the chair. Paco's six gun fell to the floor as he pawed frantically at the strap. Buck yanked harder and harder, the back of Paco's body pushed into him. He was gasping desperately for breath. Incensed, Buck jerked harder, throwing the dying man's body from left to right and at times lifting him off of the floor. "I been waitin' for this, you rotten bastard!" he growled quietly so as not to alert the other men. He squeezed tighter and tighter on the straps until Delgado's thick body fell limp, arms dangling to his side. There was no sign of life. Paco's head jerked as an incensed Buck yanked several more times to be certain of death. Exhausted, Buck dragged him over and dropped him on the chair; he slid the bloody strap off of his neck. There was a thud as Paco's head crashed to the table.

His heart racing and sweating profusely, Buck ran for the corner of the room, grabbed his Winchester and yanked the drawer open on a nearby table. He grabbed a handful of cartridges and quickly crammed them in the barrel. He hurried across the room, placed his metal gun barrel against the bottom of the windowsill and pushed the window up. He lifted a wood rod off of the frame and used it to brace the window open. The path to the pond was in clear view from this window. Beads of sweat covered his forehead as he peered at the scene outside. Shaking badly, he struggled to calm himself. Suddenly, he heard voices in the thicket near the pond area. His heart pounded as he carefully lifted the rifle to his shoulder and pushed the end of the barrel out the window. A crack shot, he watched as the men came into clear view. His hands stopped shaking. His eyes widened as the men entered the clearing, suddenly an unexpected calm came over the former freedom fighter. He leaned down and slid the barrel a little further out the window. He took dead aim and squeezed the trigger. Flames shot from the barrel. Startled by the sound, Arturo glanced toward the cabin as the hot lead blasted into his chest. He flew violently back against some thick bushes, bounced off and fell face down on the path. Not hesitating, Buck squeezed off two more shots. The sounds echoed through the surrounding trees as the second man screamed and dropped to the ground, hands covering his face as he rolled from side to side. Buck shot again; the man fell still. He moved the barrel back toward the motionless Arturo and pulled the trigger. The lifeless body jerked from the force of the blast.

Wide-eyed and excited, Buck slid the gun off of the windowsill and charged toward the door. He knocked it open with the butt of his gun and bolted down the hill toward the pond. Panting, he was almost out of breath when he reached the two bodies. He stood over the fallen men, surveying the carnage. Arturo, lying face down, showed no signs of life. The first bullet had gone clear through him. The back of his white cotton shirt had turned red with blood. Buck looked at the other man. He was lying on his side, motionless. He poked him with his gun barrel, and the man fell to his back. Blood streamed out of his mouth as his brown eyes stared blankly at the sky.

Certain they were dead, Buck ran quickly to the stable, unhitched the gate, rushed in and snatched a yoke from a fencepost. An anxious mare pranced nearby. Buck tossed the yoke on the horse's neck, led her through the gate and strapped her to a nearby wagon. He moved to the side of the wagon, untied a canvas roll and spread it on the bed. Horse and wagon in tow, he rushed back to the dead men. His stomach sickened as he lifted the bloody men and laid them on the canvas. He led the horse and wagon to the cabin, pushed the cabin door open, hurried inside and draped his arms around the limp body of Delgado. He was shaking horribly as he struggled to drag the stocky man out of the cabin and put him in the back of the wagon.

My God what have I done? he thought as he pushed the gate closed and snapped the swivel hook into the eyelet. His shirt dripped sweat as he gathered up the men's horses and tied them to the back of the wagon. He stopped for a moment to listen—he could hear sobbing coming from Jim's room. He hurried inside and rushed to his bedroom. He knelt down next to the bed and laid his shaking hand on his son's fractured body. "It's okay, son. I was just takin' a little target practice. Everything's okay now. Just try and rest."

The young man garbled out a few words. "Ya...ya okay, dad?"

"I'm fine, son. Now go to sleep." He squeezed his son's hand tenderly. The boy fell quiet; his chest heaved as tears rolled down his face, horribly disfigured by Delgado's torture.

Buck patted the boy's arm, jumped up, carefully closed the door behind him, hurried outside and jumped aboard the wagon. He cracked the leather whip, and the wagon jerked forward.

Buck bounced in the wood seat as he wound deeper and deeper into the thick woods. After several miles, he reined up and surveyed the scene ahead. A large rocky knoll jutted up from the forest floor. "We're here," he whispered as he rode forward.

Buck ducked and pushed the brush aside as wove his way around the knoll. He pulled up in a small wash area on the backside of the rocky hill. He covered his eyes from the sun as he looked up the steep incline. He smiled when he saw the heart-shaped rock at the top. He hopped down. The wood gate rattled as he pulled it open and yanked Paco's body out of the wagon. The muscles on his forearms bulged as he fought to drag the stocky body of Delgado up the rocky incline. *The brush is thicker than I expected,* he thought as he paused and scanned the rocks. He peered over a round boulder nearby and there it was—a small opening in the middle of a group of rocks. He grabbed the shirt collar of the dead man and dragged him around the rock and into the hole. After crawling several feet, his hand could feel an opening ahead. He reached inside the familiar opening and grabbed a kerosene lantern from a ledge. He reached in his jean pocket and pulled out a match. He struck the match along a rock; it exploded into flame as he reached forward and lit the lantern. The yellow light illuminated the walls of the cavern. He jumped down to the cavern floor and dragged the body across to another small opening. He crawled inside the passageway, lugging Paco behind. After a few minutes, cool air from a dark hole struck his face. This was what he was looking for. He struggled to pull Paco's body past him in the narrow passageway and push it into the eerie hole. It seemed like forever before he heard the thud of the body hitting the bottom of the deep, dark crevice.

Arms weary, Buck pushed back through the passageway and into the cavern. He hurried across the cavern and crawled through the narrow entryway and down the rocky hill to the wagon. Exhausted, he forced himself to go on. "Two more," he murmured. The ritual repeated itself until all three bodies, saddles, blankets and the bloody canvas had been carried up the rocky hill, dragged through the cavern and dropped into the deep hole at the end of the narrow opening on the other side.

"Ain't nobody gonna find them," he whispered. Totally exhausted, Buck rolled a small round rock into the hole in the wall and then stacked several more on top. He quickly wiped the dirt from the bottom side of the rocks so they didn't look freshly moved. He brushed his hands together, climbed down the rocky incline and struggled up to the wagon seat.

"Hiya," he said weakly. The wagon and trailing horses meandered back around the rocky, tree-covered knoll, traveling on until open prairie showed ahead. Once in the clearing, Buck hopped down, yanked off his hat and untied the bandits' ponies.

"Get! Get!" he shouted as he smacked their behinds with the hat. The frightened steeds raced out to the open prairie, their manes flowing in the breeze. Off in the distance, Buck could hear a thundering herd of wild horses.

A hard breeze from the prairie cooled Buck's hot, sweaty face as he stood watching the horses gallop across the beautiful grassland. His heart was heavy as he stood shaking in the dimming sunlight. He had gotten revenge for his son's torture all right, but at what price? Not a violent man by nature, he had not killed since his fighting days against Santa Anna in Texas. Yet today he had violently strangled a Mexican legend to death and had blasted his two unsuspecting accomplices to the heavens. It sickened him. He was distraught. His tired body began to shake violently, cold chills rushed through his body, his gut pushed up to his throat. He grabbed desperately for the side of the wagon as his head flew down. Bits of bacon and yellow bile blasted on the dirt trail as he heaved violently again and again. His body shook uncontrollably as he continued to extricate the remnants of the day. After several minutes of sobbing, with the smelly bile dripping from his chin, he dropped to his knees, his red, watery eyes pointing to the heavens. "Forgive me God, please forgive me!" he wailed.

Chapter 22

"Well, that's enough fun for one night, boys. We have a lot of work to do in the morning," Stanton ordered. The bargirl on his lap giggled. He playfully pulled the top of her cotton dress down and peered at her well-shaped bosom. He dropped a ten dollar gold piece into the bodice; it bounced off of her breast and fell into the blouse.

"Thank you, George." She pinched his cheek and giggled as she jumped off of his lap. George smacked her round fanny as she wiggled away.

"Naughty boy!" she squealed, digging in her blouse for the gold piece.

"It too early, señor. The girls don't want us to go," Pedro hollered, bearing a grin on his rouge-covered face.

"I know, Pedro, but we must go see how your guests are doing. It's the polite thing to do."

Pedro frowned. "Okay," he said reluctantly. Sulking, the whore planted another big kiss on his forehead and jumped off of his lap.

"See you next time, Pedro." She batted her eyes flirtatiously at the frustrated vaquero. "You're the best."

Pedro beamed at the shapely, dark-haired lady.

The other men grumbled at the shortened evening. George tossed several bills on the table as they stood to leave. The music blared; their spurs jingled as George and his rough men pushed their way through the crowd to the front door.

"Stoudenmire should be dead by now," George whispered to Pedro as he bumped through the batwing door.

"I think so," the drunken Pedro replied. "Mi amigo Paco play rough when he want to."

George mounted up quickly and rode toward the edge of town. Pedro and the boys were close behind.

"Look, George," Pedro shouted over the galloping hooves. "That's Jon's horse in front of Doc's place. Maybe he's still alive!"

Stanton roared in delight. "Don't worry, my friend— the doc's the coroner also."

"Oh good! He's the coroner also," Pedro howled.

The riders charged into the dark moonless night. The dimly lit street turned black as they reached the edge of town. An excellent horseman, Stanton rode confidently along the dark pathway; soon the lanterns that adorned either side of the big iron gate in front of his compound were in view.

As the men approached, the gate began to open. The always dependable Estela leaned back and pulled hard on the heavy gate as the men rushed in. As usual, she had waited patiently by the entrance for the men to return, opening it at just the right moment.

"Thank you, Estela," Stanton shouted as his quarter horse pranced nervously in the courtyard. "Any news?"

"I heard lots of gunshots earlier, señor. That's all."

"That's enough!" Stanton smiled.

All of a sudden Pedro raised his hand. "Quiet, everyone. I hear a rider."

Stanton calmed his steed as the hoof beats of a single rider came closer.

Pedro drew his gun and leaned toward the open gate. "Who goes there?" he shouted.

"It's Buck," came the reply. Pedro slid his six gun back in its holster at the sound of the familiar voice. Lantern light reflected off of the face of a bedraggled Buck as he rode through the gate.

Surprised to see Johnson alone at this time of night, Stanton started asking questions. "What are you doing here? What the hell happened out there today? Where's Paco and his gang?"

Out of breath from the hard ride, Buck tried to speak. "Well…when we…"

An impatient Stanton interrupted. "Speak up, man. I can't hear you!"

Buck shot a hard stare at George, grimaced and spoke. "We hid in the trees like we planned today. A short time later Jon came gallopin' over the rise just like we thought he would. We got him in our sights and started blastin' away. He dropped down hard behind some rocks, and a few seconds later he dropped out to the trail. He looked plenty dead to me, but Paco wanted to be sure, so he took aim and blasted him again. Paco still wasn't happy, so we jumped cover and ran down to plug him a couple more times when the riders appeared on the ridge."

"Riders! What the hell are you talking about?" George screamed.

"Some of the boys followed Jon. They must have smelled a rat or something." Sickened by the day's events, Buck glared at the pompous Stanton.

"How many were there?" Stanton demanded.

"Three. I recognized Cliff Stone and Ned Sloan— not sure about the third one."

"What happened?"

"They opened fire on us. We were sittin' ducks out on that trail, so we hightailed it for cover."

"They were firing from horseback, for God's sake, and you headed back for cover?" George bawled.

Buck's eyes narrowed. "I saw Cliff Stone and Ned Sloan, two of the best shots in the county comin' at us with rifles drawn. You bet we headed for cover—those two could shoot a walnut off a goat's ass from a hundred yards," a fuming Buck retorted. The other men nodded in agreement.

Aware of the shooting prowess of Stone and Sloan, Stanton backed off. "Okay, go ahead."

Buck's angry eyes glanced toward the other men. "What ya say we go inside, George—just the two of us?"

"Oh yes, yes. No use everyone hearing all of this," Stanton replied. "You boys go out back to the bunk-houses."

"Okay, boss," Pedro replied as he led the men away.

Stanton and Buck dismounted and hurried inside. Buck followed Stanton to his study and sat down in a small leather chair in front of his desk.

"Well go ahead, Buck," George ordered as he plopped into his swivel chair.

Exhausted and angry, Buck stared at the shiny oak desk top, never making eye contact with the pompous Stanton. "Like I said, we were damned surprised when Stone and Sloan rode over that hill. We were all out in the open, and we were pretty sure they recognized us, so we headed for the stream. They hit one of Paco's men before we got to the stream. Then Stone and the other guy backed off, Sloan gave chase for a short time and then gave up. A little while later, we ducked into the stream and headed for my place. When we got there, Paco ordered his men to bury his two dead compadres out in the woods so they wouldn't be bothered. When they finished, Paco shoved the barrel of his Peacemaker in my neck and demanded five hundred dollars for killin' Stoudenmire."

"What'd you do?"

"I told him to go to hell. He crammed the barrel harder into my neck and pulled the hammer back. He meant business—he said he was gonna kill me. So I dug my money bag up out behind the cabin and gave him five hundred dollars. He said he wanted it all. He laughed a real nasty kind of laugh and snatched the bag right outta my hand and cleaned it out. It had my life savings in there, over a thousand dollars. Then he and Arturo rode off. They had their money—they were headin' home."

"Why that rotten—"

Buck interrupted. "Hell, George, what'd ya expect from a man like Delgado?"

George's brow furrowed as he bent over and unlocked a desk drawer. He pulled out a metal box, popped the lid up and began rustling around inside. He pulled out a stack of cash and peeled off a thousand dollars, tossing it on the desk in front of Buck. "Here's your money. Now head on out to your place and lay low for a few days. I'll have Sheriff Cook clear things up."

Buck pushed up from the chair, grabbed the cash from the desktop and headed for the door.

"Hold on a second, Buck."

Edgy, Buck stopped by the large oak door with his back to Stanton. His hand hung over his six gun.

"I saw Stoudenmire's horse at the doc's tonight. Sure he's dead?"

"Hell yes! We filled 'im full a lead. He has to be dead!" Buck pushed through the door and hurried out.

- - - - -

"We thought something was wrong. We shoulda warned him," Cliff lamented as he paced back and forth in Doc Harper's waiting room.

"Quit beatin' yourself up, Cliff. He was on that palomino before we had a chance to do anything," Malone barked.

"Jack's right, Cliff," Ned said. "Jon heard a friend was in trouble and hightailed it out of there before we knew what was going on."

"They been in there forever," Cliff said anxiously as he plopped down in a small leather chair. He smiled and looked over at the other boys. "This is the first time I ever slept all night in a doctor's office."

"Same here," a heavily-bearded Sloan replied.

Just then the door to Doc's office creaked open. His stethoscope dangled on his chest as he stepped out to address the men. He was somber as the door clicked shut behind him; he seemed distracted.

Glad to see the doc, Cliff spoke up. "What the hell's goin' on, Doc? Tell us something!" he barked at the quiet man.

"Sorry, Cliff. I was deep in thought."

Cliff squirmed in his chair.

The doc's eyes, dark from exhaustion, looked over at the miner. "They hit him three times. One nicked his left arm, and I dug one outta his rib cage, and he took one in the back of his leg. And he's got a gash on his head from the fall into the rocks, and—"

"Okay, okay, Doc, but is he gonna make it?" Cliff blinked nervously, waiting for Doc's reply.

"Well, I got all the lead out of him, and none of the bullets hit any vital organs, but he's lost a lot of blood. And then there's that bump on his head. I'll have to keep an eye on him for a possible concussion. There's always the chance of infection, and—"

Suddenly, the door to Doc's office fell open. Jon stepped out and gently closed the door behind him. "Howdy, boys. Fancy meetin' you here."

"Now Jon, you're in no—"

The big gunman interrupted. "Doc, you dug a bucket full of lead outta me, and I truly appreciate it, but I haven't got time to lay around here. Me and the boys here got us some business to take care of. I hope you don't mind, Doc, but I helped myself to one of those shirts you said you keep in your closet for folks like me. I'm surprised you had my size." Jon grinned at the incredulous doctor. "I left twenty dollars on the table. Hope it's enough."

"Why....uh, yes....uh, that should be plenty, but you just listen to me, Jon Stoudenmire! I'm not going to be responsible for—"

Jon patted the doctor on the back. "Don't worry, Doc—I won't hold ya liable if I die," Jon laughed as he glanced around the room at the other men. "Let's go, boys."

Jon fanned his hat toward the door as the men rushed out. Trailing the others, Jon turned and grinned at the doc. "Thanks again." He ignored Doc's pleadings as the door clicked shut.

Spurs jingled as the boys jumped down from the boardwalk.

"You sure you're okay?" Cliff asked.

"I'm a little weak all right, but I'll be fine. Like I told the doc, I don't have the luxury of laying around for a couple of days—we got us some men to kill."

"Glad you're up and around, partner. We all been worried about ya, especially Cliff," Malone exclaimed.

Jon grinned at his embarrassed cousin. "Thanks," he said quietly. His expression changed. "Any of ya have an idea on where Delgado and the boys went?"

Ned spoke up. "When they saw us come over that hill, they turned tail and ran. They were duckin' bullets as they rode into the stream. I gave chase for a while and then gave up. I think we hit one or two of 'em."

"What's out that way?"

"There's one whale of a woods on the west side of the stream. It goes on and on," Sloan replied. "They probably ducked in that—"

Coming out of deep thought, Cliff interrupted his friend. "Sorry, Ned, but I think I know something that would help us."

"Is that so? Well, let's have it," Jon said.

"One day me and a couple of the boys decided to take a day off from mining and do a little bobcat huntin'. The cats had been killin' chickens and other small livestock, so we decided to try and take out a couple of 'em. We stopped by the hardware, stocked up on cartridges and headed out west of town. It wasn't long before we reached the stream near where Jon got bushwhacked. It had been a little dry, so we thought the cats might be hanging out near the water. After ridin' the stream for a while, we hadn't seen anything, so we decided to look for the nasty varmints deeper in the woods. We found a path out of the creek and rode further into the forest. There was evidence of prints, so we rode a while longer. After a while, a clearing appeared up ahead. When I looked down in the valley, I saw Buck Johnson choppin' wood up next to a log cabin. I figured he must have a lady friend that lived there or somethin'—I never gave it much thought til now. I'll bet ya that's where they were headin'."

"Can you find that clearing again?" Jon shot back.

"I think so. Ya just follow the stream until ya see a large oak tree hangin' out over the water. The path through the woods is just on the other side of that ugly oak tree. Once we find that path you just follow it to the clearing."

"Lead the way," Jon ordered.

Cliff's painted sorrel leapt forward to the front of the group; the others fell in behind. The men rode hard and fast to the edge of town and down the same trail they were on the day before. Water splashed as the men charged into the stream and raced through the shallow water. Still leading, Cliff suddenly pulled up.

"There it is," he shouted.

The men looked ahead. "You're right, partner— that's one ugly tree," Sloan exclaimed.

Cliff ducked under a long, gnarly limb hanging out over the water and climbed up the steep bank on the other side. He glanced down at the hoof prints as he plunged into the dark woods; the others were in close pursuit. After winding their way through the thick, dense forest for over an hour, Cliff reined up. Jon pulled up next to him.

"Might help to take a look at these tracks." Cliff nodded toward the path.

It was a wide part of the trail and full of tracks. Jon carefully dismounted, still favoring his injured right leg. He leaned over and limped back and forth, examining the numerous hoof prints on the trail.

"There are two sets of tracks that are always together—looks like one of the men is leading a horse. You boys must have killed one of them. I think this horse is carrying a dead body." Jon stepped across the dusty trail. "There are blood spots over here, away from the others. Looks like one of the other men could be badly hurt or dead." He glanced up at Ned. "You boys hit a couple of 'em all right. Good work."

Ned shook his head. "Two down and four to go."

"Let's ride," Cliff admonished. "I think we're getting close."

Pushing the thick brush to the side, the men charged on. A short distance ahead they dropped down into a small ravine. They struggled up the steep bank on the other side and bolted forward. All of a sudden Cliff's hand shot up. "Gather 'round," he said. The others watched as he pulled back on the leafy limbs of a black maple hanging in front of him for a better view.

The men moved up around Cliff and gawked at the scene below.

"Nice place," Jon whispered as he motioned for the others to lean in. "Can't see anybody around. Looks deserted down there right now. But it could be a trick—they could have hidden their horses in case somebody showed up, so we gotta be careful. It's wide open between here and the cabin." Jon quickly examined the periphery of the clearing. "And I can't see another entry into this dale anywhere." He drew his Colt. "Pull iron, men. We're going in. Spread out behind me as soon as we hit the basin."

Jon's big palomino jumped down the hill and sprang into the opening. Six gun held high, Jon glanced left and right as the men spread out behind him. Mud splattered up from the grassy basin as the men raced forward. Jon and Cliff charged straight for the cabin; the others fanned out and headed for the other buildings. Jon grabbed his leg and grimaced in pain as he dismounted and hit the ground. The two men burst forward; Cliff kicked open the wooden door. Jon pushed past him and charged in, hammer cocked. He kicked a couple of chairs to the side and scanned the room. Beads of sweat dripped from his forehead. His leg was throbbing. He nodded at the two open doors at the other end of the room. Cliff hurried over, pistol in hand, and quickly examined the rooms.

"They're both empty," he shouted.

Jon walked around the kitchen area. "The cabinet doors are open, and the flour and most of the canned goods are gone. Looks like they left in a hurry. Let's go outside." Sloan was just approaching the cabin.

"The gate was open, and all of the horses and the buck wagon are gone from the corral. Looks like they hightailed it outta here," Sloan said.

"They probably buried their dead somewhere around here and took off. Delgado's well on his way to Mexico by now." Jon shook his head. "Not sure where in the hell Johnson went."

"Buck's no dummy. Six horses leave a lot of tracks. He probably wanted to get as far away from here as he could," Malone groused.

Jon frowned as he spit on the ground. "I'd love to go after those snakes. I want a piece of Delgado in the worst way, but they've got a day's head start on us, and we got us a bigger fish to fry right now."

"You're right, Jon, but it ain't gonna be easy," Cliff said. "Stanton's got an alibi. Attorney Smith came down to Doc's this morning to check on you and told us that he heard that Stanton and his boys were down at the Dead End last night, and they never left."

"Hmmm…that George is no dummy," Jon replied. "Let's go have a drink and figure out how to smoke that snake out of his hole." Jon spun around, mounted up and raced back across the grassy vale toward El Cabrera.

- - - - -

The men garnered a few stares from curious townsfolk as they rode slowly into town. Tired and hot, they tied down and hopped up the steps in front of the Dead End. Ned pushed through the swinging doors, leading the way. It got suddenly quiet inside the bawdy saloon; the gamblers stopped and watched as the hard men strolled in. There were gasps as Jon came into view. With a tuft of black hair protruding from the bandages on his forehead, he limped slightly as he walked to his favorite corner table. Jon bumped several chairs out of the way, pushed to the back of the table and sat down. The others joined him. Jake hurried over to take their orders.

"What's everybody starin' at?" an uneasy Jon asked.

"Hell, the rumor is that you're dead! Pedro was in earlier, telling everybody that you got bushwhacked by some strangers on the edge of town. No big deal, for thunder's sake!" Jake bawled.

"Well, I'm not dead, so will you please tell everyone to quit starin' at me?"

"I'll try, Jon, but it's not going to be easy. It's like we've all just seen a ghost or something. By the way, I'm kinda glad Pedro was wrong!" The bartender beamed.

"Kinda?" Jon hollered; a big grin broke out on his face.

The other boys laughed heartily.

Red-faced, Jake turned to address the crowd. "Jon's alive as you can plainly see, so let the man drink in peace!" The surprised patrons shook their heads, muffled voices could be heard throughout the saloon. A few of the gamblers raised their beer mugs toward the popular men. The spinning sounds of the roulette wheel and shouts from the faro dealers soon filled the air.

Back at the table, Jake was taking orders. "Okay, fellas, are you having the usual?"

"Yep, but give Jon a double shot," Cliff ordered.

"Ya took the words right out of my mouth, cus." Jon's brow furrowed as he made eye contact with each of the men. "I don't know how to thank you boys for savin' me and then waitin' up all night and all."

"You owe us big time," Cliff joked, not wanting things to get too sentimental.

"That's for sure," Jon laughed. His expression changed as he began to talk of Stanton and the boys. "We got us a couple of big problems, fellas. Stanton's got an alibi, and he's got the sheriff in his back pocket."

"Well, maybe not anymore." Malone jumped in the conversation.

Surprised by the sudden announcement, Jon glanced left at the former lawman.

"I been meaning to tell ya, but…uh, we've been so busy and such. I just…"

"It's okay, Jack. Just spit it out," Jon growled.

"Well, one of the boys out at the mines came up to me yesterday with some interesting information. He said one of the miners saw Dave Barton shoot old Curly Harmon in the back of the head the other day. Says he's ready to spill the beans."

"You don't say!"

"Yeah, and there's one more thing. He says there was a man with Dave, and he was wearin' a badge. Says it was Sheriff Cook."

"Well, I'll be, if that don't beat all!" Jon laughed out loud.

"Yeah, and I went and talked to the miner myself. He said he was sorry he didn't come forth sooner, but he was afraid for his family. Says his family packed up and went back to Missouri, so now he's ready to talk. His name's Cal Joiner."

"Best news I heard in a while, Jack. Lunch is on me!" Jon raised his glass to the others. There were smiles all around as the men downed their shots.

- - - - -

"Who is it?" Stanton barked, annoyed at being interrupted by the loud knock on his office door.

"It's me, Cook!"

"Door's open. Come on in."

The heavy oak door swung open, and Cook rushed in. "He's alive, George, he's alive!"

"He's what?" George screamed, his face flushed with anger. George was beside himself; Cook was confirming his worst fears. The man he so loathed and despised was still alive.

"He just walked into the Dead End with Stone, Malone, and Sloan. I slipped out and rode down here to tell ya. He's got a bandage on his head, but he's alive and kickin'."

"Damn! And I just gave Johnson a thousand dollars." George pushed back from the desk, jumped up and began pacing. "That's just dandy. Stoudenmire's going to be madder than a hornet now, and he'll be coming after me. You can bet your house on that. We have to do something."

"Yeah, I know, but what?" Cook replied.

George frowned. "Hell, you're the law around here, Cook. Think of something!"

"I can't arrest a man for being shot, George!" Cook shouted.

George stormed over to the jumpy sheriff. Their faces were only inches apart. "I pay you very well, Sheriff Cook, and you're in this mess around here up to your eyeballs. So for your own sake you better think of something, pronto!" George glared angrily.

Cook's head dropped to the side; he stepped back. "Okay, okay, George. Just calm down a little."

"You heard me!"

Cook walked over to the window on the east wall. He pulled back the curtain as if looking outside, while actually he was buying time. Giving himself a chance to think.

"Well?" George yelled.

Cook sighed as he turned away from the window. "Stoudenmire's shot down two men in cold blood, and there's been nothin' but trouble ever since he arrived in El Cabrera. I will inform him that I consider him a menace to our fine community and that I want him out of town by sundown. If he refuses, I will arrest him for disturbing the peace and refusing the order of an officer of the court. It will never hold up in court, but he can't make bail until the district judge arrives in two weeks. So he'll be out of your hair."

"Hmmm…sounds good. That way he either leaves town or we got him in jail." George rubbed his chin. "Then I can bring in some more guns, chase off Stone and the others and we're back in business."

A nervous grin broke out on Cook's face.

George dropped down in the soft leather chair. "Good plan, Sheriff, good plan. Now go find Stoudenmire and give him the news, pronto."

Not anxious to implement his new plan, a reluctant Cook turned and hurried out.

Chapter 23

"Well, look who's here!" Cliff glanced toward the front door at the Dead End; his fork clanked as he tossed it on the empty dish.

The batwing door fell shut. Sheriff Cook walked in and slowly wound his way across the room toward the men's table.

"Howdy, Sheriff," Jon said. "To what do we owe the pleasure of this visit?"

"We got us a problem, Jon," Cook said, hands on his six guns.

Jon's mood darkened quickly. "What's that, Sheriff?"

The cocky lawman regurgitated the script he'd been practicing on the way to the saloon. "Seems like ever since you came to town there's been nothing but killings and trouble around here, Jon. People don't feel safe anymore. It's my job as sheriff to make sure our town is safe from a menace like you." A sly grin broke out on his face. "I want you out of town by sundown today, or I'll throw you in jail for disturbing the peace and refusing the order of an officer of the court." Cook smirked as he waited for Jon's answer.

Jon's brow furrowed. He pushed his chair back and slowly stood. "You're right, Cook. The people don't feel safe around here anymore. They don't feel safe because they got a crooked law enforcement officer—and guess what."

Cook's eyebrows raised.

"Jack here tells me there's a witness to Curly Harmon's murder, and he's ready to spill the beans. Says he saw Barton kill poor old Curly. He says there was a man with Barton who wore a badge—says it was you."

"You're just makin' that up, Stoudenmire. You're bluffin'." Beads of sweat formed on Cook's forehead.

"Tell him what the man said, Jack."

Malone's eyes narrowed to a scowl as he looked at the sheriff. "He said that Curly was glad to see ya, laughin' and shakin' your hand and all. Then when he bent down to pick up his shovel, Dave drew his gun and let the poor bastard have it right in the back of the head. After he fell, he shot him again to be sure he was dead. He says you were with Barton, and he's ready to tell all."

"Looks like cold-blooded murder to me, Sheriff. I'm sure the district judge in Santa Cruz would love to hear about this." Jon grinned at the shocked lawman.

Face flushed, Cook's eyes darted around the table at the stoic faces of the other men.

"Now take your hands off those guns, Sheriff, nice and easy. One false move, and I'll blow your damn fool head off," Jon snarled.

Cook dropped his shaking hands to his side.

Jon lunged forward, grabbed Cook's shoestring tie with his good right arm and yanked him against the table. "You're implicated in more than just Curly's murder, Sheriff. Cliff and Ned both saw your friends

Buck Johnson and Paco Delgado try to bushwhack me yesterday. You're in this ugly mess up to your scrawny neck. Stanton ordered you and Barton to go out and kill Curly, didn't he?"

Cook gasped for breath as Jon pulled tighter on the tie. "Y…y…yes, Stanton told us to g…get rid of Curly," he stuttered.

"Listen close, Sheriff, 'cause I ain't gonna say it twice. I want you outta here. If I ever see you in this town again, I'll personally blast you into the next county. You got it?" The room was thick with tension as the powerful gunman spoke.

"Y…yes," Cook said meekly.

"Now take your belt off nice and easy," Jon ordered.

Sweating profusely, Cook carefully untied his gun belt and pulled it off. Jon slid around the table and charged toward the door, bumping chairs to the side as he dragged Cook by his tie. Jon's shoulder banged into the swinging doors as he dragged the gagging lawman out to his horse. "Get on!" Jon shouted as he let loose of the noose. Cook rubbed his neck and grimaced in pain as he started to mount up. "Uggh!" he moaned as Jon kicked him hard on his backside. Humiliated in front of the shocked townsfolk, he mounted up and galloped toward the outskirts of town, never once looking back.

Jon stood watching, his eyes black with rage. Cliff and the other boys stood on the boardwalk. Suddenly, a dark-skinned man darted off of the boardwalk near the bathhouse.

"It's Pedro!" Sloan shouted.

Jon drew as he spun to his left. He cocked his Colt, pointed it skyward and squeezed the trigger. Pedro stopped dead in his tracks; smoke spewed from Jon's six gun.

"Don't move til I have my say, Pedro!" Jon bellowed. "Tell Stanton I'll meet him at sundown tomorrow here in the street. Man to man, and tell him if he doesn't show, he's even more of a coward than I think he is!" Jon shouted. The gathering crowd groaned at the prospect of yet another bloody showdown.

Pedro jumped abroad his clay and spurred her toward Stanton's compound.

Jon's expression softened as he glanced over at his compadres standing tall on the boardwalk. "See you boys inside just before sundown tomorrow." He dropped the smoking six gun in the holster and limped toward Callahan's.

His leg aching, Jon walked through the door to the boardinghouse. Katie's curly head popped up from behind the counter. "Howdy, Jon. You okay?"

"I'm fine, thank ya, Katie."

"I heard you got shot up pretty good. You sure you're all right?" the precocious new owner asked.

"Yeah. I think I just need a little rest, that's all." Jon tipped his hat and started up the stairs. He walked slowly down the hall and shuffled into his room. He dropped down in the wooden chair next to the bed. His left arm was aching, his ribs hurt and his leg was throbbing. Weak from his wounds, Jon lamented the coming fight with the powerful Stanton, a crack shot. Although not a gunslinger by nature, he knew Stanton wouldn't back down after Jon's public challenge—his pride wouldn't let him.

The die had been cast. Jon knew that either he or George Stanton would die in twenty-four hours. He leaned over, grabbed the wooden knob on the small dressing table and slid it open. He reached inside and felt around for the faded and worn Bible he had noticed earlier in his stay. He snatched it from the drawer; the thin pages flapped over as he pushed aggressively through its tattered contents. Jon had gone away from the Bible as he grew older, and he wasn't sure why. But somehow now, in a weakened state, his life hanging in the balance, he once again felt the urge to revisit the ancient book.

As a small boy, Jon had hopped up on his mother's lap in front of the fire every night after a long day in the Indiana wheat fields. He remembered how she had hugged him tightly and read softly from the Bible, a welcome respite after the almost daily beatings from his father. For some reason, even as a small boy, a verse in Romans had jumped out at him. As he grew up, it helped define the guiding principles of his life; he truly believed that God had commanded this verse to him. The pages turned more slowly. The last crinkled page fell over. His thick finger slid down the page and suddenly stopped. He struggled to read the tiny print in the limited light from the nearby window. A beam of light suddenly broke through the clouds and fell across the weathered book. A tear rolled down his cheek as he read the haunting verse in Romans 15:13: "Greater love has no man than this, that a man be willing to lay down his life for his friends."

Jon gently closed the Bible and dropped it back in the drawer. The time was coming when he would, as the powerful verse implored, once again put his life on the line for his friends. Alone with his thoughts, the searing emotions of a conflicted life flooded through his mind as he sat bruised and battered in the small boardinghouse on the edge of California. A few tears rolled down his face. His red eyes looked heavenward as he whispered, "Grant me strength Lord as I try to make the good fight." He exhaled deeply. His head gently bumped against the wall as sleep overcame him.

Exhausted, Jon slept through the next day. It was evening when he finally awoke; he yawned and glanced through the window at the evening sun. He rubbed sleep from his eyes and stood slowly, aching all over. His good right hand struggled with the snaps on his borrowed denim shirt; he pulled his shirt off and washed up. He grabbed his belt and pulled it open. The bloody jeans dropped to the floor. He stepped out of his jeans, yanked the belt free and tossed them on the bed. A quick examination of his chest and leg wounds, showed no signs of bleeding. Next he pulled a good pair of jeans from his saddlebag on the bedpost. Pain shot up his leg as he lifted it into the jeans and pushed it through. He put his other leg in and pulled the jeans to waist level. He slipped on a clean shirt and tucked it in and snapped his jeans shut. He grabbed his gun belt, buckled up and tied down.

Suddenly, a rock tapped against the window. Jon stepped over and glanced down at the street. Ned Sloan's square face was grinning from ear to ear as he and the other boys looked up at Jon. Jon leaned down, pushed the window up and shouted, "Come on up. I'm decent." The men disappeared under the canopy. Jon stepped over and unlocked the door; it fell slightly open. A short time later, he could hear footsteps in the hall. The men hurried in.

"How ya doin?" Cliff asked as he spun a chair around and dropped down, facing Jon.

"I'm sore all over. Feel like somebody's been smackin' me with a sledge hammer all night. Otherwise, not too bad."

The boys chuckled nervously.

"Any news out on the street?" Jon asked.

"Not much. Stanton's been quiet. I've had one of the boys from out at the mines watchin' his place."

"And?"

"Nobody's left that compound all day," Cliff replied.

"Good." Jon spun the cylinders on his six guns to be sure they were fully loaded.

"There was one other bit of news," Sloan added.

Jon looked toward the giant man.

"Town Board President Fred Smith watched you chase Cook outa town yesterday. He approached us shortly after you came back here and said he was glad Cook was gone. Said Cook was not the man he thought he was when he and the other board members hired him. He asked us if we knew of anyone with experience who could act as temporary sheriff until they could find another one. Cliff and I both looked at Malone."

Malone grinned. As he pulled back his leather vest, a badge appeared.

"Congrats, Sheriff!" Jon reached forward for a shake. "It's gonna help a lot havin' the law on our side."

Suddenly the men heard shouting and loud voices on the street. They stepped near the window and surveyed the scene below. Women held tightly to their children's hands as they scurried out of the way; the curious children's necks craned toward the end of town.

Jon grabbed his hat. "Let's go, boys. Sounds like they're comin'!"

The landing shook as the four big men hurried down the hall and hurtled down the stairs. Limping, Jon pushed through the door as the men rushed out for their showdown with the dangerous Stanton and his gang.

Jon's leg was throbbing. "Shouldn't have done those stairs so fast," he mumbled.

"I wondered about that." Cliff grinned at his good friend.

"It's them." Ned pointed to the edge of town.

Jon squinted into the sun as the men approached. Stanton led the parade—he appeared different, shedding his cotton pants and silk shirt in favor of a blue denim shirt and jeans. Pedro marched alongside in a brown poncho and large sombrero; a long pistol hung at his side. Armed, the other four men fanned out behind them. They looked imposing as they marched in formation down the dirt road.

"Stanton's unarmed," Malone hollered.

Jon looked closer. "Sure is. Wonder what the hell he's up to."

As they drew closer, Jon surveyed the scene. Stanton's waist was empty, but six guns protruded from the hips of the other men. Stanton looked bigger in denim; stocky and barrel-chested, his rolled sleeves exposed his massive forearms.

"Spread out on the street, fellas. Start shootin' at fifty feet," Jon ordered. Jon and the men stepped down from the boardwalk. Jon tried desperately not to limp, but his leg still hurt from the stunt on the stairs; otherwise, he felt rested from his long sleep. His gang moved to the street's middle and stopped. His anger was growing. He could feel it rising inside as Stanton and his bullies came closer. Senses on high alert, he began to focus. Jon couldn't wait for the mayhem to begin.

Heads peered out of store fronts and second-story windows; others peeked from the corner of the alley. The tension mounted as Stanton moved closer. Soon, he was just seventy-five feet away.

Jon's deep voice thundered down the street. "Any closer, George, and we start blastin'."

George's arm shot up; his men stopped. The expression on his broad face darkened. "I'm not carrying, Jon. Surely you wouldn't shoot an unarmed man."

"Not on purpose, George, but who knows? You might get hit by a stray bullet or something—can't tell." Jon grinned at the muscular mogul.

George stood still in the street. "I'm no gunman, Jon. You know that. Why, I wouldn't have a chance in a gun fight with someone like you."

"You can shoot well enough, Stanton. What's your game?"

Stanton smirked. "How about you and me, man to man, bare knuckles here on the street where the whole town can see? If I whip ya, you'll leave town. If you whip me, I'll do the same."

Cliff's head spun toward Jon. "You're all shot up, Jon. You can't do that! George is a bare knuckles fighter from way back. He'll kill you!"

Malone stepped over. "Let me arrest him, Jon. You're in no condition—"

Jon interrupted. "Keep your badge hidden, Jack. I can't pass this up."

Malone's head shook as he buttoned his duster.

"Tell your boys to unbuckle their gun belts and throw 'em in front of 'em. My boys will do the same. Jack Malone will gather 'em up and put 'em in Cook's old office." Jon tipped his head toward the nearby building.

The confident George, still smarting from the surprise beating Jon gave him at the boardinghouse, couldn't wait to take on the injured gunman. An ugly scowl covered his face as he ordered his men to unbuckle. The leather snapped, the buckles popped open, and holsters and guns hit the ground one after another. Malone and Sloan hurried along, collecting the fallen firearms and lugging them to the vacant sheriff's office.

The threat of gunplay gone, the townsfolk came out of the alleys and buildings and slowly formed a circle around the two warriors.

Jon's forearms rippled as he rolled his sleeves up. His opened and closed his calloused fingers several times, slipped off his large gold ring and tossed it to Cliff.

Cliff snatched the ring from the air.

Jon grinned at his long-faced cousin. "Don't worry, Cliff. I ain't had this much fun in a long time."

Fists doubled, elbows high, Stanton looked plenty agile as he sparred with his man Pedro.

"You'll kill him boss. I hear he's all shot up," Pedro shouted as he ducked a punch.

Stanton ignored the comment, acting as if he didn't know he was fighting an injured opponent. He suddenly spun toward Jon, fists in the air.

Jon's long arms hung at his side as he walked confidently to the center of the street. He saw large gold rings on both of Stanton's hands.

"Take 'em off!" Jon yelled, pointing at his fingers.

Slightly embarrassed, George yanked off the rings and tossed them to Pedro. He jumped quickly back to a fighting stance and jabbed the air in front of Jon's face several times.

Jon ignored the mock punches as Stanton moved in quickly, bobbing left and right to keep the badly hobbled Jon off balance. Suddenly his right fist flew forward, bashing into Jon's jaw. Jon staggered backward and then righted himself. Stanton ducked and weaved, moving quickly left and right. Jon found it hard to keep up. He threw a left jab; it bounced harmlessly off of Stanton's shoulder. George retaliated with a hard left to Jon's bandaged gut.

"Uggh!" Jon grimaced in pain as he grabbed his stomach. George raised his thick leg and let loose with a mighty kick square on Jon's head. Jon flew violently backwards and crashed onto the dusty street; his head banged hard against the ground. Blood trickled across his eyes as he lay staring at the blue sky. He was dazed and disoriented as he rolled to his side and struggled up to one knee. Moving in for the kill, George's big fist blasted into the side of Jon's face. Jon fell hard to the ground. He lay motionless, his face red and swollen from Stanton's punishing blows. He could hear Cliff shouting, "Get up, Jon! Get up!" A coarse groan went through the crowd as Stanton danced above him, waving his fist and challenging Jon to fight on. Battered and beaten, Jon was in great pain as he stared at the sky above. Suddenly, that old Bible verse came to mind. His eyes narrowed as he whispered, "I'm willin' to die for a friend, but not today."

Rejuvenated, Jon struggled on one knee and then leapt to his feet like a man possessed. The awful pain in his leg seemed to diminish as he charged toward Stanton, ducking and weaving like a bare knuckles fighter. Confused by Jon's sudden burst of energy, George swung wildly, missing by a foot. The crowd screamed in delight as Jon dipped down—his big fist flew forward and buried deep in Stanton's gut. "Oh my Gawd!" he screamed as he folded over in pain, gripping his stomach. Jon reeled around behind him, smacking Stanton's head with the side of his hand.

"Damn!" Stanton screamed as he fell hard to one knee. Stunned, the nasty tyrant tried to right himself. But Jon rushed over; his thick fingers wrapped around the brute's shirt collar. He yanked him to his feet. Eyes wide with fear, George seemed paralyzed as he waited for the next punch to arrive. Jon lifted his arm above his head. His big fist flew forward with great fury and drove deep into Stanton's gut.

"Oh gawd!" George screamed as he staggered around helplessly, dazed and disoriented by the terrifying blow to his midsection. Jon moved in closer to his prey; his fist powered forward again. Blood and sweat exploded from Stanton's face as the crunching blow crashed into his chin, knocking him backwards several feet. He slammed into a hitching post and bounced face first onto the hard dirt street. Jon stormed over and stood panting over the fallen man, fists doubled.   Beaten almost senseless, Stanton made gurgling, moaning sounds as he lay battered. Jon leaned down and yanked his limp body up by the collar; he wanted to hit him again.

Suddenly Ned shouted, "I think he's had enough, Jon!"

Eyes glazed over with anger, Jon stood shaking over the battered man. Sweat poured from his face as he pondered his next move. He saw a chance to kill this brute—he wanted to take it.   But in a bare knuckles fight, he had done all he could do.   Anything more would be murder.

Ned walked over and splashed a bucket of water on Stanton's face. Stanton's head shook and water flew as he struggled to open his swollen eyes.   Chest heaving, wet strands of black hair hanging from his forehead, he was defenseless.   Jon yanked him up to eye level; their faces were only inches apart. Stanton's face looked like raw meat. His nose was shattered and broken; his eyes had been reduced to swollen slits. Jon yanked harder on his collar. Their faces banged together. "I wish I could have killed you, you son-of-a-bitch!" he barked.

"I...uh...uh, never been hit that hard," George mumbled. "I'm finished." Jon let loose of the collar. The smallish Pedro hurried over to keep George from falling. He slid his arm under the big man, struggling to hold him up. Several of Stanton's men ran over to assist Pedro.

Jack Malone stepped forward and yanked his black vest open, exposing his badge. "I got some important news for you, George. Can you understand what I'm saying?"

"Yes...I...I can understand," he replied almost inaudibly.

"I'm the law around here now, George. Councilman Smith appointed me this afternoon. And you will be leaving town as was promised, my friend, except you won't be going where you thought you were. You're going to the county jail in Santa Cruz."

Stanton struggled to lift his head. "What the hell for?" he moaned.

"For the murder of old Curly Harmon. We have an eye witness as well as a confession from former Sheriff Cook that you ordered him and Dave Barton to kill Curly. We can also implicate you in the attempted bushwhacking of Jon outside of town yesterday. I imagine you'll be going to jail for quite a spell."

The defeated Stanton's head dropped to his chest.

Malone's brow furrowed. He flashed an angry stare at the fallen powerbroker. "You and your men have brought nothing but fear and death to this town, Stanton. You're lucky to be alive—you should be dead. Now get up!"

The men helped Stanton to his feet. Malone quickly cuffed him and stared at the other men. "I want you all out of town by sundown tomorrow. If I ever see any of you within fifty miles of this town, I'll throw your sorry asses in jail. Do you understand?"

The frightened men nodded their heads as they struggled to keep the heavy Stanton on his feet.

Battered and bruised, fists doubled, Jon stood watching in the street. He felt no sympathy for Stanton, only remorse for not having had the opportunity to kill him. He squeezed his bloody fingers open and shut as he watched the ragtag crew prepare to drag Stanton away to jail. Humiliated in front of the entire town by the beating from a wounded Jon, he was a pathetic sight. Jon limped over and punched Malone gently on the shoulder. "Good work, Sheriff. I couldn't have said it better myself."

A slight grin broke out on Malone's narrow face.

Suddenly, Jon felt a hard tug on the arm of his shirt. He turned to see the bespectacled Doc standing next to him in the street with a big frown.

"Now it's my turn, tough guy," the old doctor scolded. "You're comin' with me, ya hear me? We gotta clean those wounds and change those bandages right away, pronto, in my office. And no arguing." His glasses fell down to the end of his nose as he bumped into the big man and pushed him toward his office. The crowd roared as Doc straightened his glasses and kept on pushing. Jon grinned and walked obediently ahead of the persistent caregiver.

As they approached the office, Doc reached in front of Jon and pushed the door open. His eyes softened as he laid his hand on Jon's shoulder and looked up at the big gunman. "You're a brave man, son. I'm proud of ya!"

Jon smiled warmly. "Thank ya, Doc." The two men ducked under the door and disappeared inside.

Chapter 24

The hot afternoon sun beat down on the dry, cracked street. A pain shot up Jon's side as he dropped down from the boardwalk in front of Callahan's onto the dirt road. He quickly rubbed his sore right leg with his bruised and swollen fingers, then limped on toward the end of town. He glanced ahead at the hitching post in front of the telegraph office. He was lucky—it was shy of any horses. "Bless you Mr. Stoudenmire," a grateful lady in a yellow cotton dress and white bonnet shouted at Jon as he continued to make his way down the street. Jon saw an "Open" sign dangling on the front door of the small office. Jon winced in pain as he lifted his injured leg up the steps and walked inside.

The small desk near the front of the room seemed to vibrate as the old operator tapped away on the odd looking machine. Suddenly he stopped, rubbed the stubble on his chin as if he were thinking and then glanced over at Jon. "Afternoon," he groused. "'Nother love letter?"

Jon grinned at the old codger. "Well, I guess so."

"Logan's Crossing?"

"Yep."

"Fire away. I got me a good line to Arizona Territory right now. We better strike while the iron's hot." His scraggly face broke into a smile.

"Well...uh, okay, uh..."

The old man jumped in. "Like I told ya last time, young feller, I hear love stories all the time. Think nothin' of it. Best read it to me—my glasses broke. I'm wearin' my old ones, and they ain't worth a damn."

Jon reached inside his black vest and pulled out a neatly folded piece of parchment. He carefully opened it and looked it over one last time. He took a deep breath as he glanced nervously at the grumpy operator. After a short pause, he began to read:

> *"My dearest Elizabeth,*
>
> *Good news, darling! My business with cousin Cliff is over. I will be starting on our cabin soon. When the cabin is livable, I will wire Ed Morgan and make arrangements for your safe passageway over the mountains.*
>
> *I miss you sorely, my dear, and long to hold...uh...uh..."*

The tapping stopped; the old man leaned over and gently slid the parchment out of Jon's hand. "I take over from here. I ain't got all night."

Red-faced, Jon stood watching as the operator held Jon's letter at arm's length and began clicking the sounder. Suddenly, he stopped. He squinted as he leaned forward and checked the gram for errors. Satisfied, he folded the parchment and quickly handed it back to Jon.

"That'll be two bits!"

Jon slid a silver dollar from his front vest pocket and tossed it on the desk.

The old man's eyes narrowed as he looked up at Jon. "You don't look so tough to me," he barked. A sly grin broke across his wrinkled face as he hocked a big one into the spittoon next to his desk.

Amused by the audacity of the old timer, Jon grinned and stepped out the door. The street was bustling with activity; Jon could feel excitement in the air as he hobbled toward the stables. The bright sun felt good on his battered body as he wove his way through the wagons and buggies.

"Hello, Jon," Hank Clark shouted as Jon approached the stables. The smiling stable hand quickly hurried out the wide door to greet him. "You're a celebrity now, you know!"

"Hmmm…is that right?"

"Yep. Just got today's paper. Look at the headline." Hank yanked the paper out of his back pocket and spread it open in front of Jon.

Jon glanced nervously at the bold headline:

Stoudenmire Cleans Up County

"Oh boy—I hope Libby doesn't see that!" Jon laughed.

"You're a hero around here, my friend."

Jon frowned. "Hero, huh? Guess I never thought of myself as a hero."

"Well ya are whether you like it or not," Hank laughed. "And by the way, Babe's ready. She's been prancing around in there all morning. She's rarin' to go." Hank hurried inside and emerged a short time later with Babe in tow, saddled and ready to ride.

"What do I owe ya, Hank?"

"It's on me, Jon—it's the least I can do. Oh, and by the way Jon, Sheriff Malone brought in that Ignacio fella this morning. The one who set ya up."

"I figured he'd flown the coop."

"I guess he was packed and ready to go when Malone grabbed him."

Jon smiled at the friendly stable hand as he spun around and rode out toward the edge of town. Every muscle in his body ached as he bounced along the bumpy trail. He felt a surge of anger inside as he approached the gates to Stanton's former compound. The ever present sentries were gone; the open gates swayed in the gentle breeze. Following Malone's orders, Pedro and the other henchman apparently had fled the compound. No voices could be heard inside. Jon glanced down at a bevy of tracks heading south from the former fortress. "Good riddance," he mumbled.

Jon's stomach knotted as he rode over the rise near the river where he had been bushwhacked by Delgado and his gang a few days earlier. He felt sick as he glanced down at his dry blood stains on the large rock. He quickly jerked away from the disturbing scene and rode on down the path. When he reached the stream, Jon eased Babe into the cool water for a drink.

A strong wave of emotion came over Jon as he gazed ahead at the trail to Vinegar Bend and his cherished vineyard. For the first time, he realized that he was going home. *My dream is finally coming true,* he thought. *No more fighting, no more bloodshed, no more killing.* He was overjoyed at the thought of the bright future that lay ahead for him and his beautiful Elizabeth. For once in his troubled life, he would have the peace he so dearly longed for. He would have a life with the woman he loved.

Jon glanced down at his wounds, taking stock. The round blood stain on his leg hadn't gotten any bigger since Doc had cleaned his wounds the day before, which was good. Doc said his leg could be healed up completely in a couple of weeks. A brownish scab was all that remained of the flesh wound he had taken to his left arm. He carefully unsnapped the buttons on his shirt, pulled it apart and examined his chest. The new bandages were clear of any blood. Doc said the soreness in his ribs might continue for several weeks. But that was okay—if his leg and arm healed on time, he would be able to finish the cabin by late summer. His ribs should be all right by the time Libby arrived, removing any lingering remnants of his violent days in El Cabrera. He wanted desperately to be a whole man when he was reunited with Elizabeth.

Jon carefully dismounted and dropped into the shallow stream; beads of sweat dripped from his forehead, his heart raced as he unstrapped his saddlebag. He dug around inside the bag and pulled out a leather pouch, the same leather pouch he had emptied on a hilltop just east of El Cabrera on his way into town. It was time to renew his pledge to Libby and once again put his guns away. He struggled to unbuckle his gun belt, his fingers still sore and swollen from his nasty fight with George Stanton. He grimaced as he untied, carefully folded his guns together and pushed them into the pouch. Then he folded the flap down and yanked the leather strap tight on the bag. Feeling vulnerable, a sense of panic rushed through him as he stood gunless and alone by the river. Then, as suddenly as it had begun, the feeling stopped, and a sense of calm came over him. He collected himself for a moment and then stuffed the leather pouch deep inside the saddlebag. He carefully lifted his injured leg up to the stirrup and mounted up.

"Those guns will never see the light of day again...God willing," Jon whispered as he spurred Babe down the trail to his vineyard paradise. The haunting call of a raven filled the air as the intrepid warrior disappeared into the dark shadows of the thick forest.

ABOUT THE AUTHOR

An avid student of America's early frontier, R B Conroy has turned his passion into another compelling novel, **Return of the Gun**. *Return* is his second novel and a stand alone sequel to his popular first novel **Devil Rising**. In addition to the books mentioned above, Conroy has also written short stories about America's west. He resides in Leesburg, Indiana with his wife Cheryl, where he's hard at work on his next project.